BLACK DOVE

ALSO BY COLIN McADAM

A Beautiful Truth
Fall
Some Great Thing

BLACK DOVE

Colin McAdam

First published in Canada by Hamish Hamilton in 2022

Published by Soho Press, Inc.
227 W 17th Street
New York, NY 10011

Library of Congress Cataloging-in-Publication Data
Names: McAdam, Colin, author.
Title: Black dove / Colin McAdam. | Description: New York, NY :
Soho Press, Inc., [2021] | Identifiers: LCCN 2022012563

ISBN 978-1-64129-422-5
eISBN 978-1-64129-423-2

Subjects: LCGFT: Novels. Classification: LCC PR9199.4.M38 B53
2021 | DDC 813'.6—dc23
LC record available at https://lccn.loc.gov/2022012563

Interior design by Janine Agro

Printed in the United States of America

10 9 8 7 6 5 4 3 2 1

for my family, and to the ghosts

CONTENTS

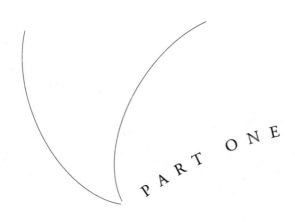

PART ONE

A Story

1

LAST DECEMBER THERE was one leaf left in the neigh-bourhood. It was hanging high from the tip of a branch, curled up and wrinkled like a little man who knew he was going to fall.

Oliver stared at the leaf from his bedroom window in the morning and looked beyond it to the skyline of the city. He lived in a tall and narrow old house on a stained and busy street, in an area that was not the nicest part of town but prob-ably not the worst. Stockyards full of cattle used to be around the corner, and nearby railroads still carried freight trains that groaned half-awake through the night. He had lived in that house since he was born.

His room was at the front, at the top, his dad's was below. There was a third room that his dad used as a study, where he sat every day writing books.

He was always writing something. Some days Oliver sat down with him quietly in his study and waited to hear a story. He would look at his dad's phone or imagine he was riding his bike while he sat there. He wasn't always good at sitting still.

Even when his dad wasn't writing he was making up stories. He told them to Oliver at bedtime or when they went for long drives. He told them at breakfast.

"I have a completely unbelievable story for you," he would say. "Totally unsuitable for a child."

He made things up while Oliver ate toast, and even though

the stories were never quite as advertised, Oliver appreciated the noise and the distraction—anything that kept his mind away from the day ahead at school.

When he left the house he looked up at the leaf and kept the sight of it in his mind. Twenty minutes to the school's main gate, through the doors, down those corridors of slogans and judgment, Oliver was as uncomfortable and unwelcome as that leaf in winter. The boy with no mother. Smaller than everyone in his class. Funny ears, no crack in his voice and no friends left to walk next to.

It was after school that Murdoch liked to hunt. No matter what the school day threw at Oliver, it was the time after the final bell that he most dreaded. Murdoch waited near the doors or he hid near the gate. Sometimes Oliver was faster than him, but it made no difference in the end. Three blocks from the school Murdoch punched him in the face till blood dripped from his nose, both of them out of breath. No one was around, so Murdoch wasn't showing off—he wanted to punch that face no matter who was watching.

To different people Oliver pretended he was in the Chess Club or the Code Club or any after-school activity that would keep the teachers from wondering why he hung around. Once the janitor was finished cleaning, Oliver snuck into his store-room with a lockpick he'd made with paper clips. He hid in the corner behind a tarp and waited in there with the light off in case the janitor came back.

Silent.

He liked the quieter superheroes. The ones who worked at night or who fled their good deeds without saying a word. And not just the ones who used silence as a power but the ones like Black Bolt, who was quiet because his voice was too powerful. Blackagar Boltagon. He underwent rigorous training to let nothing escape his mouth, because if he made a sound, even in his sleep, his voice would destroy things: cities, battleships, planets.

Quiet in the cubicles when they came knocking. Feet up on the toilet seat and the smell of everyone's piss.

"Come out, little Mickey. I want to show you something."

The storeroom was the safest.

Oliver stayed till five thirty and unlocked the door when he was sure that Murdoch had left the school grounds. In the winter it meant that he always walked home in the dark.

"Zebras are actually pretty strong," Oliver told his dad. "A lot of those animals that get chased by lions, like water buffaloes and wildebeest, are actually super strong. It's only sometimes they get eaten."

His dad thought that Oliver stayed behind at school to run or to read. "I like your facts," he said.

"But the night is also when none of them can sleep," said Oliver.

He had his favourite routes home. There were streets near school where the houses were bigger, and at night their lamplit living rooms looked golden. He saw paintings on the walls and polished tables that were proud with milk and wine.

He used to be friends with Murdoch—at an age, five or six, that he couldn't see clearly anymore. Murdoch's parents had one of the nice houses on Glenlake and a TV as big and bright as summer. He and Oliver played after school and their moms had been friends, but it was like Murdoch got picked for some team that would always win and Oliver got passed over. Murdoch grew tall, and his mom was calm and elegant. He was going to be either a doctor or an athlete, he had a laptop and an iPhone, sharp eyes, and he acted like Oliver was some kind of dirty secret, some part of his past that he was ashamed of and wanted to disown. It was like he wanted to let people know that he had nothing in common with him.

Beyond the streets with all the nice houses, things got a

little too quiet. Near the empty lots and unmended fences it was easy to have the wrong thoughts. Oliver was too old to be afraid of the dark, but he was aware that behind him there were ghosts, and above him the trees leaned forward, taking hold of birds and old seeds and trying to find lost memories.

Every now and then he took Keele and Dundas, the busier route, to have a bit more company. He tried to keep his eyes forward. Avoid temptation. He could steal candy if he wanted. He'd figured out a way to steal toys from the Dollar Store—you just waited till it was really crowded and all the employees had to work the cash. None of them cared about the merchandise anyway. Which also meant not much of it was worth stealing.

If he turned to the windows in the dark he caught sight of himself. Saw again that he was short, a kid. His hat was only chest-high to the people with business on the sidewalk, and the future waited down the road as some cold, unknowable thing. Sometimes the world seemed full of people who said, "You'll never succeed like we have, Oliver. You'll never know what we know."

THERE WAS A man in the neighbourhood named Iron John, covered in hair, who lived at the Peacock Hotel. He collected cans in bags and sometimes screamed prophecies about the sun becoming a bladder of blood that would burst and spray people's faces.

The cans brought him thirty bucks a day if he was brave enough to wander as far as the stockyards to collect them. The box stores out there with the garbage bins full of lunchtime drinks and dumpsters near the grocery stores. People buying lumber and televisions, nobody noticing the smell, the stink of death from the rendering plants. He felt like he was at the end of the earth out there and the smell made him afraid.

He never slept. He filled his bags with cans and shook them, and the cops asked if he'd taken his meds. A conversation in his lips all day, people talking through him, movies in the sky and the girl who smiled at him once, where are you. Calling for the memories and on the bad days he screamed so hard he had lesions in his throat.

At the Peacock Hotel he kept a secret, the skin of a boy. He'd found it in the alley behind the bar near Heintzman, looking through the dumpster they forgot to chain some nights. Not in the dumpster but beside it. Dropped like a bag, a wet leather suit. Some things made him quiet.

It was moist when he picked up the skin. Fresh. Smelled like nothing, damp enough to make his hands wet, and warm in the folds. It dried as he stared at it, shadows up and down the body. The streetlight in the distance helped him understand. One arm and then another, he held the skin up by the shoulders, the head flopping down, some weight to it at first but light, getting lighter as the breeze blew.

It could be a real ghost.

He let go of one shoulder and lifted the head, stretched it out against the streetlight. A body had been in there, a life, holes for the mouth and eyes, looser skin at the cheekbones, marks where personality might have been. He put it in a bag with the cans and brought it home.

The life slipped away from it the more it dried. It was fragile and made him sad. In bed he laid it on top of himself and it comforted him through the coughs and mumbles, moans through the walls from the other yearning mouths at the Peacock. After a year the skin had dried completely, went from a creamy yellow to white, then grey. He still laid it on top of himself and whispered to it, forgot exactly how he had met this boy's ghost or whether he could help in any way. It grew brittle and waxy like vellum, and the trace of the face looked tragic.

John went to that alley every night as part of his route, and one night he saw a boy who looked familiar. The cheekbones under the woollen cap.

On his meds he didn't see the world as clearly as this, the red halos around the streetlights and the sun inside everyone, screaming.

On his meds he might not have seen this boy.

The back door of the bar opened every now and then, people stepping out for a smoke. But otherwise this alley was quiet. Iron John hid behind a car and watched.

The boy took his hat off, his coat and shirt. Old clothes like John wore. Looked around. Smelled the air. One dim bulb above the back door of the bar, lights at each end of the alley and whiffs of beer and garbage. Iron John could stay as still as a tree. His hair covered his eyes. The boy looked straight at him and paused, kept staring towards him while he took off his boots, pants, underwear.

Pale.

A noise came out of John as he stared.

The boy walked naked to the building beside the dumpster and rubbed his head on the brick quoins, like a cat spreading its scent. Scraping. John heard it, the itchy sound, felt it in his teeth, the ache, wanting to get out of his own skin. The boy rubbed the top of his head up and down the corner of the brick and reached up, fingers in his hair finding the split he'd made. He turned in Iron John's direction and pulled his skin off slowly, inch by inch from his crown. Didn't blink, like he was in a trance, waiting, disappearing, and the same boy, the newer version, climbed slowly out of the skin, pink as a scratch.

John was talking but he didn't know it.

The most private thing you could see.

He pictured the old skin he'd found, at home in bed. Could he fill his room with new friends. He'd had snakes in his brain since he was a teenager, and when he took his meds he asked his friends, Whose hands are these.

Yellow snakes, brown, and this pale one. The emperor.

The boy went back to his clothes and took a knife out from his trousers. He walked slowly, new and naked, to Iron John.

"Used to be a store here, you could hold the snakes," mumbled John, quickly. "Let me hold you, said the prince. I used to be a prince. Let me hold you."

HIS MOTHER LEFT home before Oliver turned nine and she died shortly after. She put a trellis on the front of the house to encourage the growth of vines, but she never planted the vines. His dad said she gave up on a lot of things.

Oliver remembered crying the night she left, lying on his parents' bed and not being able to stop. At first there were dreams of the street outside collapsing in on itself, Oliver digging down to find her. His dad said she chased sweet things and sweetness got the better of her.

But the basic facts were that she was an alcoholic, and she didn't feel strong enough to be a mother. She hid bottles of vodka in the bathroom cabinet, in the linen cupboard, all over the house, and his dad kept finding them months after she had gone.

He kept some pictures of her in his study from a long time ago and said that people used to tell him he was lucky she liked him. Oliver looked hard at the photos sometimes, trying to see deeper, her eyes bright but smudged like old coins. He was thinking more about her lately and didn't want to. His dad said she was the first in her family to go to university, had all kinds of possibility. Took cool photos and got some published in magazines around the time his dad published his first novel. But some kind of darkness started growing in her, "when everything should have been happy. I used to feel so good just looking at her, and then, I don't know, I wondered for years if it was my fault, but something just got ahold of her. I wanted to cure her sadness. All that promise, the joy that should have followed." Oliver saw a line in one of his dad's books: *Whether it's the booze that makes the clouds or the clouds that make the booze* . . .

When he looked at her face in pictures Oliver sometimes heard her voice.

"Mom slept a lot, didn't she?"

"Near the end she did. Before she went."

Sometimes he remembered her clearly and most of the time he wanted to forget. Flashes behind his eyes of the woman in the photos. A smile. A pair of white pants, something blue about her at night and a feeling like he might drown. *I love you so much.* His dad said the last time he saw her she was almost dead, in a hospital, blue sheets and dripping IVs. Oliver's memories could be triggered by a smell, his dad having a whisky before telling him a story. He could feel her leaning over him, tucking him in, crying and a wet mouth. More swollen than she was in the pictures. *Do you love me?*

He had an almost clear memory of a day in summer when she took him to a swimming pool before he could swim. He must have been little. He could find a birthday feeling when he thought of her that day, like anything could happen. "Let's have some fun," she said. They went to a shop full of bottles and she bought one with a crown on it.

In the changing room she said they'd go for ice cream after. "Maybe see a movie." Smiling at him when he put his goggles on.

He made a friend in the water. Sunnyside pool full of all kinds of people, and everything was too bright. He remembered standing in the shallow end, afraid to go deeper, staring at his mom as she slept on a towel. Transforming. He poked her leg and waited for something to happen, and knew, was he too young to know already, that the movie and the ice cream weren't going to happen. His new friend tried to get him to swim out deeper. He looked back to his mom and she was gone.

The problem with some of his memories was he couldn't be sure what was true or what was told to him by his dad. The story his dad told him was that he got a call from the people at the pool. *Is she your wife? We think she's sick.* A lifeguard found her passed out in one of the stalls. Her and dad fighting at home, all night. He remembers shivering, but maybe that was in bed at night, swimming out too far, the smell of chlorine and alcohol while she tucked him in. *I love you so much, Oliver. Do you love me?* she said. Blue hugs, like the pool was hanging over him, telling her he loved her and trying to stop her crying. She kept saying it. *Please tell me you love me.*

What he remembered about their days was how she changed all the time. Asleep when he went to school, fun when he came home sometimes or mean, and at night someone different, bigger. One afternoon she was asleep on the stairs, looking like she'd fallen, and he was afraid to go to her. It filled her up, this damp grey light. Took over her body and made her face look heavy. A different mom with metal under her skin.

When he walked home from school he saw a woman in one of the nice houses laughing at a joke her husband told. There was a lot he didn't understand about what happened between his parents. Whatever it was that took over her, maybe that's what walked behind him some nights. Reaching down, blowing across his neck. Hiding up there in the alley or between the houses. All it would need was for him to make the wrong choice, walk across the tracks, stop somewhere or think the wrong thought, and some infection would turn him into a person he didn't want to be. A drunk who didn't care.

His neighbours' house had stone lions out front and a tiled picture of the Virgin Mary. When their window was open he could hear the woman crying and praying, and he used to think the house was haunted. Up the road was Pelham Park Gardens, a tall apartment building hiding among townhouses where there were shootings and screams on summer nights. Oliver's dad had talked about some of the houses in the neighbourhood—theirs and a lot of the others were over a hundred years old, from when the railway was built and the workers needed homes. Lots of red-brick Victorians, some of them owned by the city and boarded up. He'd seen a family of six raccoons crawling out from under the roof of one of them. On Dundas Street was a rooming house where strange, sad men looked up at the night and whispered things only they could understand.

"People worked hard in this neighbourhood," his dad said, "and then when there was no more work, once the railways were built, the younger ones couldn't fill the shoes of their parents. They didn't know what to do and some of them got lost. It's history. In a city like this, history writes a kind of destiny from one street to another. Some people come here fresh and make a house something new. Some are born into it, and the house makes them."

"There's history in my blood," said Oliver.

Like most parents, his dad said, "You can be anything you want."

When he got home from school, Oliver sat at his desk with a reading light on. Sometimes he read comics, sometimes he just stared at the ceiling. He knew every mark and crack in it, and imagined he was floating in space, looking up at a cold moon, nothing underneath him but the chair of his spaceship. *I can confirm that there's no life up there*, he reported. Later at night in bed, staring again, his hand low on his belly, under his pyjamas, waiting for something, his voice, his body, to change.

He didn't mind being in his room, knowing his dad was downstairs. Those things back there in the dark were no longer chasing him, the trees, ghosts and hungry mouths. If you never turn to the ghosts, you won't see them.

He got up from his bed and called downstairs for company.

What you need to know is that Oliver loved his dad. And his dad loved Oliver more than the clouds love whatever holds them in the sky.

"YOU LOOK LIKE you need a story," said his dad.

"Maybe," said Oliver.

"Let's brush our teeth, and I'll tell you one before bed."

His dad's stories weren't always perfect for a twelve-year-old. Not a lot of spying or bloodshed, and Oliver was probably getting too old for bedtime stories anyway.

He lay in bed and his dad sat next to him. "This is a story about a flower," he said.

Oliver sighed.

"This was the first flower. The first flower on earth."

"It's still a flower."

His dad was quiet for a moment.

"Do you know that some of the world's most powerful chemicals—all kinds of drugs and poisons—come from flowers?"

"Maybe."

"Plants and seeds and flowers," said his dad. "For thousands of years people have been healing and killing each other with flowers. They dry them and grind them and turn their chemicals into pills and potions. They fight wars over them. A lot of the pills and drugs have names with *exes* and *zeds*, but they still come from flowers. From the ground."

Oliver turned on his side, away from his dad. His silent way of allowing him to continue.

"And the most powerful flower of all, the rarest, most

dangerous plant ever studied, was this first flower that I'm telling you about. Two of its petals rise like wings whenever night falls. It is the most dangerous because it makes whoever finds it unimaginably strong. It takes away fear. If you can find the flower, you can do anything you want."

"What's it called?" asked Oliver, with his eyes closed.

"The Black Dove," said his dad.

"MORE THAN A hundred million years ago, there were flowers underwater that carried their own seeds, and the first that emerged from those dark soupy waters was the Black Dove. It was the first to bloom on land, and the hardiest.

"Everything wanted to eat it. And everything wanted to eat the creatures that ate it. Picture a dinosaur eating the flower, and another one attacking that dinosaur. They fought and soaked the ground with blood, and insects ate the blood-soaked ground, and birds ate the bugs and soared up to the sky with the blood of the ground in their bellies. That was how the Black Dove spread.

"It bloomed and died and rose again, and the creatures who ate it found some kind of triumph, in friendship and fights and dark corners. Children stood tall in the face of tigers. When humans took over the earth they told stories about the Black Dove.

"Not everyone knew how to grow it or find it, but words and books passed on the secret to some. Boats, travel, buildings, cities. Everything came from fearlessness and creativity, the pupils in our eyes like black flowers."

Oliver closed his eyes more tightly to the darkness around the house, and he may have heard the rest or he dreamt it.

"Picture a girl, Oliver, younger than you, living in a time when everything—clouds, tools, thoughts—was heavy. She was found squirming in a sack on a cobblestone street by a hungry man who hoped the thing squirming was a dog so he could swing the sack against a wall and eat it.

"Murderers walked those streets hand in hand, and liars preached for money.

"The hungry man fished the baby out of the sack and cursed, but he figured if he couldn't summon the taste to eat her, he could, at least, sell her.

"The girl was bought by an innkeeper, who sold her to a candlemaker, who traded her for a bag of fat to a man who sharpened his fangs with a file. He had a sister who couldn't have a baby, so he gave her this one, and the sister gave the girl a home for her first nine years.

"So there she is behind your eyes, her little face burdened with cark and care, as some people said in those days. No matter what depraved and beastly thoughts people hid behind their doors, they expected virtue and perfection outside, especially in girls. To make her a model of righteous behaviour, the sister of the sharp-fanged man beat the girl regularly and sent her out for work.

"She stood with a wheelbarrow near the doors of slaughter-houses at night, and took away skins and offal. Any part of an animal that few people wanted, the girl piled onto her wheelbarrow and carted to a man outside her city who paid her for every load. He paid her poorly, but he fed her from a grill that burned red and gold, a pinprick of light in the night's swart cloth. Swart means black, Oliver.

"It was protein from that man's grill that kept the girl alive. He fed her crispy corners of pigskin, a fatty knuckle or two. And so she had the strength to work like that every night, to lift the handles of her barrow and roll fetid refuse towards that tiny fire of hope, that flame that gave her just enough strength to hope for strength to hope.

"She brought what little money she made back to the

woman who raised her, who grew daily jealous of the little girl's strength.

"And was she beautiful, this girl? Does it matter if she paced with the grace of a gazelle which panteth for the cooling stream? If she was dark or fair or tall or broad? All I can tell you is that as a woman she had a smile that miners dig for. She had a light inside that explained our search for gold. She carried confidence and strength and a love for all mistakes, and if you can walk tall with constant forgiveness, and curiosity that never dies, you will be beautiful no matter how you look.

"And her curiosity took her through nights of evil and dearth, of men saying thou shalt not kill and stabbing each other's back. They watched the girl driving her wheelbarrow in the dark and they raided her goods. They held knives to her throat and draped those skins and intestines on their backs, but through the attacks and privation she said to herself, 'There is a better place, I know it.'

"Now coal, Oliver, is made of ancient plants. Swampy forests that lived and died. From all the layers of dead vegetation came those hard black nuggets we call coal. In every piece is a history of flowers and trees that once thrived. And if you think of those stories over millions of years, you can imagine all kinds of flowers that were buried and transformed."

"The Black Dove," said Oliver.

"The Black Dove. He didn't know it, but the man who cooked those scraps of protein for the girl every night was using coal that held the Black Dove. The first flower, from when it was strongest, had been crushed into the carbon that glowed in his constant fire.

"And the smoke of the Black Dove caressed his food. Its heat made the girl's body fearless.

"'This will make you strong,' he always said to her, handing her morsels from his grill.

"He gave her advice: 'Know your letters. And know this move,' he said.

"He taught her a move of self-defence which he called the Hunting Birds. He showed her the precise points on an adversary's body, where if she struck him with the tips of her small fingers, she would take his breath and run before he could harm her.

"And by the light of the man's grill she learned the shapes of letters.

"Signs in the city came alive. The North. The South. The Gallery of Oceanic Wonders.

"And just like you, Oliver, she read. Letters bloomed across the page, filling her eyes with wonder and strength, and confirming her belief that there was indeed a better place than here. And as she girded herself for her travels in the dark, she said to the man: 'I want to go to the ocean.'"

2

OLIVER AWOKE ON a Saturday. On the weekends he and his dad watched a lot of TV. In fact, his dad watched TV every night, through summer, spring, winter and fall, until everything in his room, the books, the curtains, his face, turned a really pale blue.

"She left a hole in our life," said his dad. "That's why you dream of her going down beneath the street. She isn't down there."

"I don't want to talk about it."

Oliver sat on the couch with him. Time passed in silence more and more these days, his dad remembering himself at that age and how he often didn't want to talk. Oliver could be almost manically chatty sometimes, but over the past year he was quieter, and his dad tried to figure it out. Be a friend. Questions getting larger every year as a parent. If you don't feel loved by your mother, can you still feel love.

They stared at the TV, watching something about the planet falling apart. On the table was an old-looking book, open to a page with an etching of a flower. Oliver leaned forward and looked at it.

"Is that the Black Dove?"

His dad looked away from the TV for a moment and thought.

"No, that's just a flower."

"Does it really exist?"

"Sure. You see it in parks, gardens. You see poppies, right? Doesn't mean people are growing opium."

"I don't know."

His dad looked back to the TV.

"Can we look for it?"

They sometimes walked to High Park on the weekend. Some of the woods were big enough to make it feel like it wasn't in the city. There had been a thaw overnight, and a fog hung low in the branches. Everything was dripping or bubbling, and the bark on trees was almost black.

Whenever they were there, Oliver thought of his friend Charlie. They used to ride their bikes in the woods, and every year their jumps had been getting higher. Charlie moved away last spring.

"How does that story end? About the Black Dove."

"It doesn't," said his dad. "Stories never end. They stay in your head and they make you who you are. Part of you, anyway."

"But what happened to the girl?"

"I'll tell you later. I thought we came here to look for it."

"I looked for the Black Dove online and all I saw was a restaurant and an old movie. There's nothing about a flower."

"You can't find everything online," said his dad. "You can't find this." He took off their gloves and held Oliver's bare hand.

Oliver looked around to see if anyone was watching. Everything black was standing out more than usual.

He looked up at his dad and saw a change in his eyes.

"What are you thinking about?"

"Stories," said his dad. "I want to write a good one."

"What's a good one?"

"I don't know. They have to feel true, even when they're not. And the only true stories for me are sad ones. I want to write a story that's true, that has a happy ending." He got down on his knees and looked at Oliver. "I want you to be happy," he said.

3

HERE IS A cup of letters.

You can tell what drugs the city is taking by testing its waste. If you start at the top of Jarvis in the rain you can follow the water south and drift eastward over streets already soaked with spit and greasy characters, the whole place looking for an ear. A storm sometimes quiets the fuck-ups and seekers.

The rain turned to snow and the man walked solid looking everyone in the eye. The academics and the residents of boytown, couples on dates. He wandered far from his store sometimes. Moss Park where needles and razors whispered at your nape and the army of wise nothings, never wanted, who held their mouths open under life's empty bottle.

He was almost saved near here. A tosher looking for coins in the sewer. He has climbed below, seen the brick tunnels and gagged on the stink, followed the path which he now walked above, ankle-deep in the buried creeks. Tonight he got wet from the snow.

Stories used to be told of a herd of wild hogs who lived under here, a pregnant sow slipping down into the sewer from the market and raising her progeny on the city's waste. In storms or when the sluices were raised the surge of water could sound like frightened pigs.

And the tale of a rat who took the shape of a woman, lurking down there and seducing the men like him who hunted for treasure in the sewage. What a thing to imagine. They said her eyes were like mirrors, claws on her toes, that she was blessed in accordance with Hogarth's line of beauty and if you gave her the time of her life she would make you rich and protect you from other rats. Rich among the bodies of dogs, and vegetables down the sink.

Depending on which branch you choose, the sewer will tell you about each neighbourhood. Under Summerhill, Rosedale, the effluent speaks of wine and antidepressants, mercury-rich diets of Chilean sea bass, lawyers and cheats whose long days of coffee and cocaine are spelled out clearly amidst the letters of DNA.

Farther south where the branches converge you find the true mess. The humbling. Genetic tales too confused to make any sense of, the only things clear being illness and addiction, what's going wrong with the city.

He thought of the three boys, made in his likeness, their strength the product of learning others' weakness.

Past the hotels and churches to the old wet well at Eastern Avenue. Here the flow of sewage is passed to the treatment plant and here you can climb down a manhole and gather most of the city's secrets. He took cups from his coat and filled them. Sealed them for his lab.

Rush into me. I want to understand.

4

SUZI LAY IN her parents' bed and wondered if she was real.

Sometimes, just before closing her eyes, she felt a kind of weight at the top of her head. Something pushing down. Not a bad or really heavy feeling, but some kind of sense of a force above her, above the world, a cloud of metal. Not quite scary. Completely impossible to describe.

She felt it just now. Not asleep or awake. A pressure on her brain. Probably a growing pain. You get those in your legs, why not in your head, but it wasn't even a pain.

The ceiling was bumpy. Popcorn.

She moved her fingers on top of the blanket and felt the cotton yarn. That was real. The bed was real. If it wasn't she'd be on the floor. She closed her eyes and tried to get the feeling back. That's what convinced her that it wasn't scary. She wanted to feel it.

The bed disappearing for a second, the room, her body, nothing but the cloud, metal noise, soundless hum, rising. She chased the feeling and it grew and she chased it more and the more she looked for it the less she felt herself, the less she felt anything except whatever it was, that pressure.

Am I real? That's not exactly what she was wondering.

She just felt small.

The bed was too big, she wasn't used to this house yet, her world had changed. Everything could change. So many possibilities out that window, and that she was even here on earth, never mind in this bedroom, seemed totally . . . fragile. How many chance events had to happen for her parents to meet, for them to like each other, for her to be alive and wearing this shirt. This shirt felt so important when she saw it. When she convinced her mom to buy it.

Who cares about a shirt.

Everything's small and fragile.

That feeling in her brain, the pressure. Maybe that's what it feels like for a mother to give birth. Maybe that's what was happening now. When you grow you give birth to yourself.

She got up and wandered next door to her bedroom. Before they moved here Suzi rode her bike over to take a look at the house and street. It wasn't as far from her old house as she'd thought. Maybe twenty minutes. She pretended her bike was Hermes, the talking motorcycle in *Kino's Journey*. Going to explore different cultures, places where people lived to work and places where the only purpose of living was to make people happy.

Her parents had packed boxes and fought every day over where they put things and who had last seen what, and there was an effort among the three of them to decide what was important. What do we need to take with us. And her mom cried every day, leaving the old house behind. She took pictures down from the walls slowly like she wanted to take the walls along with them.

"It's where you grew up," she said to Suzi. "All your memories."

She remembered the story her mom told her once about how she had decided, when she was pregnant, to walk out into the world and smile at everyone. Figured it would open people up or reveal some happy force that was hiding in their hearts. Make herself feel good about bringing this baby into the world.

The first person she smiled at was a woman, and the woman scowled back and said, *Do I know you?*

Suzi whispered to Hermes when she got to the new house. *This is it.* A little red-brick place with toothpick columns in a row of little red-brick places.

She'd drawn pictures of her bedroom before she saw it. Originally a bed on stilts with a desk underneath, then one of those drafting desks like designers have, in the middle of the room, a queen bed, light coming in from a huge window. Plants everywhere. She drew one of those long lamps that start on the floor in a corner and reach over to another part of the room, as if the lamp is being kind and stretching to where it's needed.

She smiled, looking around at the truth of it.

There were marks on the walls, nail holes, handprints from the people who used to live here. Tiny. Nothing unpacked. Just enough room for this twin bed and her old desk. Even her bookcase was too tall for the ceiling.

Kino looks for the beauty in everything.

She was still excited, even though the room wasn't what she had imagined. That day she rode her bike over here it felt like the sun was filled with honey and she could almost see the whole thing, *almost*, what the scene would look like: a swell in the music that makes the hair on your arms stand up, right when the girl on her bike rounds the hill. Animation making the road move and not the bike. The sweet sun, fear and worry in the picture doing some kind of battle with . . . what . . . with something surprising, unknown. The colours of it all making you ignore that some things, the houses and the fish warehouse, weren't so pretty. Then you get the close-up of her eyes, bigger than her eyes in real life. She could see the eyes clearly but she probably couldn't draw them. They'd have to be totally open, almost blank. That kind of blank that shows there's actually too much to draw. Memories and thoughts and even a little disappointment, all of it pushed to the back where you know it's there in the drawing but you can't see it. What you see is her whispering to Hermes and the eyes show a new beginning. Possibility.

Her mom said it was going to take a while, for all of them. To get used to new rooms, new streets, new friends. New school.

Suzi took it as a time to think. She looked around her room. *Is this real.*

ON THE WAY back from the park they walked along Dundas. His dad bought Oliver a Snickers which he planned to have at home.

They lingered outside a store they had often walked past, sometimes stopping to look in the window but never going in.

ALL U.R. NEEDS A. PRINCEPS, said the sign.

"Have you been in there ever?" asked his dad.

"No."

Oliver wanted to get home to eat his Snickers.

"Have you noticed it's never closed? It's always dark but it's never closed. Want to go in?"

"No. Let's go home," said Oliver.

His dad stayed looking into the dirty window of the shop. It was no more than ten feet wide, the smallest storefront on that stretch of the street, but it was on the corner and the window had a slight curve. It might have been welcoming if it hadn't looked so weird. A wooden carving of a pig with a human face was dangling front and centre from a worn old string. Behind it were crates of detergent, and paintings that belonged hidden in someone's attic. There was a plaster mask with no mouth, a lobster made of rusty steel, three guitars, a mirror frame and a dead plant.

"What do they sell?"

"All our needs," said his dad. "We should go in someday."

There used to be more stores like this along here, ones that seemed odd, that weren't flashy or that focused on things from a different era: a radio repair shop, a used-appliance store. Blockbuster Video. Now most of the stores were about to turn into apartment buildings, or they sold expensive clothes and furniture and coffee. If you were a kid you were either not interested or not welcome in most of them, unless your family lived on the nice streets, like Murdoch's. He always got Converse at the skateboard shop a few doors down from here, and Oliver was afraid of seeing him.

"Let's go home," he said again.

Murdoch's father made money with car dealerships. Nice cars like Jaguars and Aston Martins. And he was on the Business Improvement Association, making the neighbourhood nicer so more restaurants and stuff could open and better people would live there who wouldn't have to see needles on the sidewalks. Oliver heard Murdoch boast that his dad had made thirty thousand bucks one weekend and that he put it all in stocks of AI tech. "He plays the system, my dad. Smartest guy in the building."

Oliver looked up at his father outside the shop window. His ears were big like Oliver's, but bigger. A bit of clear snot was hanging from his nose.

They didn't have much money. His dad said his first books brought in a bit and they got the house when the neighbourhood was really cheap. He bought used clothes for Oliver—decent brands, but old and dorky and Oliver didn't know how to make them look cooler. He knew there had been times since his mom left that his dad was artificially cheerful, when money was really tight and he tried to show Oliver that everything was going to be okay. He kept his mouth shut if his dad came home with clothes for him, some awful pair of cords or a hat that smelled like someone else's head. He did stuff around the house to help out, like the laundry and vacuuming, even though he hated most of it.

He thought about all that when he hid in the janitor's storeroom the following Monday. He sat in the dark, in a steel bucket behind the tarp. One of his worst nightmares was having to clean for a living.

The janitor was a nice man. He probably wouldn't have minded if Oliver hid in there. Sometimes he came back and Oliver froze while he searched for whatever he had forgotten. He heard him say "I've locked you, I've locked you, I've locked you" from outside the door when he left. Oliver could pick the lock to open it, but he couldn't figure out how to lock it again from outside, so every morning the janitor probably questioned his own memory.

He fell into a half sleep behind the tarp. Dreamt it was an animal skin. He had hunted for his family and was nodding off by the fire. Head bounced and he remembered where he was.

The schoolyard made him shiver when he thought about it. A place to run through now, never to hang around in. Murdoch liked to trap him there and say things like, "You wanna see a real cock, Mickey?" Standing there with a circle of people around, his pants open, his penis a man's. His favourite thing, him and his friends, was to chase Oliver, corner him, force him to be somewhere he didn't want to be. Oliver could see in Murdoch's face some kind of question when he was finally trapped, sometimes. When Murdoch actually had to do something, to hit him or show him something he didn't want to see. Like the chase was everything, like he knew that each new thing he did to Oliver would have to be worse than the last, and part of him didn't want to do it. Oliver felt some kind of strength when he thought about that, seeing vulnerability in Murdoch, but it wasn't real strength. It wasn't enough to make him stand up to him, or to keep him from fearing the next thing. And when Murdoch beat him up when no one was around . . . No one told the teachers that Murdoch carried a two-hundred-dollar knife.

Oliver took his beatings. He took the wedgies. Sometimes he fought a little. Hanging by his underwear from the hooks in the change room. He struggled a bit, but it wasn't fighting back. The fear of the beatings was sometimes worse than actually getting hit, and once it was happening he felt a kind of relief. Like he didn't need to pretend to be something anymore. That was the thing that almost made him sick when he had time to think about it later. Throwing out his underwear so his dad didn't see the rips and the blood. How he felt relieved hanging there, like it was meant to be. Like he deserved it.

He had made the lockpick with two paper clips and his dad's multi-tool. One of the clips was a tension wrench and the other raked the lock. He knew he hated cleaning, but he also knew he liked to make things.

His dad said people were expecting to evaporate these days. Turn into some sort of bodiless substance that could live online. But they would always be bodies. Forever. And bodies needed chairs. Places to store food. Things to light up the darkness. "There's no shame in making a bed or a toaster. And if you can make them beautifully . . ."

Oliver sat in the bucket with the tarp an inch from his nose. A lockpick wasn't the most beautiful thing to make, but it kept him away from Murdoch.

HE CALLED CHARLIE on his dad's phone, sent him messages and set up chats, but he never heard from him. He followed what he was doing through pictures Charlie posted, but it was starting to feel like his friend was slipping away.

Charlie lived on the other side of the country now, where there were mountains and the faces of new people.

He stared at his homework and gave up on it. Saw his reflection in the window. No light across the street.

Calling on people. Never getting called on. That's how the world was divided. People who had friends and people who waited for one.

It was pitch-black by dinnertime. He put his boots on at eight.

"Where you going?"

"For a walk."

His dad encouraged him not to be a kid. Didn't need to be looked after all the time. The chances of getting killed or assaulted were higher at home. He had stats. He also went out and left Oliver alone sometimes, staying close by being apart.

"Wear your hat."

"I will."

"Take my phone."

"Then you won't have one."

He untied his boots when he was down the street a bit. They made a heavier sound like that.

Maybe he'd make it all the way to High Park. He'd been there a couple of times at night, in the winter. Teenagers in the play structure vaping and giggling. It was built to look like a castle. Kids sat up top and made out. Wrote their names in the wood with knives. Down there at that end of the park the kids were all rich, probably butter knives they stole from the kitchen.

Oliver walked past the Watkinson Parkette, closer to his place, swings and slide that no one ever used, adults from the halfway house sitting on the benches and smoking.

Things were quiet tonight. That feeling like everything's waiting for snow, tightening up. Colder than the middle of winter for whatever reason. He shrugged and listened to his boots.

If you don't have friends to call on, you make your own world, that's how the world got interesting. He'd read a book about bodysnatchers. The people who dug up bodies from graves and sold them to scientists. To him they seemed like the ultimate quiet types. Sneaking around at night. They dug from twenty feet away, made tunnels, sometimes took the bodies out from the end of the coffin while the funeral was still going on.

They were the ones who helped us understand. Cured disease. He slapped and rubbed his arms while he walked. They maybe had friends between themselves, family. But they were shunned by the rest of the world, and they were the ones who saved it.

The zoo in High Park had been cleared out in the fall. All the animals taken away. He thought he might go there tonight, but then he remembered. Some animal had got in, or some people thought it might have been some crazy animal-hater. Ripped apart the peacocks and the caribou.

Oliver closed his eyes and saw a white light behind his lids, from the streetlights. Blank. He wanted to put colours there. Feathers and pretty faces. There were girls in his class he thought about, wasn't sure how to think about. Smiles in the sky, some hot blue fire in his chest. Michelle W, Maeve and Christina. He touched fingertips with Maeve in gym passing the medicine ball down the line. Looked in her eyes for a second. That was the most he could do.

He walked a little with his eyes closed. I dare you, he thought. Whatever's out there in the dark. Come and get me. Werewolves. What scared him the most were people without heads. He opened his eyes again. Seeing people lose them in movies. How their bodies behaved normally for a second. He'd heard something on the news where a guy was walking on the sidewalk and the wing mirror of a truck came by so fast it cut his head off.

Cold was under his neck now. The sounds were different in winter. That was the thing. Quiet. Nobody opened their windows. In the summer you heard music from cars and people washing their dishes. Walk through the neighbourhood and you heard people living. In the winter it seemed like even the cars were whispering.

It was only near the end of last year, after Charlie took off, that he started getting picked on by Murdoch. People changed. He couldn't see it clearly at the time, but he could see it now. Once Murdoch picked on him a couple of times, everyone else started drifting away from Oliver, ignoring him or standing in those circles and laughing while Murdoch talked shit. He started feeling like he stood out all the time, and when he knew the answer to something in class—when he knew it deeply and knew that no one else knew it, and it almost hurt to keep it in—he didn't raise his hand because it would only draw attention.

Some of the bodysnatchers he'd read about became really successful, not just from being good at digging up the corpses. Their trick for getting more bodies to sell was to start killing people. They got kids drunk with rum and threw them down wells. Mothers and poor people. Killed a young guy with clubfoot and nobody missed him because everyone thought he was useless.

A bus sped past from behind and scared him.

He was only a few blocks from home. Little boy out where he shouldn't be.

"Do you want more of the story?" said his dad. "I can tell you how it goes."

OLIVER LAY IN bed and closed his eyes.

"When the girl was ten," said his dad, "she stood before the sister of the sharp-fanged man, who'd tried to be her mother. 'I've had enough of you,' said the woman to the girl. 'Your words. Your nights of learning. You should be grateful to me for taking you in, not trying to be better than I am.'

"At that moment the girl resolved that if she ever lived to have a child, she would show that she understood these truths: no one has a choice to come into this world, and those who are here already should try to make it better.

"She said to the woman, 'I've read of places where apples don't taste like dust. Where milk is clean. We can go there together, and soon I can care for you.'

"The woman lifted the hem of her muddy dress and showed the girl her feet. They were made of cobblestones like the streets and she could barely lift them.

"She softened and said to the girl, 'You go. This city has been killing me all my life.'

"In the years to follow, her sharp-fanged brother read her letters from the girl. His teeth cut his lips as he read, and the woman cried with pride when she learned of the struggles her daughter overcame.

"The girl left her wheelbarrow with the man by the grill, who filled her pockets with coins and cured meat, and she followed a sign that said WEST.

"The West was the first page of a book, the place where people journeyed when their stories had all gone wrong and they wanted to write anew. Books had told her that if she chased the falling sun, her day would never end.

"Her journey took her from Ur to Uruk, to Kish and a city called Err, where everyone made mistakes," said his dad.

"Men in armour lifted her onto horses with gloved hands, and she fought but her fingers were nothing against their iron. For years she was enslaved to noble families across the Near East, learning the customs and wasteful ways of the rich. When she wasn't exhausted she read and learned new languages. And stories in every language told her that if she dreamed and strove, her dreams would come true. But they didn't.

"'I want to go to the ocean,' she said to the winter moon.

"The Black Dove bloomed beneath the windows of a noble-woman in Ebla. She made the girl tend her garden and whipped her with its stems.

"The noblewoman didn't like the way everyone looked at the girl, or how she caught herself trying to copy the girl's rich smile in the mirror.

"But the Black Dove leaving welts on her skin made the girl's smile even deeper. Her fearlessness kept her young and looking for surprises.

"Coal fires burned. The flower brought progress to worlds she couldn't imagine. Men captured lightning to make electricity. Factories crushed the bodies of children but soon set them free. Soon women and children could read at night while machines burned coal through the day.

"She was put on a ship as a slave at twenty and saw the ocean through a crack in its hold. She reached out to touch it, but a chain pulled back her hand."

THE NEXT EVENING his dad carried on with the story.

"She worked on a plantation," he said, "where the Black Dove covered the land. She picked its tops and put them in a sack and her day wasn't done till she had picked two hundred pounds. Its seeds filled the air and made her choke. The flower made her work harder and more defiantly. She picked five hundred pounds and spat at the feet of the landowner. He feared her strength, and cursed her.

"'You will get everything you want, one day,' he said, 'but you will choose to watch it go.'

"His days of being allowed to own slaves were numbered, and he worked her harder than ever.

"She awoke one morning in her cot to the man resting a gun on his shoulder. 'You're free,' he said to the room full of labourers. In anger he shot at the ceiling and blew a hole out to the sky.

"Across the land the slaves roamed free. A huge man tried to hold her in a forest but she uncaged the Hunting Birds. He fell to his knees and she left him gasping, and as the years passed in towns of plain talk she worked and quietly said, 'I want to go to the ocean.'

"'Join us!' shouted men with megaphones on horseback. 'The sun sets in the beginning! Ride with us to the sea and seed a sweeter garden!'

"They rode horses through the town for two days, shouting invitations to join their caravan heading west. She stood on the porch of the café where she washed dishes and listened to the riders. There were women among them who shouted about fruit that grew from cracks in broad roads and a sun that always nourished. 'Come and live by the ocean!'

"She stepped off the porch in her apron and got onto the back of a horse. She held the waist of a woman in front and gently swayed towards a sense of liberty and peace. She daydreamed about meeting a friend who was born to be her friend, about starting a family and having a child who might take a while to know what to do with the fire that burned within him.

"The caravan gathered horses and scores of wagons, self-driven carts that whispered silently as if they didn't have engines. Everyone talked about what lay ahead, their problems and how they would be solved.

"And she met that friend, a man who said he had dreamt of her all his life. Her eyes were a comfort and a feast to him and he told her, 'If you are with me I have my West.' He talked about the Black Dove and that she looked like she possessed it.

"'I've held it,' she said.

"'They say it grows everywhere under the western sun.'

"With her head on his chest, she whispered, 'I want to go to the ocean.'

"The land was bigger than anyone knew, and they crossed a pitiless desert. A horse broke free from a wagon and they watched it run till night fell.

"She swelled through the journey and had a child who immediately became their hope. They loved that boy and yearned ever harder for the land of lemons and flowers. Stories abounded about this western world, about a valley where ease was made. Fantastic inventions and ready-made friends, and work that involved no labour.

"They said that children had machines which took them from here to there faster than feet could dream. Light and words could be sent through wires, and medicine lifted people out of their bodies up to cities in the clouds.

"At night they rolled past the moonlit carcass of the horse that had broken free. Its nose had been bitten by a snake. The woman stared ahead, and the land beneath the moon looked white as an empty page.

"Many of the horses began tiring and the chatter and stories stopped. A fever began to spread through the caravan, and the woman, weak from bearing the child, was among the first to suffer.

"She had visions of a crab, a cancer that fed on hope. Oliver. It was a murdering . . . indiscriminate crab that mocked their dreams and ambitions."

His father stopped. His voice was trailing off and he chose his words more slowly.

"They put the woman among the other ill, in a wagon

separate from the rest, realizing that the fever spread immediately from touch. The driver of that wagon grew weak.

"The man visited her, carrying their son, whenever the caravan stopped. He and the baby both ached to be with her.

"'Please don't bring him near. You both have to be strong,' she said.

"People began to die.

"The driver collapsed in his seat and they didn't know who would replace him.

"'I will drive,' said the man, but with all her strength the woman said, 'No. You have our son. He didn't choose to come into this world, and we have to make it better.'

"The only hope was for the healthy to ride ahead. To find answers and help from the valley of inventions.

"The fastest horses were fitted to the other wagons, and the ill were left behind.

"'I want to stay with you,' said the man. 'Death only hurts people who don't follow dreams. I've wanted you all my life.'

"'Your son is our dream. I will find you,' said the woman. 'I have overcome worse than this. I know I will go to the ocean.'"

His dad lay down and stared upwards.

"Did she swim?" asked Oliver.

"The man rode ahead with their son. It seemed to the woman as she watched the disappearing wagons that the curse of the landowner was coming true. 'You will get everything you want, one day, but you will choose to watch it go.'

"One of the sick had volunteered to drive the wagon, but when the woman felt it stop she knew that he had died.

"With all her might she sat up. She was the last in the wagon to move.

"The wagon cover above was completely still, and she lay back down. When she closed her eyes and slept, the crabs began to appear.

"She heard the sound of their legs on the canvas canopy and saw their shape when the sun shone through. Hundreds of desert crabs, gathering for a feed.

"She hauled her body over the side of the wagon and tried to stand on the dirt. For a moment she got up on all fours, but she collapsed facedown.

"Through her fevered eyes she saw two shapes in front of her on the ground. Beyond her reach was a desert flower, and closer stood a crab.

"The flower was the Black Dove, Oliver. The sight of it conjured strength, and sent a rush of healthy blood through her body. Memories of shaking off tyranny and knowing, in her bones, that there was always a better place.

"'I want to go to the ocean,' she said.

"The crab came closer to her face. 'A long time ago,' it said, as it reached a claw to her cheek, 'this desert was the ocean.'"

Beasts

1

NEIGHBOURS SAW A kid, a young guy, maybe a teenager. Handsome. One said his clothes looked weirdly old-fashioned, baggy dark pants and coat, wore a beanie or a watch cap.

The woman was making her morning coffee. Nine o'clock. Saw herself in the mirror in the kitchen and didn't think she looked too bad.

It was only last week that she felt she could breathe again, first time really since giving birth. A proper schedule now when the baby had a morning and afternoon nap, a chance for her to shower, watch something, sleep without a mouth on her.

Even from the knock on the door she knew she had to help him. She could just tell. A soft knock like he wasn't selling anything.

"Hi," she said, not expecting a kid. She corrected herself in her head. A young man. She was holding her housecoat closed.

"I think I used to live here," he said.

"Really?" She had bought the place five years ago from an old Serbian woman who said her kids were grown. Lots of Eastern Europeans who moved away. Babic. No. "Mrs. Babovic? Was she your grandmother?"

"I lived in this neighbourhood."

Something strange about him, for sure. His accent or his eyes. Beautiful eyes. Like she was on a slide, just looking at him.

"Are you visiting?" she said. It was a school day.

"I'd like to visit."

"Would you like to come in?"

"Yes."

He took off his watch cap. Someone in a movie. A strong kid working on an old ship, an orphan, maybe someone she had a crush on when she was a girl, a silent blue-eyed boy. She almost touched his face.

"What's your name?" she said.

He held his cap in one hand and gently reached for her wrist with the other.

"Amon."

A sharp or a burning feeling.

"Ouch," she said. Pinpricks of blood came up where his fingertips had been on the soft side of her wrist. "That wasn't very nice."

"I know you," he said. He reached for her wrist again, and this time she got used to the pain. Settled into it. A too-hot bath that becomes just right.

She had a baby because she wanted those eyes. That white so pure. Kids help everybody start all over again. The longer he held her wrist the more she felt she knew him. He didn't deserve it. Something terrible had happened, and he didn't deserve it.

"I have a baby upstairs."

"I can smell," he said.

"We can spend time together while she sleeps." She took his hand and led him to the kitchen. The burning again from the touch. She'd never had this feeling before. A little ill. Trusting so immediately, but knowing she shouldn't. Maybe once. But that was romance. "I'm making coffee. Would you like some?"

"No, thank you."

Too young. Her fingers left a smear of blood on the mug.

Thirty-five was the year everything changed, she thought.

She hadn't been prepared for that. A midlife crisis was supposed to be in the forties somewhere, but here she was at thirty-five feeling like a teenager. Wanted to quit the firm, go into private practice or just travel. Single moms are tough as nails, but she felt herself swooning into some kind of softness. Maybe it was just hormones. She forgot about him for a second, and when she turned he wasn't in the kitchen.

She sat out in the living room with her coffee, and he leaned back in the armchair across from her.

"Do you like this or is it not your kind of place? Maybe I shouldn't have changed it."

He looked around with those beautiful eyes. When they pointed upwards she liked them the best, the white so clean it was almost blue itself. The essence of *looking*, the innocence. Kids aren't shy about staring.

Was she blushing?

"You know, when I think about it, I feel like I know you, too," she said. "Maybe there were pictures of you that a neighbour had."

She had done a lot to the house since she bought it, but there was a lot she still wanted to do. Paint the dark trim upstairs. Put down lighter floors, birch or white oak. Restless hours when she wanted to do so much but the days just drifted in a haze of milk.

"Where do you find these clothes? Vintage like that. I *love* those pants." Wool, dark blue or black. She leaned forward to look closer and her housecoat opened.

"How old are you? Thirteen? Fourteen?"

"I'm old," he said. His hand was on the back of hers as she rested it on his leg. That soothing pain again. More understanding. More blood. I've never felt closer to anyone, she thought. She saw him scared at night, holding up a knife, now brave, not wanting to fight but able.

"You've been through a lot, haven't you?" she said.

He didn't seem sad about it. How can he have seen all that but kept his eyes so clean.

The past few months she'd felt a lot of confusion. Getting up every two hours to feed her. So dreamy sometimes, not knowing night from day, being awake at four in the morning like she hadn't since university, dozy but also being *really* awake, looking at the world, thinking about all the hours she should have seen, wants to see, so much life already wasted. Couldn't go back to work in two months, no way. Clear moments, and then back to the blur.

She had a sip of coffee.

"Do you want to sit on the couch?"

"Yes, please."

So quiet at this time of day, all you heard was nosebreath and sighs. The sound of their clothes settling on the upholstery. He sat up next to her and didn't mind when she ran her fingers through his hair, just stared forward with that smile, not quite a smile, that look of sweet contentment.

"Your mother must adore you."

"I don't remember."

She could see a blank space where his mother should have been. There should have been all kinds of friends. She tilted her head and kept looking at him.

He was a place to visit for a second, the room disappearing entirely. A forest on a hill where there was constant danger but good people who protected you. Dark and deep. She wanted to be saved by him. Build some kind of a den or a cottage and wait for him to come home. Go on trips to unmapped lakes.

"What do you want to do?"

"I'm hungry," he said.

She kept dreaming. Beautiful darkness that would never get old. You'd never quite get used to it. She sat up straight and opened her housecoat, put her arm around his shoulder and chest and eased him down. He shifted to get comfortable and she cradled the back of his head. Felt heavy, but those eyes looking up at her . . . Every day would be an adventure. Anticipation. I've been waiting for you all day, my love.

There were dogwood bushes beyond the porch that never changed, a pretty green in winter. Sweet kiss when he first put his lips on her nipple, and then a sting. He closed his eyes. Gold and cream.

Everything hard in the room began draining. Water in the plaster mix started sweating from the walls, glue from all the furniture. A tropical swell. Rains coming. Tears in his eyes like an alligator's.

Let it come, salt, then milk, then blood.

She cursed at the bite at first, like she sometimes did with her daughter. She wondered who he was, how he could have ended up with his mouth there. But he was fastened. Jaws clamped. He took out his knife, reached into her chest and held her heart like wet velvet.

What it would feel like when he came home. All the waiting over. The deepest touch. No more worry about the future, what the world would be like for her daughter. Unimaginable comfort and excitement. He squeezed her heart and the world went dark.

His jaw started moving. A car drifted past and he felt the light in the room changing. Darker clouds or daylight blowing and a tick, tick, tick of the furnace. The baby monitor lit up and he heard the baby stirring. Calm sounds as though she might drift back to sleep.

Neighbours saw him arrive but no one saw him leave. Like a golem. From the earth and back to it. Fearfully and wonderfully made.

2

THE DAWN BROUGHT a day of beasts and dark miracles.

Oliver had dreamt about the girl in the story. Most of the time he slept badly or had nightmares, but every now and then his sleeping mind was good to him. Dreams of kisses or punching Murdoch back, being able to fly just a little higher than everyone's head. Last night the girl in the story didn't die in his dream, like she did in the desert. She jumped from a ship when she was twelve and moved in across the street from Oliver. Coolest girl in the city and she waved from her window at night. He was walking with her when he woke up, hand holding hers, going to a movie where everyone in the crowd turned and saw how lucky he was.

When he got up and glanced out the front window, the neighbourhood looked different. A water main had burst overnight, and the street in front of his house became the river it used to be. Two parked cars had washed sideways down into a dip where they filled with murky water and the street was drowned until the people from the city came and closed off the main.

The water was draining when Oliver walked to school. He imagined it as a visitor, coming up from wherever it sprang, searching for things in this upper world to take back down with it.

When he got near school the good feeling from his dream

was gone. He began to move quickly with his head down, as he always did. If he ever heard his name called he ran, expecting to be chased.

But the sidewalk and main gate were strangely quiet, and he couldn't help lifting his eyes. A crowd of kids, parents and teachers, standing near a tree looking upwards.

He thought about going straight inside the front door, but he was curious. Trying not to look at anyone, he made his way to the crowd and stared up into the tree like everyone else.

"It must have flown from the zoo."

"That's not from the zoo. I know every animal at the zoo."

"Is it a crow?"

"When have you ever seen a crow that big? It's a condor."

"That's not a condor. You don't get condors downtown."

Oliver had trouble seeing it until it moved its head. Deep within the branches of the spruce tree, dark against the trunk, was a bird that stood as tall as a teenager. Oliver pushed forward.

The bird had blue-black plumage and yellow eyes that seemed to pierce all human nonsense. It had an upright stance and muscularity, a gigantic, dark nobility, as if an eagle, human and raven had conspired to raise the perfect prince. It was big enough to lift a child with its talons, and was clearly looking for a meal. Aside from their questions about what the bird was and where it came from, almost everyone beneath the tree was quiet.

It began calling. Oliver watched its throat move, and its hooked beak opened, but no sound came out. It did this repeatedly and looked around as if perplexed by its own silence.

"It's quiet," someone said.

Oliver made out Murdoch in the crowd and thought about slipping away. Something about the bird made him feel safe—a strange comfort in knowing there were eyes that could humble a bully.

The bird looked down at the crowd, aiming its yellow stare

at a girl with a white pom-pom on her hat. Its entire body became
intent on her, and it continued to scream silently.

People covered their heads when it dove through the
branches, gasped when they took in the scale of its wings.
Oliver heard someone scream, "No!"

The bird flew away with the girl's white hat in its talons.

"I've never seen anything like that," said Hornby, the science
teacher. "No idea." He looked down at the hatless girl. "It must
have thought your hat was a rabbit."

Oliver could still hear the bird pumping its wings. He
watched it against the grey sky. Massive. Imperial. What call
was trying to escape it.

He kept staring as people made their way to the doors.

As he looked up he felt whiplash in his neck. He turned his
cheek in time to keep his nose from hitting the ground.

"Bow to your king," said Murdoch.

HE FELT, AS usual, that something would happen after
school. Kept thinking about that dark bird circling in the sky,
stared out the window through class and imagined it as he sat
behind the tarp after the final bell. The paper clips of the lockpick were good for cleaning his nails, and he thought of talons
with his eyes half-closed.

The janitor let himself into his storeroom unexpectedly and
made Oliver jump. The steel of the bucket he sat in made a loud
noise, and the janitor pulled back the tarp.

"Hello," he said. "How did you get in here?"

"It was open," said Oliver.

"But I locked it. I know I did. Are you the one?"

"No."

"Stand up out of that bucket. That's no place to sit, it's horrible. Are you the one who opens this door all the time?"

"I don't have a key."

"Well, you can't be in here. You'll make yourself sick with these fumes. What are you hiding from?"

Oliver was quiet.

The janitor stared at him. "Way I see it, this is the worst room in the world. But you stay if you want."

A door banged in the hallway.

"Or there's a way out where we take deliveries. You know that door? Through the basement and up the other side. No one will see you."

Oliver got up and walked close to the wall in the hallway. He saw a few students at the end wearing gym clothes, and he hurried to the basement stairs.

Murdoch always played basketball or hung around the gym with his friends until at least four thirty. The clock in the hallway said 4:35.

Furnaces in the basement were burning and shouting and made Oliver walk more quickly. When he pushed out into the cold he looked up and the sky was dark. Freezing rain. He stopped and searched for the silent bird.

Heard his dad giving him advice on how to be calm.

Think of a kind giant, and his favourite pet. I'll be your giant.

He walked his normal route and defied the rain. Some of it came down as snow. The girl in his dad's story walked next to him, her face like the girl's in the window across the street. He gave her a red coat and tried to remember that feeling from his dream, how soft and electric her hand felt.

"My dad said your mom used to hit on him," said Murdoch. "Getting drunk in our basement. Whole bottle of vodka to herself and rubbing her crotch on his leg." *She's a drunk* is what he kept repeating.

Just the two of them months ago, out of breath on this corner in daylight. Oliver had to lie down for a while on the sidewalk.

It was the shame of it. Of being punched and picturing her like that. Dogs run for shame when they get knocked by cars. They don't run home. They don't know what happened. They just run to some safe corner where they try to figure it out.

He felt an artificial courage with that huge black bird in the sky. Justice circling up there, eyes with a smarter view of this world. One day people like Murdoch will get beaten by something bigger, by the people who they beat on. Stories told him so. He clenched his fists in his pockets and headed for the busy road.

"Hey Mickey, don't walk alone at night," shouted Murdoch. "Out with the drunks and bums."

He felt something hit his back, a basketball, and he stumbled. Murdoch was ten feet behind with Jonathan and Carmine, the three of them picking up their pace for a bit of easy sport.

He ran without looking back. Without looking to the side, without thinking.

A bus clipped his backpack as he ran across Annette Street.

FROM THE TARMAC, he looked back. Murdoch held his arms out to hold his friends as they stared with open mouths.

The bus hadn't stopped.

Oliver's head had hit the street, and he felt dizzy.

He got up in the middle of the road and cars slowed down.

A woman shouted, "Are you all right?" and Oliver started running again.

He could hear the boys laughing.

Up the road he saw stores and other people. The dizziness made him trip.

He did it without thinking.

The door was on the corner and the store was always open.

More pigs with the faces of people hanging from the ceiling.

The stuffed head of a deer with fangs.

"WHERE'S OUR FRIEND?"

"Is he your friend?" asked the man.

"Mickey!" said Murdoch from the door.

"When is his birthday?" asked the man.

"Today!" said Murdoch, laughing.

"Get out of my store," said the man.

IT WAS DARK in there. A dim old lamp on the counter by the cash register. The walls covered by objects in deep shadow. Animal heads and street signs. Glass jars on wooden shelves.

Oliver leaned against a counter, feeling wet.

"You'll be all right," said the man.

He had locked the front door when he pushed the boys away.

"Sit up here and let me look at your head."

He led Oliver to an old wooden chair and turned on another lamp behind him.

"I'm going to take your hat off. You're bleeding."

Behind him the man stared at his fingers with Oliver's blood on them. He rubbed them together slowly. He disappeared and came back and, gently, he pushed Oliver's hair aside to try to find the cut.

"It's not bad," he said. "Heads bleed more than other parts because they want us to attend to them."

Oliver found his bearings and looked around the store. Each of the pigs hanging from the ceiling had a similar woman's face. On the wall above the door was a gigantic lobster, its claws pointing downwards.

The man could tell Oliver was looking at it.

"Lobsters never age," he said. "They just keep getting newer. They slough off their exoskeleton and get bigger, and the bigger they get the more attractive they become. The more powerful. They can live like a boy, forever. It's not alive, if that's what you're wondering."

"Was it real?"

"One of the biggest ever caught. Forty pounds. As long as a child. A smaller child than you."

The man poured liquid from a bottle onto a piece of cotton and swabbed Oliver's scalp.

"Are you selling it?" asked Oliver.

"It was probably a hundred years old. And if it had never been caught . . . who knows? Everything in here is for sale."

The man took Oliver's hat to the back of the store. He dabbed the blood with a Q-tip.

Oliver gingerly reached behind his head to find the cut, but couldn't feel anything.

"Your head is fine," said the man. "All healed." He knelt in front of Oliver and put the wet hat on his lap.

The man wore a pair of thick glasses and the light made it hard to see his eyes. They seemed wide apart and bright, and his gaze was a bit off-centre, as if he was blind or too uncomfortable to look directly at Oliver.

"I want to give you something," he said. "You were obviously fast, to outrun three boys."

He went to a shelf and came back to Oliver. "This is a cheetah," he said, holding up a small figurine. "The perfectly designed running machine. Do you know that a cheetah's back paws stretch forward to its head as it runs? Imagine having that eagerness. But everything can be better, you see."

He held the figurine closer to Oliver. "I made this one. It's just a little longer than a normal cheetah. A little narrower, a little more perfect. So it would be even faster, you see? Put it in your pocket."

Oliver got up.

"Those boys are gone," said the man.

"How do you know?" asked Oliver.

"I can see."

He took his glasses off and handed them to Oliver. The smart lenses showed footage from cameras of the nighttime street in front of the shop. Snow and rain falling, no one on the sidewalk. Cars were gliding silently. The man took out a phone and changed the images projected onto the glasses, other glimpses of the neighbourhood. Some place that looked like a farm in the country. People in coats walking home from work and coming out of shops. He stopped at a man who walked alone, and made the image larger with his fingers.

"Businessman. Serious." He took the glasses off Oliver's face. "Most people go through life completely unaware that what they see through their own eyes is nothing like the whole story."

3

HIS FATHER SPENT the morning writing. Half-built scenes and old yearnings. A sense of fear creeping in more these days. Paying the bills, the world moving on from the aesthetic he was raised in, organs quietly aging. Still such a fire in him, but burning on what. He wrote every day the way kids sing in the dark to keep their fears quiet. It's not real singing.

The radio was on in his bedroom, for company. All night and all day. Sometimes there was laughter or some heightened emotion among the DJs that made it seem like there really were people in the house with him, having a good visit.

He stood up and looked out the window towards the fish warehouse on Osler. Brown snow and everyone shrugging. There was a blue-and-red light in the scene in his head, warmer than what he saw out the window, but the scene was giving him an empty feeling.

Spend your life imagining people, maybe you won't know them.

A couple in a hotel room. He was trying not to feel lonely by summoning old ghosts. He wanted to write about what it had been like before Oliver was born. The story was not that the child changed everything but that everything had already changed. All the guilt he'd felt over the years for not really knowing her, either not wanting to see who she really was or making her into a character instead of being brave, being *with her*. He wanted her to be an artist, find her promise, not linger over her injuries. The drink and painkillers were in her, took hold of her, long before either of them knew it.

In those early days he had book money. The start of a promising career. Any excuse to travel and go to hotels. They had picnics on hotel room floors in different cities, and god she had a spirit. Practical hands and a shape like one long muscle. Anxious and always thinking, right *there* physically but her head somewhere else, worse as the nights progressed . . . the look of someone always wondering what was beyond the rise.

The couple in his story are going to drink champagne in the afternoon, celebrate something. A raise. No. She gets a good part in a TV show. Finally. A breakout role. Probably nothing to worry about anymore. The man says, *What do you mean, probably? Everything's going to be great.*

He needs to set the scene. She's wearing underwear and his T-shirt and the door is sealed tight to the draft.

Sometimes he stared at the words he wrote, like meaningless marks. How do they go from letters to meaning to story. Abracadabra comes from the Aramaic: *I create as I speak.* Letters are a conjuring. Mystics making monsters from incantations.

He got up again and wandered the upstairs without really thinking. Head was spinning a little. The radio hosts talked about a song. *It's not really a classic, but, man, once it's in my head it's in there. Like nothing else.*

Totally, said a woman.

He sat on his bed. Oliver used to stand on the bed and his dad would jokingly shout, *Lie down!* Gently push him backwards so he fell on the mattress. Oliver couldn't get enough of it—he could do it all day when he was three, even when he was eight or nine.

And twelve. He moved closer to the edge of the bed. What is a twelve-year-old. Most of the boys he saw in the schoolyard were bigger than Oliver. Filthy mouths. Some had incipient moustaches. All on the edge of adolescence but they rolled and jumped and ran like puppies, innocence still governing their limbs while the storms gathered. Storms he saw in Oliver's eyes when he was silent.

When he looked in the mirror he thought of that Robert Graves poem where he lists the scars and flaws of his face. *He still stands ready, with a boy's presumption, / To court the queen in her high silk pavilion.*

His queen.

Imagine if your childhood is taken away completely, how it haunts you when you age. That universal idea of innocence, not a single good memory. All your natural inclination towards love and curiosity being replaced by simple fear, and your fear creating habits, subterfuge, every day running from something. She said she would kill herself. Kept a kitchen knife in the top drawer of the dresser, in case there were intruders. *I'll use that knife one day.* Having Oliver only reminded her of the things her brother did to her. Her father.

He leaned over the banister and wondered.

Could he do it.

Falling down the stairs probably wouldn't be enough, but could he do it, dive right over, snap his neck, give up. No more worries about money, meals, dentist, every day the same struggle.

"Oliver? You home?"

The radio.

For whatever reason he always wanted to see what would happen next. He couldn't wait. Even if there was some shitty surprise or misery. Having a kid was like a constant invitation. When she left, when she was there in that hospital bed, face swollen from running at the window, he came home to the babysitter, who said Oliver had wet his bed. That he had cried all night. It could have been awful, could have raised the question of why the fuck any of us carry on: is washing sheets all I have while the love of my life wants to die. But there was something about the simple act of cleaning up, holding him, knowing we're just little animals and I would do anything to protect my boy.

Oliver was a miracle. She drank a bottle of vodka every day while he was in her womb. Six weeks premature. He shouldn't be alive.

The surge was there, and he typed.

A couple knowing that some kind of threat was hanging in that blue-and-red hotel room, city lights coming in while the day fades. Champagne becoming vodka or gin, and they start arguing because they're unconsciously afraid of something coming.

You won't keep the part if you drink too much, says the man. *You'll forget your lines. You'll get fat.*

I drink to make this more interesting, she says. *Life with a writer. Your problem is you don't know me. Spend your life imagining people, you won't know them.*

He felt the chill of standing on the edge of a fight.

Disappointment.

He sighed and closed his laptop.

Tired of his small concerns.

There has to be something new to write, he thought. Or some old belief to open his mind to again.

Something fantastic. Forget memories, realism.

The stories of his childhood, the ones he wanted Oliver to read. Back to basics. How reading got him here. The first time he saw her eyes, a shouting beggar in his heart.

He turned in his chair and talked to an imaginary Oliver.

"The story didn't end. Like I said. See. She stood up in the desert and looked at the crabs crawling over her feet. Do you know what happened to her next?"

"No."

"She lunged in her fever for the flower, took it and gathered strength. Because the flower helped her see what wasn't there. It helped her wonder.

"That's what gets lost when you get older, Oliver, the ability to wonder. When you get hurt. You stare at the desert and see things burned, no hope. But she took the flower and breathed dreams into her chest and saw that behind those rocks there were people hiding. People who were simply scared. And that the rocks themselves weren't rocks, they were piles of fruit. Peaches, pomegranates, lemons.

"Was it a time to smile? Her husband and son, she knew, were gone. Either too far on their own journey or too precious for her to put her hands on. She was cursed. She'd been ill and seen how weak she was. That for all she had wanted as a younger woman, she was just this flesh, this girl who had been through too much. She felt she couldn't help anyone. Realized all she could do was keep herself alive, and the only way to live was through visions. Maybe through meeting those people behind those rocks and trying to see things in other hidden places. So she didn't smile, but she didn't think about what she'd lost either. She chose to yearn instead of grieving, to imagine, and the force of wonder kept her looking for something, if not the ocean: something.

"The sand became scrub, became woods and the fabled valley, and she caught a train that dipped and rolled her to a city past mistakes. Past scrap heaps and twisted rebar, through the purlieus where the unlucky sold unwanted goods and sipped cancer from their taps. Down there on the platforms sat men on mobility scooters, oxygen strung through their noses, coming just to watch the trains go by.

"How small it looked, and the dramas in each of those heads so quiet from her window on the train.

"And the train travelled onwards. A girl, just like her, appeared on the seat beside her, and they rolled through pastures and a greenbelt towards the city proper, deeper into the valley. 'Look at those horses,' she said.

"Black and brown horses whose sweat made them shine. The horses ran next to the train down city streets and she felt them in her blood, felt herself on their backs as they got hotter and ran up palace steps and leapt. 'Horses don't just run,' she said to the girl who wasn't there anymore. 'They can catch fire.'"

FOR TWO HUNDRED years, men like this have stood on that plot speaking the same half language of want and dissatisfaction, gonna get and got got, hands of government men and cops reaching up through the cracks and holding their ankles, and all they could ever do was squirm and kick. Streets once soaked in drink, with workers who could quote no poets.

The Peacock Hotel had been across the way for two hundred years, an inn, waystation, scene of rebellion and collapse. These men whose names weren't known to each other talked about the disappearance of Iron John and his bag of cans. Waiting for the liquor store to open at ten, one of them feeling like the iceberg was pressing the back of his eyes. Iceberg that this city crashed on, got stuck.

I'm smarter than you, he's thinking. Seen this guy every day for who the fuck knows and he's known he was smarter since he met him.

"Cops mighta took him."

He spent last night with a girl whose body was like a man's.

Police had been through John's room and gagged at the smell. Piece of rotting leather on the bed, cut in the shape of a person, and the chairs facing each other, piled with scraps, a party for who knew what.

Before the liquor store opens the sidewalk is made of thin glass. You can't move quickly or take on any weight.

"I seen him maybe two months, who knows. Cops are cleaning things up for winter. I might go in. Who knows."

They stood here squeezing fists in cotton pockets when it was minus forty. How many winters. Shouting at night with the fight in them. Courage when the moon and the float were high, calling the coyotes from their bedrooms to come and eat the rats.

Girls had disappeared at the Peacock since the Peacock opened its doors. They walked in with no dreams and got lain upon facedown, man after man after man, until they were pushed through the floor and the next one below, buried with the flowers that hadn't looked up for centuries. And boys went missing too. Lost in the stink of manhood and the stubbled costume. More and more were missing.

Part of each man here wanted to say *be careful* to the other.

Whether he was taken to jail or crushed up for gelatin on Mulock, the absence of Iron John was a warning, written in oil on the streets and the white-and-red lights of pharmacies. Take what flesh you can and feed yours.

Five years ago this liquor store was a parking lot where the girls bent over at midnight. Before that were tenements that were built to fall down. Matchstick studs and walls of paper. Everything was temporary until now and it struck the one man as some lost dance or language, those errors that brought him here. Above this store was a great white condo. What would it take to pull this down. No fire or fist would be strong enough.

Suzi walked by the two skinny men who both asked her for change. "Darling."

She smiled a little smile.

He looked at her and thought *old enough*. There's trouble tonight. Once he gets the float up.

She was still trying to figure it out, this neighbourhood. Lots of people begging, older women saying *stay in school, sweet-heart.* Her parents said the area would be full of kids her age, but most of them were younger, houses a bit cheaper because everything was rough around the edges.

Her dad was proud of buying their place. They'd been renting the old house for twelve years, and all he had been saying for as long as she could remember was *we've gotta get into the market, gotta get into the market. We're nothing if we don't own.*

And then the funny part was he'd been hating the house since they moved in, while Suzi and her mom learned to love it. Small and not much to look at on an ugly street.

They'd been living in Bloor West where all the houses were the same and it looked like everyone had been trying to do the right thing for too long.

The men watched her pass and the smart one asked the question to himself: What do you do in a world where everything's for sale and you've got no money.

He kept watching the girl. *Come back in an hour and I'll charm you.*

"I fuckin dare you to come back," he said.

The stupid one said, "No! Come on, man. That's just a girl."

SUZI'S PARENTS PUT her in soccer and gymnastics and swimming and guitar, and the swimming she stuck with until two months ago. Practices every morning, summer evenings too, and a meet on every weekend. She had a crew of friends who all lived the same life, everyone's hair turning green from the chlorine and their ears always full of water.

At her old place she had the swimming friends and the neighbourhood friends, the kids of her parents' friends, and weekends were busier than school. And then they moved here.

Every house was different. Some rundown, others pretty. Her parents replaced the numbers on their porch with letters to spell them out, trying to make it look more elegant.

It was just far enough away that she wasn't seeing the neighbourhood friends. Just enough time passing for her to ask questions she hadn't asked back then. What if I don't want to do those things. Every weekend lost to swimming, all of next summer, everyone expected to get better all the time. What if I'm not as good as you think I am.

Her dad was the one in the house to push her, both her and her mom. Hiking on weekends and brain puzzles instead of conversations. Timing them when they ran.

After she quit swimming she saw a change in the way he looked at her. Smiles not as bright, that little frown when he looked at the stopwatch.

SUZI TALKED TO Oliver on the sidewalk once. She lived across the street from him in Charlie's old house. He was on his bike, stopped and staring at her house when she came around from the back. And she was smart-looking or something that was enough to make him uneasy.

He almost took off.

"My friend Charlie used to live here," he said.

It looked like he was blaming her.

She wanted to get her bike and see if he'd go for a ride, but he looked angry. Something dark in him. He was hunching over with his arms folded, one foot on a pedal making the bike stab forward.

Where did Charlie go.

What's your name.

What do you guys do on the weekend.

She had questions but all that came out was, "I guess he doesn't live here anymore."

Oliver pumped the pedals and rode away like a kid in a movie saying fuck you. Like someone who was too used to hearing what he didn't want to hear.

At night he could see the light in her bedroom window, like he used to see Charlie's, and sometimes he thought she was looking back at him. She thought the same thing.

Her place was a two-storey row house and his was three but it felt like their bedrooms were right across from each other. Each of those houses across the street had a skinny white column holding up a little porch roof that two of them shared. Charlie used to say he could hear his neighbour snore.

"HE'S JUST STRESSED." That's what Suzi's mom said about her dad. "The move's been hard. He's not sure we made the right decision, all the money for the house. He wants you to be stronger than him, I think."

Maybe it was a reaction and not a real change in her. Maybe it was her dad's fault really. If he didn't push her she would be excellent. Before stopwatches she ran as fast as she could. When she told him she came fifth in the two hundred metres at school, he gave her that face again. Saying "That's okay" like a parent is supposed to, and clearly feeling the opposite.

"I like coming fifth," she said. "I like other people who come in fifth."

"Why?"

"I don't know. They're probably good at something else. Or they've got bigger things to care about."

She felt it when she read now, the things she chose to read and the anime she was drawn to, drawn away from. Bigger things, mysterious things, no more *Sailor Moon*. No more playing with other kids just because they were kids or because their parents knew each other.

In bed she chased that feeling. Falling first and then racing somewhere. The pressure in her brain, the cloud that told her she was a speck among small things, thrilling the heavier the pressure got, because when she lost it, when she wondered what just happened, she realized there was so much more she didn't know, so much to get out and look for.

When they moved she put all her stuffed animals in a garbage bag and her mom cried again. The bag was down in the basement of the new place, her mom keeping it just in case. Maybe some days Suzi would want to go down there and not grow up just yet, hold her one-armed teddy. Grow up however she wanted to.

The good thing was her parents were always at work. She hung out in the basement. She shot baskets in the neighbour's hoop in the alley. Streetlight making a circle around her. If this one goes in I'll make a new friend.

OLIVER DIDN'T WANT his dad to worry, so he didn't tell him what had happened. "Code Club went late," he said. "I learned to count to a thousand in binary."

He didn't want to talk anymore.

"Are you okay?"

"Yep. I met a new friend. At Code Club. I'm just tired."

Up in his bedroom, he put the figurine on his bedside table and got ready for bed. He stared at the cheetah before he turned the light off. A cheetah faster than a cheetah. A boy faster than three boys.

The next day he didn't hide in the storeroom after school. As soon as the bell went he bolted for the delivery exit, past the furnaces in the basement and out into a sunny and cold afternoon. He walked the long way around the school and found his way to the main road.

When he saw the store he slowed his pace. ALL U.R. NEEDS. He glanced sideways at the collection of strange objects in the window, the metal lobster, dead plants and guitars. Today they didn't seem so strange. The man had looked after him, given him a gift and healed his head.

Normally Oliver would be sitting in a bucket at this time of day with a tarp an inch from his nose. His dad had a passage pinned on a wall in his study: THE MIND IS ITS OWN PLACE, AND IN ITSELF CAN MAKE A HEAVEN OF HELL, A HELL OF HEAVEN.

Forget the mind, Oliver thought. It was best to be outside. Best to be out of a bucket. He opened the door to the store.

He started speaking as soon as he walked in. "Hello?" Stepped beyond the doorway. "It's the boy from last night. Oliver."

He couldn't see anyone, and felt self-conscious. Nervous. No lights were on. With the door closed, the store was just as dark as it had been last night.

"Are you open?"

His eyes took in more objects as he wondered where the man was. Lots of old books and glass containers that looked like they belonged in a doctor's office or lab. Shoes lined up on the floor under shelves, and the shelves all loaded with typewriters, porcelain figures, hairbrushes. A wet-dog smell and the must of an old man's suit.

Oliver stepped tentatively and the traffic sound faded behind him. Heard a clicking, like mice. Fingers on a keyboard. An old staircase had been drywalled over and in the nook beneath it was the counter, where the man sat with his face lit up by a laptop. There was a patch of white on the side of his hair, a perfect rectangle.

"Hello," he said, without looking at Oliver.

"Hello."

"I have a knife here." His hand rested on it. "Gravity knife. It's illegal for me to sell." He closed the laptop. "Do you want to hold it?"

He handed it to Oliver.

It was heavy, closed, no evidence of a blade.

"It was a paratrooper's knife. If you were stuck in a tree. Your parachute. You'd open this." He took the knife back gently, flicked a lever with his thumb, and the blade slid out when he held it upside down. The sound of a fight beginning. "You'd cut the lines of your chute. It's very sharp." He rested it on the counter. "You can hold it."

Oliver picked it up, afraid of the blade even though the end looked blunt.

"Oliver."

"Yes?"

"You said your name was Oliver. They said your name was Mickey. Allele Princeps." He put his hand on his chest as though he was announcing his name to someone who didn't speak English. "It's a *cee* that sounds like a *kay*. Princeps. Latin for captain, or leader, or someone in charge of his and others' destiny. When I was a boy I wanted to call myself Joe, after G.I. Joe, although my favourite was Golobulus. Leader of the Cobra-La."

Oliver looked towards the door.

"Let me see your head." He stepped out from behind the counter.

Oliver held on to the knife and tentatively pulled off his hat. He felt the man's fingers parting his hair and touching his scalp.

"It's a miracle. Isn't it? My salve. I've tested it on myself often. On little nicks. I cut my finger clean to the bone the other day. Put the salve on and watched my skin heal up like I had closed the curtain on a night's bad dream. No pain either."

He and Oliver stared at each other.

"There are times in life when you think all is lost, and suddenly a door will open."

THE STORE WAS much larger than Oliver had thought. Princeps gave him a soft drink in a glass and took him on a tour. They passed a small, dark kitchen where he had got the drink and went into a room larger than the one in front. The ceiling was a bit lower and it was just as dimly lit.

There were stacks of old doors leaning against a wall. Complete wooden and marble mantels, ornate bathtubs, chandeliers lying unlit on the floor. Enough structural and decorative pieces to build an old mansion.

"I won't show it all to you, but if you want to tell your mother about the range of goods I sell, I am open every day."

"My father," said Oliver.

"Ah. Dad does the shopping."

"No. We don't buy much," said Oliver.

"Poor, eh? That's too bad. I've been rich and I've been poor, and I far prefer being rich."

Oliver was unable to think about much besides how delicious his drink was. He stared at his glass after every sip.

"Do you like that?"

"Yeah," said Oliver.

"I made it. I'm glad to have someone to share it with."

Princeps stopped walking just as they were reaching another open doorway. "Come back to the front of the store, Oliver. There are things you will find more interesting."

In a display case near the counter were more figurines like the cheetah that was now in Oliver's pocket.

"Here's a gorilla with a friendly face." Princeps reached into the case and held up the little gorilla. "Gorillas are vegetarians. Of course they have little arguments among themselves sometimes, but they are very gentle souls. Why do they look so mean? Why the fangs and frowns if all they eat is salad? If gorillas had friendly faces they would be far more popular with people. They wouldn't be hunted or threatened. You can have this one."

Oliver thought about having no money. "I can't . . ."

"Of course you can. You can have any of these little animals. No one wants to buy them."

Oliver looked harder at the array of figurines. It looked like a miniature zoo, but when he looked closer there was something unusual about the gathering. Exaggerations here, reductions there. A snake with arms.

It seemed more fun than a zoo.

"Did you make them?"

"You would be surprised what I can make. Leave the knife on the counter and you can come back and play with it anytime."

EACH DAY AS school ended, Oliver faced that choice. Sitting in a bucket or running to the store. Princeps was a bit weird but he seemed generous. Friendly. He made his own soft drinks. A man who created. Oliver's father would like him. His dad had drinks with guys like that all the time, regular drinks with friends once a month who were all borderline failures but who made things. He hadn't told his dad about the store yet. If he ever had to tell him where he really was after school, it was better to say he was in the store than in the janitor's closet.

An old-fashioned bell rang above the door when it opened.

"Why do we keep things from our parents?" asked Princeps. "If our parents knew everything, they would own us. We would be no different from them. There would be no future if we all stayed the same. Do you love your father?"

"Yes," said Oliver.

Princeps looked beyond him. "I'm glad to hear that," he said quietly.

For a week Oliver spent an hour or two there before walking home. He could feel uneasy at times. Weirdly tired. The dim light made him trip or walk over things, and if he stood among some of the narrow shelves it was impossible to see beyond them. The shelves weren't arranged in rows, so if you were led by your curiosity from a toy to a book to a bizarre little skull it was easy to end up feeling trapped for a moment in a maze.

"That's a squirrel's skull," said the man, coming out of nowhere. "It's yours for two dollars."

He usually sat on a stool by the counter, in front of the computer that was brightly out of place. He stared and typed and seemed oblivious to other things, until he would suddenly appear and announce the price of an object. Oliver wandered and asked questions, and whenever he went deeper into the store the man stood close to him. Noises from somewhere distant, the basement or back rooms, like angry cats or raccoons fighting.

"This was actually two old houses, joined at the back across the alley. Where we're standing, here, used to be open to the outside, but it was closed in years ago. My family home. I lived here as a boy."

They stood among the piles of doors and scattered chandeliers, the bathtubs and pedestal sinks.

"Who buys this stuff?" asked Oliver. "All the doors?"

"Anyone without a door. I get builders, people fixing up their houses. There's nothing strange about it. There are old houses in the neighbourhood, and people like these old doors and things to help them pretend that they can bring the past back. Make it better."

On one of the walls was a massive chart with illustrations of all kinds of hands. Human hands, ape, monkey, pictures of fish and fins and talons of birds, circled with handwritten notes.

"I like the idea of continuity. You can look at your hands and think they make you different from a lot of other creatures. What could look less like us wise men than a fish? But that's where our hands come from. Hands that made tools which have helped us to believe that we have nothing in common with fish. I like these ones here, the hominins. Big changes came there. Our hands themselves became tools with the longer thumbs. Clever ancestors liked bone marrow, you see, and their hands changed slightly so we could be better butchers. And it has always got me wondering what changes might be next for us. When our hands keep reaching for the things we want and trying to understand, the blind seekers in us, these paths from our brains to our fingers." He held up his own like claws. "Always wanting new things, aren't we." He glanced at the doors and chandeliers. "Some of the old things too."

The store was quiet unless Princeps was chatting. Oliver never saw customers. He paused before he went into the store and looked at the window display. Why *would* anyone want to come in, he wondered.

"People come in when they need to," said Princeps.

"I can tidy it for you. I could put new things in the window."

"You're very kind. Very well raised. Do you want to work?"

"I could help you."

"I don't want you changing the window. I don't want you changing anything in the store. But you could do some things that would help. I actually have three boys, but they live in the country. I miss young people during the week, you see. Perhaps if you did a few things around here, I could talk to you. I could pay you, in fact. People can be kind, Oliver, but it's always best if you get money out of them."

At the end of the week, Princeps gave him twenty dollars from behind the counter. Seemed like a lot. "Tell me what you are good at," he said. "You're obviously good at running. You are thoughtful. Not the tallest boy in the world. What are you good at?"

"I don't know."

"Come on, now. Modesty is old-fashioned. Boast a little."

"I can make things. I made a lockpick."

"Excellent! Show me your lockpick."

Oliver reached into his pocket. "I made it from paper clips."

"So you are cunning. You know how to find your own way into places."

"I can imagine things."

"Fools can imagine things. Billions of people imagine they will be saved by kneeling to certain gods. Do you admire that?"

"I don't know."

"Do you imagine the right things?"

"I did a drawing of a motorbike with no wheels. Like a hovercraft. It takes in air and it blows it downwards so it floats."

"That's the spirit! Transformation! Bring me the drawing. There is nothing that cannot be better, Oliver." Princeps stepped closer and stared at him. "I thoroughly believe that everything will be better one day soon."

EVERY NOW AND then a sound from deep within the house made him look towards Princeps, who never appeared to notice. Oliver looked over the bookshelves. Ratty paperbacks and medical books. *A History of Snakes*. More stuff about lobsters.

A pile of papers lay perpendicular, holding up a row of books, the edge of the papers wrapped by cardboard or thick brown paper, titles handwritten in pencil.

The Holland Marsh.

The Tale of Allele Princeps.

"That's me," he said, over Oliver's shoulder. "That's my story. Work in progress."

He took the papers off the shelf, as if he was keeping them from Oliver. None of his business.

"My dad's a writer."

"I'm not a writer. I just need to tell my story. Some of my secrets, for people like me to hear. Everyone has something to share. No? I sense your modesty again. I bet you think you haven't lived enough to tell a worthy story. I'd read anything anyone had to say."

He smiled at Oliver and folded his arms across the papers.

"You can read anything you want from the shelves."

Oliver did sit and read for a few afternoons. He found an old leather chair whose arms were cracked and scaly, a lamp above him. It wasn't unlike what he did with his dad at home, but there was something about reading with a stranger . . . he felt more curious about what Princeps was reading on the screen, more self-conscious about his own book. He read *Black Bolt*, and worried it didn't seem grown-up enough.

He caught Princeps staring at him.

He showed him his drawing of the hoverbike and was surprised by how absorbed Princeps became. He took a pencil and said, "Can I?" Drew lines with comments and calculations. *Titanium engine?* "Do you know there's a metal called microlattice? It's strong, but light enough to balance on a dandelion. That's what you'd want to make the frame out of. Or aerographite. Have you heard of that?"

When Oliver said no, he caught a look from Princeps. Not disapproval, exactly. A look that made him want to learn what the man was talking about.

"I want to consider your drawing longer. Make more notes. This could easily fly. It's all about preparation, isn't it. Knowing everything that can go wrong, so you can always avoid it."

HE WASN'T THERE one day. The store was open and dimly lit as usual, but when Oliver called for him all he heard was the boiler, something banging in the basement. He took a few steps, put his fingertips on the glass counter. Looked around as he went deeper and started to feel nervous.

Part of him got excited when he stole stuff from the Dollar

Store. He could take anything he wanted from this place. Princeps didn't know his last name or where he lived. The gravity knife was on the counter.

When he left the store he watched a teenager walking a dog. The thing about having stuff, knives and toys, was you needed someone to play with.

"I was in the country," said Princeps that Wednesday. "Seeing my sons. Tending to things." He gestured at a pair of muddy boots near the door. "You can come in here whenever you like and make yourself at home. Come here with your father."

"Don't you worry about things getting stolen?"

"No. It's the people who are valuable, not the things they might take."

He gave Oliver a drink.

"I like repopulating the place. I never thought I would come back here, to this house. I left when I was around your age. It's full of bad memories." He was smiling. "I have ways of forgetting, you know? Are there tricks you have sometimes for not seeing what's in front of you?"

OLIVER LOOKED AT his hands while he sat in his bedroom. Imagined the weight of the knife. Paratrooper cutting himself loose. Landing on the ground and ready to fight at close quarters. He squeezed his fists and made his body tense. His jaw. Like when he thought about fighting Murdoch. Whole fights played out while he was showering or cleaning up his room, he could feel them in his bones and teeth, grabbing his neck, eyes getting wide. *I'll fuckin kill you.*

His hands looked small.

On his desk were photos printed from the internet of seabirds that had died from eating plastic. Bottle tops and Playmobil wigs they had swallowed thinking they were fish.

He had to do a project on the environment. Every year since

kindergarten they had to do something like this, some kind of presentation acknowledging that everyone was going to die soon, the earth was going to burn, unless we changed. Pictures of actual mountains made from garbage in India. Coal stacks and lithium flats, kids harvesting computer parts from poisonous landfills. These pictures caught his eye, shocked him, the birds dead and greasy, little piles of plastic where their bellies once were. If a clown had a dinner party—some maniacal clown with a few clown friends—that's what he would put on the table, an albatross murdered by toys.

He didn't exactly picture himself saving the world, but he liked the idea of making something, doing something, fighting. Or figuring out a way not to fight. He didn't really want to kill Murdoch. Just wanted him to leave him alone.

"WHERE IS YOUR mother?" people asked. Teachers, before they knew the truth. Family friends who hadn't heard, and all the clerks in stores who found it strange to see Oliver shopping on his own. Those old men on the corner who whispered at the moon.

"Where's that lady who held your hand?"

"You look a lot like her," said his dad. "In the early days when she smiled I felt like everything would be fine. Just fine."

There were songs and sights that made Oliver remember her and he forced them out of his head. Made himself sing other songs, twitch his muscles, think about other things, never getting rid of that feeling she was behind him.

People talk about how important mothers are. Everyone has a mother. You know moms. They'll always be there for you. They feed us and make us grow and hold us with undying love.

Earth mother.

Glassy eyes and swollen. That was his real mom.

Complaining. Scaring him. At night when she cried on the other side of doors, when she came into his bedroom with a wet face and asked over and over if he loved her. He didn't know that person. Like she was possessed or someone had stolen his real mom. Crying about what she could have been, how much better she could have been, how she'd be better tomorrow, you'll see. Oliver trying to be good for her, do a chore or say something right to make her happy.

If you loved your mom and your mom loved you, you wouldn't be afraid of her. That's what he was remembering. He was afraid of being held by that person at night. Afraid of her being mean those times, just randomly mean, like when he showed her a picture he took and she said, *That's crap.* Mumbling around and pushing him away from the toaster when he tried to make his own breakfast.

Murdoch called him Mickey because that's what people called the bottle of vodka she carried. Bringing it in her purse to parties, trying to dance with Murdoch's dad. It wasn't Oliver's big ears or being scared like a little mouse.

Mickey waited at school because she forgot to pick him up, his teacher getting angry. He sat on a summer curb with a headache, the smell of hot tarmac making his head worse, or better, some kind of poisonous comfort, waiting for her to come out of the bar behind him. The one on Dupont that he crosses the street now to avoid. She gave him a bag of chips to eat while she was in there, and when she came out she walked behind, a vampire in the daylight, frowning and slurring, *Go on. I don't like the look of you. Go on.*

You can count rocks and sing songs to yourself while you sit there, pretend your feet shoot lasers at the gaps between cars. You can imagine a real vampire walking behind you and think of yourself as brave. *Don't look at my face.*

Oliver couldn't tell his dad that he was afraid of what was in his blood, because his dad was in his blood. But his mom was in there too.

AWAY.

That old lady shuffling along the block, her face black and cracked like an old bull's knees, sixty, seventy, eighty, who knows: she was someone's daughter.

Held in hands as a trophy or an apple, not put on a knee like a boy. Go out, my son, and do your worst, even unto these daughters, my own.

How you went from an apple to that, because you couldn't get away.

From the arms that drew things to you, regardless of where you stretched them. Every inch of you admired. Your eyes, your legs, your elbows, owned, by father, lover and brother, wherever you moved you were theirs.

Did you get away?

That place where you could sip from the stream and forget.

See the girl down there, now on the street, and think that could have been me. Backpack full of sketches. White hat and joyful colours, that jump in her step was just like yours, and you wonder, please, why do girls stop skipping.

That could have been you, and what will she become?

Like you she dreams of Venice. Her taste of pain not as deep as yours, the headaches you got whenever you were needed. But she still wants to know what's out there. Looking up and out while she adjusts her backpack.

He thought about getting back to his study, at least to get ideas down, but he kept watching the girl across the street. When they moved in he was going to go over and introduce himself to her parents, but who does that anymore. He remembered seeing the girl and wondering if she would end up as good a friend as Charlie was.

Everything so heavy sometimes, but look at how she skips.

Maybe she does a project at school on how it is not the sons but daughters of chimpanzees who look beyond the horizon and wonder. Who walk to rival groups and see if they can find a new home.

Maybe unlike you she will feel no shame in being liked.

Maybe it's not my business to imagine, he thought. The man looking down from the window.

All drawings and dreams go to that place, away, where the world is not like this.

"HAVE YOU EVER heard of the Black Dove?"

"A black dove?" said Princeps. "I like the sound of that."

"My dad said it's a flower, looked like a bird. Something like the first flower that ever grew on earth. It made you strong if you ate it. Dinosaurs ate it, and kids ate it. And this girl— That was part of a story, but this flower sounds real. You don't even know how it makes you stronger, but it came out of the oceans and everyone has always been looking for it. It's like a drug."

"A flower. Interesting. Do you want to be stronger, Oliver?"

"Maybe."

"Those boys who chased you. Who doesn't want to be stronger, eh? I'm not sure anyone knows what the first flower was. But you can read some of these books. Look online. Ask your father."

"I think it's just a story," said Oliver. "He tells stories."

"You never mention your mother." Princeps went behind the counter and shuffled through a drawer. He came back with a tape measure and unspooled it.

"She died. I don't remember her," said Oliver. "Just little things. She left."

"She left you?" He wound the tape measure up, holding the centre between his fingers.

"She made herself sick. Alcohol and pills and that stuff. Dad tried to look after her but she said she wanted to go, so she's gone."

Princeps stared at him. "That's not the sort of thing you read in kids' books, is it? Mothers love you forever. Or if they have to go it's because they have cancer. Do you miss her?"

"I don't know. I think I was sad when she left. I just don't think about . . . I don't remember much."

"Forgetting is an important part of survival," said Princeps. "You want to forget the pain. Maybe she wanted to forget the pain."

"What pain?"

"Of living. Not getting what she wanted. Childbirth. It's all pain. I know it. Failing. Knowing people hate you for your mistakes. Those boys chasing you. Pain. You probably want to know why she drank. Maybe there's a reason."

"I don't know."

"Does your father keep secrets?"

"He wants to tell me everything. I don't want to hear it. She left us." He didn't want to say more. He remembered Princeps mentioned sons and felt defiant. "Where's your wife? Your kids' mom."

"Oh. I'll tell you one day. She's not here either." He unspooled the tape measure again and put it around Oliver's head.

"What are you doing?"

"You're proud, aren't you. I can see it. If your mother wanted to leave, then to hell with her. I can see it." He wound up the tape measure and put it on the counter. "One can tell a lot from measuring heads. Do you know that? Predictors. The world is full of predictors these days. All these algorithms telling us what we like. Some of them are right, aren't they. Doctors would have measured your head when you were born and they might have predicted this young man standing here. A smart boy, wanting to be stronger. They might have predicted some of your weakness. Your mother was probably drinking while she was pregnant. Your head is a little small. Is that something you'd want to change? If you were stronger, what would you do?"

"I don't know."

"You have to know things if you want to be strong. What would you do? Walk taller?"

"Yeah."

"Like you're above everything? You could see things coming?"

"I wouldn't be afraid of anything."

"There are some people who are afraid of nothing. Imagine having their blood, eh? Or finding that flower." He sat down on his stool. "Being able to forget all pain. Doctors measure heads because they understand destiny. Genes are destiny. We can eat lots and get fat and strong, can't we. That's our choice. We can change a few things, but destiny is in our blood. We can't control what our parents give us, so we like to pretend that we can change everything later. So who are you going to be, Oliver? A doctor might have measured your head when you were a baby and said, 'He's going to be slow and five feet tall.' Is that who you'll be? Or do you dream of strong arms, swimming in dark seas?"

His mind was fast but he was talking calmly, sitting across from Oliver. Like he was a coach or an uncle. Like a friend.

"If you come back tomorrow, I'll show you a secret."

4

PRINCEPS GESTURED FOR Oliver to follow him. They walked farther into the store, past the room with the chandeliers and doors, down a corridor that led to the back of the attached house.

"It might sound strange, but I like to know that you've suffered. I liked hearing that you lost your mother. I have felt that pain too. The weak may not have strength, but they *understand* it. Just like the poor know the value of money in a way the rich never will. And when you have that understanding, what will you do with it? That's what I wonder, Oliver. What can you do with your need for strength?"

The walls were painted a deep blue, mottled with browns and red, sticky. Two doors stood on either side of the passage and one at the end.

Oliver had assumed that Princeps lived here, in this house at the back.

He heard a sound like the bark of a puppy that surprised him, calmed him—it made him think there was a normal home back here.

"Do you have a dog?"

"I've had many dogs," said the man.

He used a key to open one of the doors on the side and went in before Oliver. "Wait here." The sound of an alarm being disabled, louder yipping and barking. Princeps came back out.

"You probably like wizards, don't you. Werewolves and things like that. Dragons. Everyone loves dragons."

He stood with his back to the door. "When we go in, I'll have to turn the light off. Don't be afraid. It has to be dark for you to see what I want you to see."

Princeps pushed open the door and Oliver briefly saw a mostly empty room, something yanking and slithering in a corner. A chain dragging. The barking became relentless, layered, as if dogs were calling to each other from different points in the room.

Behind Oliver the man shouted, "Now, now. It's all right." He turned off the light.

The barking stopped briefly when Princeps lit a candle. "Now, now," he said again. "This is my friend Oliver."

As his eyes adjusted to the darkness, Oliver followed the movement of Princeps to the corner. The flame from the candle was just enough to cast a shadow, and the barking had changed to the sound of panting and licking. Oliver hung back and saw Princeps kneeling down.

"Good boy," he said softly.

Oliver made out what he thought was a puppy: a dark coat, standing on its hind legs licking the face of the man. Princeps turned to Oliver and said, "Come closer."

"HE'S A FRIEND," said Princeps. "My friend. Be nice."

Oliver knelt close, and by the small flame he saw dark, deep eyes, a searching black snout. The barking had stopped but sounds were filling the space like a confused conversation. Question marks, coughs, timid whines and something strong above all. Demanding.

"Put your hand to him," said Princeps. "If you act afraid, he'll sense it."

Oliver leaned forward and felt the wet nose. A sneeze. And then a tongue.

"There," said Princeps.

A puppy's tongue, licking as if Oliver's hand was chocolate. He giggled a little over the tickle, and leaned his other hand in to touch the head. He'd wanted a dog all his life.

As Princeps moved the candle, Oliver saw more. He saw the tongue licking his hand and he recoiled without thinking.

There was a bark and slight panic, but Princeps made soothing noises. In an even tone he said, "Bring your hand back. Don't let him question his trust."

"The tongue," said Oliver.

"It's forked. He can smell with his tongue as well as with his nose. Tongue of a dog and a reptile. Now he knows the smell of you. As a friend."

The tongue was licking Oliver's hand again. Eager noises grew as he couldn't get enough of the hand, and underneath them was a purring, a sound of contentment as if he was relieved to have company. With dogs you can feel like you're their answer. All their searching and sniffing, and all they wanted was you. He loved them. And cats if they acted like dogs. Loyalty and goofiness, needing affection and giving it. Savagely protective. They had all the best parts of people. And they could be beautiful. This one was beautiful. But there was something else . . . the purring, the chatter like a whisper now, the tongue.

Princeps moved the candle along the body and Oliver saw deep markings—black spots surrounded by slightly lighter lines.

"It's called ghost striping. I gave him the coat of a black jaguar."

He tried to understand. "You . . . what breed is he?"

"He's nothing you have ever seen."

A stub of a tail, wagging. Oliver ran his hand slowly along its coat, soft and loose. Scruff for a mother to take hold of.

Princeps handed him the candlestick.

"He's afraid of the light," said Oliver.

Whispers blew the flame. Something was happening here. What else was in this room. The animal was sitting up, eyes suspicious of the candle, and those noises. Oliver put his hand out towards the black chest, they were coming from in there. The murmurs and suspicions, some kind of chattering parliament, all inside that body somewhere. Calm when Oliver put his hand against the chest.

"He was half that size yesterday," said the man. "I'll show you how he eats someday. Siberian tigers grow ten feet long and eat fifty kilos of meat a day. I expect he won't be far off that."

"You said he was a dog."

"No, I didn't."

"So he's a tiger? What's he called?"

"I don't know, Oliver. I don't name things."

"Yeah, but what's . . . does *he* have a name?"

"For a collar? He doesn't need a name. Give him one if you want."

They both stayed low on their haunches as though they were looking at a discovery in the dirt.

"Does he live here?" He petted the scruff and wondered how big. "Like, can I . . ." He thought about feeding him, playing.

"Well, you're friends now. You're the only person who has seen this. And if you come back tomorrow, or the next day, you'll see changes. Like I said . . . even I don't know how big he'll get."

The more they talked the more energized the animal became. Like he wanted to be a part of it, or just wanted Oliver's attention. He leaned forward and licked Oliver's face. Stood on his hind legs and lifted the heavy chain he was attached to.

"Where did he find you? You want to play." He draped his paws over Oliver's arms and chattered again, moved his back legs as if he was dancing.

"Okay, okay."

Very sharp teeth.

"I've never seen you laugh," said Princeps.

"You can talk," said Oliver. "Can't you."

He tapped those jowls with his fingers and it bit, nibbled. Dropped the paws and it sprang back up. "What are you trying to say."

The man picked up the candle from the floor and Oliver stayed standing, holding the paws.

"Ten feet is not much less than there to here." Princeps, from the door, talked to Oliver's back. "You see? He'll be big. And like every young body he needs his rest. We should leave him soon."

"Can I see him tomorrow?"

"Of course you can. But there's one more thing. He's not afraid of the light."

He flicked the switch and blew out the candle. Fluorescent light and a concrete floor, boxes and junk in the corner.

Oliver held the paws, but his friend was gone. The chain stiff, risen and staring like a snake.

The paws were in his hand but he couldn't see them. He got scared and let go.

The chain stayed taut and barked.

"He's going to be beautiful," Princeps shouted. "The greatest hunter that ever lived."

"He's invisible," said Oliver. The barking was scaring him now.

Princeps opened the door all the way and turned off the light again, the bulb in the hallway making a rectangle on the floor. The creature stood at the edge of it, up on his hind legs and barking.

"He can be seen at different frequencies. Weak creatures that rely on their eyes will never see him coming. I want you to look at him, Oliver! Go back to him for a second, and decide for yourself. Do you want to be hunted, or do you want to hunt?"

5

THERE ARE STORIES about king cobras being able to remember the faces of people who tried to kill them. They were recognized as the smartest of the snakes, with memories and a need for vengeance.

Amon came home with pockets full of meat. The kidneys and stomach of a baby. Always a spectacle to see him rise. He ate every two weeks and shed his skin a few times a year. Coiled in the dirt by the heating stack in the basement, he slept facedown and didn't move for days. Then slowly, impossibly, he rose spine-upwards without the help of his hands, his waist pulled under and forward, knees and shins like rubber. It wasn't just a vision of him rising but of something perfect. A virus. No remorse or apology or sense of anything beyond its purpose. Click of the joints, and he walked.

Through his fingertips he delivered venom that brought on visions and paralysis, at the same time his fingers understanding the flesh he touched—its memories, the tales in the DNA of the person about to die.

King cobra. Hamadryad. Snake who eats snakes. The Naga in Hindu mythology were beautiful grandchildren of Lord Brahma, serpents who could take on human form. They became so powerful that Brahma banished them to the underworld and ordered them to bite only the evil or those who were destined already to die young.

When he rose from the basement he drifted through this neighbourhood of the weak and aspiring. Schizophrenics, junkies and professionals. The correctional service ran a floor above the old post office on Keele with ten beds for child molesters and rapists who couldn't find welcome in the local halfway houses.

He dragged his fingers along the bricks and windows of stores and knew he had lived here before. This neighbourhood was home. Leaving trails of poison along the buildings and seeing the lives that had rubbed against them. His fingertips led, like a serpent's tongue, to the Jacobson's organ near his brain, so through them he could smell as well as see whatever he touched. Neighbourhood of suffering.

AN OLD MAN named Henrik Aagard of Norwegian stock volunteered to work with the inmates at Keele. He made them coffee and understood how much they wanted to be seen as the people they could have been, before they made their choices. Some were in their sixties and seventies, many still had crimes to look forward to. He bought workboots for the younger men, the twenty-six-year-olds finishing their last six months for assault. All it took for some was a stranger like Henrik to give them subway fare, a little attention, and they could make it through the day. Not think about going to the playgrounds, the little girl they left up north with panties stuffed in her mouth. He bought them coffee and took the able men up to Mark's Work Wearhouse.

They all believed that everyone could see them. Visible for their crimes. "Pull your shoulders back," he said. "Not everyone knows what you did." The man who took a shotgun to his wife in bed, better to kill her than tell her he lost his job. Henrik didn't judge. Not really. What he did was learn about himself, about society. Where do you draw the line. Here was a building full of pedophiles in the middle of a now expensive neighbour-hood. Have they paid their dues. Kids walk by here all the time. What if they really did see what these men had done. Will everyone understand that everyone needs help.

He lived alone in that little apartment for fifty years, Henrik. Maybe he liked their stories. Lives he hadn't led. Walking on the edge of morality, or well over it, hearing what these people had done when they were younger. What they still wanted to do. "The boys are like little birds. Electric little birds." Some of them told him all about their crimes, and many pretended that all they saw was the future.

"Life is about choice," he said. "There is no such thing as destiny. You think you should turn left in your car, turn left. Doesn't matter if your body is saying turn right! You have choices. Go to work. Don't go to the schools and the play-grounds. Just stop."

He drank akevitt on the weekends, more of it than he used to. Helped with the pain in his back.

AMON WALKED THE alley off Indian Grove and then out along Dundas. He liked to kill in private. It was some kind of journey back home. Are you my mother. My father. Choosing houses he liked the look of. There was something he wanted to return to, but he couldn't remember what. Asleep for two weeks, dreams of a golden snake, a golden river poured molten down a jungle hill, cities built around it and burned, history of hunger from the world's first gut. Mothers ate their children if they didn't leave the nest, and fathers ate the mothers, jaws clamped behind her head as she rolled and rolled. Hunger that burned so rich it felt like love. In private, in their houses, he could take them apart with his knife.

The crowds on Dundas were a blur of prey. His smile was tight-lipped. Asp staring back at the beautiful queen. His feet moved, but in his mind he was gliding. Slowly. Even though he was upright he felt the movement across his belly.

The snow was here for good. Henrik was stopped with a cart full of groceries, opening the door to his walk-up over the Vietnamese restaurant. Blond brick buildings where a bar once stood, these all built in the seventies as affordable housing. The smell of the restaurant made the boy slow down.

Henrik had one hand on his cart and Amon touched the back of it.

Whose memories.

A mother with a dirty mouth. Fingernails. Walking, terrified, to a group of men around his brother . . .

The old man felt ice in his chest and throat, turned to the boy and fell dizzy. Sliding down the door and sitting on the sidewalk. Melted snow seeped into his pants and woke him up. He always wondered if there was kindness in the world. Was he truly kind.

A boy stood over him.

"Will you help me? I . . . I've fallen."

People passed by on the sidewalk and hunger burned hotter in Amon.

"I must have gone faint. I need help."

The boy took his hand to raise him up. Squeezed a stream of venom.

In Norway, Henrik's uncles took him hunting and showed him how to skin a reindeer, butcher it in the woods and not spoil the meat by piercing the bowels or bladder. There was a terrible taste in his mouth. Chemical. A flood. He peed his pants like he did in the woods. Felt sick when all those surprising reds and purples spilled out of that reindeer.

"I'm going to be sick," he said. He vomited in the snow beside his door. Tried to find his bearings, one hand on his cart. He was a little boy again, feeling like he had to be a man.

"I will be all right," he said.

People changed their paths along the sidewalk, swerving from the old man being sick. Henrik looked up. Parable of the good Samaritan, *passed by on the other side*, he thought, spitting.

"I'm cold," said Amon.

He was a strange boy. Enchanting.

"You *must* come up. Help me with these. It's warm in my apartment."

Henrik pulled the cart into the entry. Crucifix at the top of the stairs. He closed the door behind the boy and lifted bags out of the cart.

"Can you . . ."

So hungry. Amon smelled urine in the old man's pants. Cancer. His tongue tasted tumours and anthracyclines, morphine in the blood of old folks at the New Horizons Tower. He had fought with cats for the flesh of their dead owners.

"Nobody else stopped," said Henrik. "An old man . . . Take these, please . . . An old man being sick on the sidewalk and nobody stopped. Except you."

He was feeling a little stronger. Confused. The back of his hand was numb and cut but he was lifted by this kindness. Who has ever helped him like this. He led the boy upstairs, who kindly carried his bags.

"I have chocolate. And money! You deserve a reward."

Their boots were loud on the stairs.

He had been coming to this door for fifty years. No other apartments in the building. Smells from different restaurants over time. A sign with BERGENSFJORD on the door, the sign his father made with the name of the ship that brought them to Quebec. Bold boy on the prow, calling for adventure. What was that movie . . . *Titanic*. No. Scared boy. Seasick.

Heartbroken.

Henrik hesitated at the top step and wanted to speak of

things he had never told anyone. He was dizzy. All those years of listening to wretched confessions and never honest about himself. My first love was a boy like you. I don't go a day without thinking of him.

He neared the door.

The dogs.

"I hope you don't mind dogs. They're very friendly."

He had three black mouth curs, tall and healthy. Arne grey in the chops. Misunderstood, loyal as children, sweet strong pariah dogs who would quit or lose a fight. Great with kids. Henrik bought his first ten years ago, and he shouldn't have had three in such a small apartment but the walks kept everyone healthy.

There was much to talk about today.

"You'll see," he said.

When he put the key in the lock the dogs were barking. Not their usual greeting, not just smelling a stranger. A question crept up Henrik's spine as he opened the door. Something bad.

Amon had limbic reactions, movements his reason had no control over. Hissing. He dropped the bags.

The dogs were on him before Henrik knew what was happening.

Ben was hanging from the boy's upper arm, trying to pull him down, and the boy was twisting.

"Stop!"

Freya, the gentle one, latched on to the crotch where his genitals should have been. Her front paws stretched, jaw clamped, trying to pull him open. Amon put both hands on her shoulders, pulled, as if he was feeding himself to her, waited for the change in her eyes when the venom hit.

Henrik felt sick again. Like he was punched and couldn't breathe. Muscled dogs, something stronger, some fatal twitch. Arne barking as he never had, lip lifted over teeth the man had never seen. Some evil chasing him all his life. Betrayal.

"Stop! Everybody!"

He thought stupidly that if he could feed the dogs . . . the groceries there on the landing . . . everybody sit down and eat . . . He held Ben's collar and jerked it.

"Get down! Ben!"

Blood was soaking Freya's coat, down the back of her neck. Leaking from the boy's groin. Or was it Freya's blood. The boy was hissing. Squeezing Freya's neck from the top. As if he didn't notice the other dog hanging from his arm, a hundred pounds hanging over the stairs. He should have pulled the boy right over.

The dogs were drinking his blood with their tongues while they kept their jaws clamped. Poisoned blood that made a pink froth. Legs starting to freeze.

Henrik looked at the boy. His eyes were too open, showing no pain, like the eyes of someone about to laugh. Looked down and felt the numbness move deeper through his body. Freya walked with him to bed every night. He could hear her starting to cry.

The oldest had been barking all this time, waiting for the young ones to bring down the kill. Amon watched him running, up the back of the one between his legs. He tried to get his knife but there was still a dog on his arm. Reached across his chest and dug his fingers into the ribs of that dog, venom into his lungs like smoke. He felt both of the dogs getting weaker. Fangs pierced his shoulder, near his neck. His blood.

Henrik sat down on the floor in the apartment. The door open to the scene on the landing. His arms were too heavy, couldn't lift them, couldn't feel his legs. Some kind of slowing down, even when he was panicking, trying to get the dogs off . . . wanting to. Was this a stroke. He was paralyzed. The chemo drugs had side effects. The vomiting. There was an incredible pain in his left hand. Swelling like it was going to explode.

He sat completely still and watched his dogs eating a boy. Quieter now. Ben and Freya looked limp, teeth hooked onto the boy's clothes. Hanging there. Only Arne growling. He had the boy pinned against the wall, his back paws twitching and trying to get purchase on the boy's belt as he clamped on his neck.

Henrik wanted to cry, call for help, but he couldn't move. This feeling. He knew he was in trouble. Watching Arne feed on the boy. It wasn't fear for the boy anymore, or feeling ashamed of his dogs.

They were all going to be killed.

He saw the boy's neck get thicker. Those eyes wide open.

The boy started spinning with his hands on Arne. Slowly a couple of times and then rhythmically. Three dogs attached to him, bumping on the door frame and the landing walls. Like a machine, car wash, something furry and ridiculous, but the sound, the hissing. It wasn't coming from the boy's mouth, but from everywhere. Invisible wires, airwaves hung with dying dogs, wind of fire around them, cooking.

Ben got knocked from the boy's arm on the door frame and landed at the man's feet, dead. The oldest on the boy's neck closed his eyes to keep from getting dizzy. Around and around.

Henrik saw them fall.

Amon rode dead Freya down the stairs like a sled. Sunk his teeth into the big one and dug his knee into the belly as he landed.

Yelp like a skidding tire.

PRINCEPS GAVE OLIVER one of those piles of paper. *The Tale of Allele Princeps.* Said it would help him understand things. Said it was another secret and he shouldn't tell anyone. "There are things in there a boy shouldn't read. But maybe nothing should be hidden." Oliver put it in his backpack, which he kept at his feet at lunch. "I'm trusting you with it."

In winter they all ate together in the gym. No escaping to the parking lot to eat when it was minus thirty. Oliver sat at a different table, his back to Murdoch and the others, but he could still hear everything they said. Day after day, the stories building and changing. Those laughs that sounded like they were mocking something, even when they weren't. The boys who rule the world.

Murdoch and Jonathan were the oldest kids in the class. Yesterday they'd been talking with Thomas, in a way that everyone could hear, about orgasms. Who'd been jacking off for longer. Murdoch had been at it since he was eleven. He had a girlfriend, Jodie Hawkes, who was older, over on Runnymede. Almost fifteen.

Jonathan's dad was a lawyer on Bay Street, and Jonathan liked talking about the cottage in the Muskokas, his dad having dinners that cost thousands. How he overheard his dad tell someone on the phone that he had to get Russian hookers for his clients. Orgasms. All he wanted to do was talk about what they were like, egging Murdoch on to tell his stories and saying *gross* whenever he heard them.

"She makes me jack off and I put it into this little perfume bottle of my mom's," said Murdoch. "I took it from Mom and it still smells like perfume. Jodie doesn't believe that I'm, like, almost thirteen, and she's getting me to prove stuff all the time. So I'll be ready for her. It's hard to cum in this little hole. The opening."

They all laugh.

"Fuckin gross," said Jonathan.

Oliver felt them rising behind him. Ducked down closer to his table. No food left. Nowhere to hide. What was going to happen today.

He was strong as steel in his dreams, sometimes thinking he could kill them all. But in times like this, these split seconds just before something was going to happen, he knew he wouldn't do anything. Wouldn't be able to. Just put his arms up and wait for the beating to stop. Try to smile while Murdoch made fun of him. Smiling was meant to drive bullies crazy. They want you to cry.

You're sure it's going to rain sometimes, clouds dark and brown, but the storm just hangs and drifts. Rains somewhere else. The boys passed. Nothing happened to Oliver, and he breathed.

He spent a lot of lunchtime in the fourth-floor bathroom. There was something weirdly comforting about it, the smell of it. Those pucks they put in the urinals, disgusting but familiar. Deep heat from old radiators, paint dark green and thick. Dim lights. There were springs on the stall doors so they all stayed closed, and it was quiet because the nicer bathrooms, renovated, were on the lower floors of the school. Murdoch had found him in those too often.

A lot of the graffiti had been there as long as Oliver could remember. The talking penis, phone numbers, JD + SH, hearts and arrows and the private stuff that barely made sense. *Brenda smoked a razor.* Oliver came up here during class, sometimes missing as much as twenty minutes, nobody noticing he was gone. Spent as much of the lunch hour as he could in here, reading or just closing his eyes, wondering how his afternoon would play out at the store—whether he could get another glimpse of that creature that so far hadn't been explained or named.

"You are the only person who has seen this," Princeps had said. Purrs and whispers coming from that thick warm body. Puppy kissing Oliver like a friend. But not a puppy. What was it.

He looked at himself in the mirror before he went into the

stall. Looked for hair on his face. Sometimes the light in there could make the blond stuff look darker. He'd seen a teenager on the bus with hairy fingers. Seemed like a luxury, too much.

What would he look like with a beard. If he had a girlfriend, what would he do with her. Someone his age. Some of the porn he'd seen had terrified him. Penises like medieval weapons. Holes. Things even a doctor would gag at. He got nervous sneaking a look on his dad's phone, put it on private and saw this angry storm of pink and red, moans like something worse than pain. Sadder. When he got near those talks about sex, like at lunch hour, he felt himself getting nudged into a pool he didn't want to swim in. Too many bodies.

What if they were sitting in his bedroom doing homework. Would he say can I kiss you. Imagine if she said that.

He took his backpack into the stall. The papers from Princeps and his dad's old tablet that couldn't get most of the internet anymore. He'd downloaded his favourite comics. Black Bolt, King of the Inhumans. There was the newer version that he liked the beginning of:

He is a king, but he wakes in filth and darkness.

A place worse than this bathroom.

Oliver had mapped out all the appearances of Black Bolt. *Fantastic Four* 45 to 48, 50, 52, 54 and so on. The B versions in *Thor*. Hundreds of them for decades, little, what, like black pearls, those rare ones you find—Blackagar was hidden in a lot of other stories, but that first one in *FF* 45, that was one of Oliver's favourites. Those first few. He loved the old-fashioned language of them, like when the Thing was in fights. *Yer breathin on my baby blues, buttercup.* And the setups. *But now, let's change our scene for a moment, as fate toys with her many mystic human strands . . .*

Next Issue: The Shocking, Mind-Staggering Secret of . . . Black Bolt!

He's a mystery in issue 45, just someone Crystal keeps talking about. Oliver liked to see himself as Johnny in that issue, *the quick-tempered teenager* who happens to be the Human Torch. Johnny's restless, his thoughts going everywhere, and he takes a walk through midtown, finds himself in a slum neighbourhood that's going to be torn down for a housing development. And he sees her, a girl, a vision, *like something out of a fairy tale*! What's she doing in that neighbourhood?

Turns out she's Crystal, one of the Inhumans, and they admire each other's hidden powers. They meet Lockjaw, the massive dog with antennae, whose master is Black Bolt. And they go under the city to the realm where the Inhumans are waiting for the human race to pass.

Lockjaw made Oliver think about the creature he'd seen at the store. Creature. He was real. He was going to be big. Invisible. Impossible. When Oliver thought about him last night he felt special, felt he knew something those assholes didn't. A secret. A new friend or something deeper than they could ever imagine. He felt a shiver like after he peed. A thrill. He took his pants down but kept his feet off the floor.

Someone came into the bathroom. Little kid. You could tell by the sort of quiet way he moved, deliberate or self-conscious, still going through the rituals his parents taught him. Wash your hands.

If you want the full story about Black Bolt you have to go to a few different comics. His parents were royalty, and he was exposed to the Terrigen Mist before he was born. He was strong and could manipulate electrons and all that, but it was his voice that was most special. Even as a baby, if he made a tiny noise as he slept he would bring down a city, so he was locked in a soundproof chamber and learned the discipline of not speaking. A kind of prisoner to his own voice. Couldn't even grunt.

The little boy had no idea Oliver was in the stall. He rushed like he was scared of being alone.

Oliver felt warm, comfortable.

Was it two different tracks, two different worlds, one for love and one for sex. Johnny the Human Torch liking the look of Crystal. He fell in love with her right away, thought she was full of stories he either knew or wanted to know. Oliver traced Crystal's face with his thumbnail. That wasn't sex. Johnny loved the look of her, but it didn't mean he wanted to fuck her. Or maybe it did. Maybe it wasn't two different tracks, but sex was the track and love was the train. Or the other way around.

Oliver looked down at his penis and shook it. Pulled up his pants. Rested his feet on the ground for a while and stared at the tablet with his pants open. Drawings were so dark, you could just make out the lines of red in Black Bolt's prison.

He has been bound.

He has been chained.

The bathroom door was kicked open and Oliver knew them right away, those laughs.

"Let's see it!" said Jonathan. "Take it out!" Trying to whisper.

"No way," said Murdoch. "I'm showing Jodie! Make your own. Fff."

"Fuck."

Oliver could see them through the crack. Standing where the kid had been. He needed to pee again, or worse. Hold it. Hold it.

"What are you gonna do with her?" asked Jonathan.

"Today? I don't know. I'm always waiting for her at the park. It's fuckin freezing."

"Yeah, but when you see her. Do you whip it out?"

"No way! It would freeze off."

"No. The bottle. When do you show it to her? Let me see it."

Oliver tried to see them through the crack. His heart felt

like a scared rabbit in his chest. Bowels burning. Needed to go. They were standing sideways by the urinals, zipped up. That's what he liked about the stall doors all being closed—if you didn't see feet, you thought you were alone. He kept his raised above the floor and tried to stay quiet. Not a sound. Black Bolt couldn't even breathe aloud when he was punched, the sound would kill innocent people.

Murdoch was holding up a little glass bottle for Jonathan to see. "So gross," said Jonathan. Like someone pretending he doesn't want to be tickled. "Will she keep it?"

"I don't know."

"Maybe she'll drink it . . . That's so fuckin gross."

"Wait," said Murdoch.

They were quiet.

Oliver held his breath.

"Anyone in here?"

He wished he had that knife. *Brenda smoked a razor.* What does that mean. All these people coming in here to cut their thoughts into the paint. He could swing his backpack. Heaviest thing in there would have been the tablet, but that was resting on the backpack on his lap. His keys. You could stick keys in people's necks.

"You should just fuck her," said Jonathan.

"I know. I'm going to over Christmas."

They were looking in the mirror now.

"I'm not scared," said Murdoch. "She's the one who's scared. She pretends she isn't. Says she's done it a lot, but I don't know. I think I'd be her first."

Oliver couldn't see them now. Please go, please go. He knew that bottle would come out. If they heard him. They'd make him drink it. Pour it in his hair. His eyes were closed and he was willing it not to happen. Pictured all the invisible things, electrons, darkness, breathing in quietly to gather them.

"We do a lot of other things," said Murdoch. "I don't get

nervous." He sounded like a different boy for a second, younger. The opposite of what he was saying.

"I need to practise kissing on someone," said Jonathan. In a serious way. You could hear some kind of caution, or shame. Weird silence around their talk.

Oliver's pants weren't done up. He could burst out the door and run. Maybe they'd stay up. Do up his belt while he ran, leave the backpack and tablet. Princeps's story. His thighs were starting to cramp from holding his feet up.

It got even quieter, he realized. Nothing. Were they kissing. Something wet. That tap always dripped. He couldn't hear anything else. Took a little shallow breath through his nose and really tried to freeze his body.

Nothing. While he was sitting there thinking, they must have left. He waited another thirty seconds or a minute. Relaxed. He leaned forward, resting his feet on the ground and let out a sigh.

"Nowhere to run this time, Mickey."

They leaned over both sides of the stall.

Oliver jumped up and heard something crack. Did up his pants and froze, holding the backpack.

"Little Mickey," said Murdoch. "Sneaky."

"What did you hear?" said Jonathan. "Were you spying?"

"Little mouse. Were you drinking in there?"

Murdoch pulled his ear and walked him out near the sinks.

"What were you looking at?"

Oliver held his backpack as tight as he could.

"Give me that," said Murdoch.

"Hiding in the stall looking at porn. Fuckin perv." Jonathan's mouth was right on Oliver's ear.

"Fuck off," said Oliver.

"So quiet," said Murdoch. "What did you say?" He was trying to pull the pack from Oliver, yanking so he pulled him with it in jerks.

Oliver held it as tight as he could. The papers. The tablet. It was an old piece of shit that was probably broken now. *His.*

"Fuck off!" he shouted. Jaw clenched. Holding tight. Shouted as loud as he could. Cities crumbling, planet bursting.

Murdoch pushed him back into the corner of the bathroom, letting go of the backpack. "I'm tired of you, Mickey. You're always sneaking. You can't spy on people like that."

"Where you gonna go?" said Jonathan. "You gonna run away and tell people's secrets? That was a private conversation." His dad the lawyer. He pushed on Oliver's face. Pinned him against the wall and mushed his mouth so he couldn't say anything. Oliver tried to kick.

Jonathan was pushing harder on his mouth, twisting the side of his face against the wall. Like when you really want someone to shut up, or to take something back.

You could feel them thinking. A second there before the punches came. *What are we going to do with him.* This is the worst place I could be, thought Oliver.

He relaxed. They could feel it. No more kicking or swearing. Submit.

Murdoch punched him in the ribs. Didn't hurt.

Jonathan grabbed his hair with both hands and brought his head to his knee like a ball, goalie using his knee instead of his foot. Let go and send that thing flying. Oliver's head bounced up. Jonathan's knee hit the socket above his eye and Oliver heard a crack before his body gave way. Back of his head came down on the floor.

When he woke up Murdoch was saying, "Why'd you do that? He's bleeding."

The light was making noise around them. Jonathan and Murdoch were standing over him, some scene from a movie, two parents looking down at the baby they don't want.

Oliver panicked, not knowing where he was. His backpack,

keys. He sat up and saw his tablet on the ground, its screen cracked.

Murdoch was jamming his finger into Jonathan's shoulder. "I'm not getting in shit with you. I'll tell the principal you did it. Or his dad. If they ask, it's *your* fault."

"You were looking at porn, weren't you? You gonna tell on me?" Jonathan stared at Oliver. "You gonna tell?"

Oliver put his fingertips above his eye, where he suddenly felt the pain. Saw his blood.

Jonathan stood closer.

"Let's go," said Murdoch.

He watched them walk away, like a dream. This movie he was in. Parents walk away from the baby and the baby stands up. Holds on to the sink for balance. Looks into the mirror and sees he's not a baby. He's all grown up. An old man bleeding into his eye.

He hated that guy in the mirror. Remembered him from childhood, the little loser who got beaten up all the time. He turned on the tap and looked up again. Rubbed the blood into his cheek. Both cheeks now, a little makeup.

He was getting into some kind of character. Stood back and watched himself. Hiding in the bathroom. Remember how that kid succumbed, relaxed. Go ahead and hit me.

The cut above his eye was deep and he tried to hold it together. More blood squeezed out. He smiled a weird smile with the pain. Wanted to barf on the mirror. Should he walk the halls like this. Go to class. Freak people out.

Poor me.

He filled his hands with water and tried to wash his face. His dad would help him. Everything rushed in. His dad would help. It felt good to know that.

He sat down on the wet floor again with his back to the wall. Took a breath.

Teachers would track them down, Jonathan and Murdoch. Put them in a world of pain. They could be arrested, couldn't they. That's assault. Doesn't matter if it happened at school. Or is it his word against theirs. Thought about Jonathan's dad again. How would Oliver's dad help him.

I fell. Playing hockey at lunch.

His dad with an image of him as someone with friends. Days full of play and learning.

Oliver tried to remember what happened. Why did he deserve that. He did nothing to those guys. Ever. Now he had to decide if he should tell on them. It would just make it worse.

No more. Say you're not gonna let them do that again. That's enough.

He looked at the tablet on the floor, imagined taking the cracked screen to Jonathan's face. Dragging the glass across his skin. One scar deserves another.

The quiet superhero. Black Bolt sitting on a piss-soaked floor. He heard the bell ring for class and waited to be found. Blood trickled warm down his face. Come and see what they've done. Take me home to my dad.

He sat there for a while. Dizzy when he moved.

As the movie continued you could watch Oliver, the abandoned baby, float out of the school. He was sitting down but he started rising like Aladdin on his carpet. Along the ceiling, above the lockers, everyone in class now and his teacher just assuming he was in the bathroom, again, sometimes with kids this age you just don't ask questions.

He was set down outside the school in loose boots and the sun had its back turned, busy in another country. The cold entered his cut and drifted through his body. You could see that in the movie. The snow making him hurry, pick up his pace. His breath coming out like steam.

There was a place under the city. You just had to find the

door, or find someone to take you there. Go and have a long look around, learn what other people don't know. Tell your dad about it someday and impress him.

Before he opened the door to the store, some big sob grew in him like an explosion under the sea.

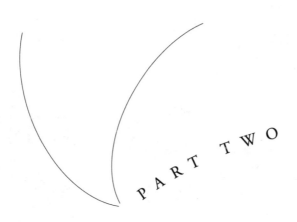

PART TWO

The Tale of Allele Princeps

1

I ALWAYS THOUGHT that spring was the great destroyer. An earth-shaker covering the ground with dirt and debris, all my quiet memories shattered by a bomb of crocuses and flies.

I believe that the world is about to change its foundation, as they say in the socialist song. *We are nothing, let us be all.*

I am writing to you quiet ones, basement-dwellers, the ones who keep reaching for the golden fruit that the rich have eaten for centuries.

The bloom is coming. A bomb.

It was spring when I played with my brother on the tracks near here, both of us escaping the teeth and nails of our mother who told us we were worthless. We had a small father, and people always wondered where Amon came from: a tall boy with black hair, a jaw growing square, a decency and a volcano in his heart.

If my brother had lived you would have known him. A leader. A captain. He showed me that the garbage beside the tracks wasn't garbage, it was either a glimpse of history or something that could be changed. He was the one with imagination, with athleticism and bravery. I was born with Waardenburg syndrome, which gave me strange patches of white in my hair and odd eyes, and my brother had a milder case: his eyes were lambent and beautiful. I did not exactly want to be like him, I just wanted to be with him. He was my hero.

Our mother bullied our father into the attic and had visitors every week. She beat us with the back of her hand or anything nearby. Her visitors gave her gifts, and she had a special laugh for them, showed a face to the world that she never showed to us.

I got migraines as a boy and was often sick. If I didn't make it to the bathroom in time to throw up my mother would hit me for the mess I made. We both went to school with bruised faces and cauliflower ears, and got into fights to make it seem like those marks didn't come from home. Somehow her anger made us unafraid of anything in the world, except of her anger. My brother was the strongest boy in the neighbourhood and our mother was the only thing that ever made him cry.

I would like to tell a tale of genius children who rose like cream, who found their calling and honoured their upbringing despite its difficulties, but my brother was lost in a red mist and I have become this thing. We were kids who played in garbage because we were frightened of our house. We played where we shouldn't have, but I believed that as long as we had each other we would be fine.

Some people know me as a scientist, and know the good the garbage did me. It was my playing with bacteria that led to LOBSTR. I have knelt in puddles in the woods and called for everyone's secrets.

Twenty years ago I was a junior researcher at the Genomics Institute. I studied the role of RNA in how bacteria defended themselves from viruses, and played a small role in discovering the series of DNA repeats and the mechanisms used to edit our genes.

Tools for editing life's mistakes. So many diseases are the result of genetic errors. One letter misplaced in the 3.2 billion that make our code, and a life can be ruined. Blindness, cancer, muscular wasting, children who can't stop bleeding. All of it can be cured by putting the right letter in place of the mistake. That's what those technologies were: correctors.

But LOBSTR is perfection. I am now able to change the course of a life, long after it begins, to redirect living organisms from failure to glory, regardless of their genetic makeup. I found a way to fuse the genetic sequence TAGG to my creations, so their cells create telomerase just like lobsters do. Telomerase keeps cells from dying, so all my creations keep blooming. Lobsters get killed by predators, by each other, by weather. But they don't die from within. When they die they know nothing but youth.

Imagine staying a boy forever. Always curious. Always eager. Always getting stronger.

My colleagues at the institute knew little about me. I kept my head low and worked from Monday to Sunday. Some may have whispered that I had no life, if they whispered about me at all.

EVERYONE CARRIED KNIVES when I was a child. If I close my eyes I see evenings before dinner, flashes of silver dancing all over the neighbourhood as children tried to cut some kind of opening in the air. Our mother made us sit at the table on weeknights and used her dinner knife on our arms and faces, the flat of it slapped across us if we slouched or forgot to wash our hands.

I have no memory of her eyes. No doubt she directed them at us, hot and judgmental. I must have cowered so often that I never dared look back. I never stood up to her. I tried to understand her contradictions. How she said she wanted what was best for us, and hurt us every day. She sat us on a stool and stood behind with heavy scissors to cut our hair and give counsel. She knocked our heads into place and shook us, advising us on life as if she cared where we were heading. "I won't tolerate filth," she said. She used the blades to scrape the darkening hairs on Amon's lip. "I won't clean the messes from your filthy dreams." He got in trouble at school and she hit him across the ear every day.

"They're always ringing," he told me. "I can't hear."

I think of the silver in the air and the sound in his ears as the same. He found no peace.

The trains were a refuge to us both. They were a relief on those days when she had visitors and told us not to come home. Dormant boxcars kept the rain off. Sometimes there were wardens who chased us away, but most of the time my brother and I could sit at the open door of the box and look at the night. For a while, especially in winter, we were never bothered.

Beside the tracks we found boards from old apothecaries, beer bottles from long-gone railway workers, a comb that he said was old. "I bet we could build a new city just with stuff that's thrown away," he said.

We found shirts, pants, dresses, some of them tangled in bushes or soaked deep into the ground. We pulled them up and laid them flat, and imagined people stripping down and running away from their lives.

He never made any promises about looking out for me forever. In fact he said the opposite. "I can't always be there for you." But if other kids pulled out knives when they fought us, my brother pushed me behind him. Usually his height and presence alone were enough to end the fight.

We spread the clothes we found on the floor of the boxcar, and one evening the car jerked forward and started moving. We had been thinking of people shedding their identities, and it was as if the engineer had read our minds. We looked at each other in a way that said, *Let's see where it takes us.* Someone had decided for us that it was time to try another life.

Our mother was that thing in the sky that we all feel looking down on us, we creatures born with questions. Should I do this. Will everything be okay. Her leather finger snuffed the candle of the sun and pushed everything in our way. It nudged the back of the train and made it glide slowly through a landscape that didn't change.

The boxcar was simply being moved to a different siding and the journey was less than a minute.

It was a lesson to Amon that we couldn't go anywhere new. "This is where we'll always be," he said. I remember him watching a commuter train shoot through those yards every night, following it with his eyes till it disappeared.

I have thought for years about creating the perfect boy, and know that no matter what colour eyes and hair I give him, what height and iron bones, if there's a weakness in the genes, a sadness, he will amount to nothing.

That spring he said, "I'm not a kid anymore." He was about to turn fourteen. His hands had grown and I could tell more clearly from his face what kind of man he would be. At night in bed he said, "She makes me think about her." When she had had a few drinks, or at some unpredictable moment, she did things to us that I won't write down.

On the dark web, hobbyists have written, shared videos of their failures. I have heard moans from their basements, their doomed creations and chimeras drowning in soups of agar. Unicorn foals collapsing on absent knees, duplicate organs and stillbirths. The wicked husbandry of hopeful people.

What gene can we target to cure a broken heart, asked one.

AT THE GENOMICS Institute, at night after all my superiors went home, I gave myself the role of Creator. Genes are the first and final text, the true alpha and omega. Everything on earth, from viruses to Michelangelo, is made of the same four letters: GATC. It's how they are put together that gives the world its variety, that gives each creature its plot.

There, in that lab, I realized that I could change the story. I could make animals better. And I could create new ones.

I thought of Geppetto with his little block of wood that with some simple whittling became the boy Pinocchio.

I started with the humble mouse and worked my way up. One of my colleagues brought her cat to work every day. I played with him in the lounge and took his blood. I learned his story and could see its turns—the same long walk through this thinning garden that every creature takes.

I experimented with telomerase, and his muscles not only grew visibly, they kept growing. From a pet to a king.

"What are you feeding this guy?" someone asked my colleague as she sat with the cat in the lounge.

"I don't know!" she said. "He's getting too heavy to carry."

I had thoughts of self-sufficiency. All individuals having no need for others, no need to be carried or helped. We talk all the time about bullies, in schools, on the news, at the office. How do we stop the bullies?

We can't stop bullies. But we can give strength to the weak.

AS THE WEATHER warmed, my brother and I were often not alone on the tracks. Travellers, hoboes, drifters, people who had been discarded from the lives of others were all finding rest in those boxcars. Rest or mischief.

I was afraid of some of them. Their eyes were buried deep beneath muck and clumps of hair, and they smelled like animal truths that our cities have tried to build over. Even when they stepped out for the day, their smell remained in those boxes.

But my brother wasn't afraid.

A shirtless man drinking from a bottle said to him, "I see

you. You wouldn't know it to look at me now, but I was a hand-some boy like you there. Football. There's girls in your future. I got notes from girls saying they're dreaming of me."

"You don't know me," said Amon.

"Yeah, I see you. I know you. I'll show you parties. We have beautiful parties. You're just like me."

I had seen that man sitting on the edge of a box on a cold evening. He had long arms, skinny and weak-looking, his body covered in wrinkles and lines as though he had been written on by some mocking pen. That wasn't what my brother would become.

They talked while I kicked around on the tracks. At school we were taught about battles and grammar, and it seemed to me that real life wasn't mentioned. School was about how people ought to talk rather than how they really talked. Sto-ries of what people did on the earth, not what the earth made them do. Rocks and dirt, flowers lending colour, I wanted to understand it all, the small neglected things and what elements made the world whole. I looked around and saw Amon lis-tening intently to the shirtless man.

When we started for home Amon said, "He says at night here terrible things can happen. 'Glorious' is what he called them. 'You can learn and make some money,' he said."

Amon spat, and I copied him.

"Those clothes we keep finding, that guy says those aren't there because people bought new outfits."

"We shouldn't come here late," I said.

"I'm not afraid."

There was no warm corner in our house, no reading light or books. Our mother knew nothing except how to make people feel weak. I still believe that if you can pinch and push and belittle others according to your ignorant whim, you will have more power than any genius or hero. We lay down to the sound of her shouting at our father. We straightened our backs, even when we heard her in our sleep.

"You think you're cute," she said to my brother. "People tell you you're a good-looking boy, so you think it's true. You're not. You're a burden." She struck him after each declaration.

"Stop," he said.

"You're a weakling like your father. This house needs a man."

She buried my face in my brother's dirty sheets. "Keep your face there and heed me. Tell me you won't be a fuckin dreamer."

Knuckles and rings and daily screams that came from a bright sky in hell.

"All I do is pick up after you! Both of you! Weak little mopey faces and filthy sheets! You vex me! Get out of my sight!"

She locked us in for two weeks and then locked us out.

"I'm staying on the train," said my brother. He told me he would live there forever.

COULD GEPPETTO MAKE the perfect boy? Free from the flaws that cause Alzheimer's and immunodeficiencies, a double-muscled warrior? The difference between the Pinocchio story and what I have done is that Pinocchio had to endure a journey of terrible experiences, he had to suffer to understand suffering and he had to *learn* to be a good boy by denying his mischievous nature.

I can eliminate suffering from the beginning. Gather everything I believe is excellent and bring it to life.

Early on I looked around at all these people with advantages, with luxuries they took for granted, and how they always found a way to hang their heads. Not a world of bad genes, entirely, but I realized that, like my colleague's cat before I saved him, everyone was dying from within. Depression is the body's quiet recognition that its cells have faded and blown like burnt fireworks.

AMON RAN AWAY and I missed him terribly. I hadn't realized until then how he was my only friend. I was eleven. He was my island in a sea of misery.

Our mother had grown up in Ireland, poor, the eldest girl among seven children. She had had to be a mother to them and never had a childhood herself. All her life besieged by hot pans and clothespins, illness, dirt and needy mouths, all promise of romance and beauty smashed like the last china cup. "I want knights, not little bastards," she said. We were two boys who reminded her of her disappointing marriage.

I was even more afraid to be in bed at home. I had accidents like my brother did. She raged and tried to force me to tell her where he was. She feigned tears and said, "I only want you boys to be prepared." She locked me in the house.

My brother wasn't made for his short life in the wild.

The commuter train shot through those yards and he watched it like a star that he could wish upon.

"Please don't come here," he said. He gave me his black watch cap that he wore on cold nights, and I put it on. I kept it in bed with me for comfort.

Some nights I escaped through the living room window.

"Please. I can't look after you."

"What happens here?" I said.

His face was pale as a bone. He gave me money that I thought he had found by the tracks. Ten-dollar bills balled up in his pocket.

The hoboes and rejects lit burn barrels in the yards. They drank and laughed the wrong kind of laughter and the wardens drank among them. Everything was rising, the flowers, weeds, sparks.

"You need to go."

Everyone thought I was weak because I was young.

I see the shirtless man in my dreams still. Long arms,

knuckles below his knees, dragging a bottle over railway ties with a rhythmic tink and threat.

I heard that sound of glass in the lab, thought of ancients fusing obsidian over campfires, my Erlenmeyer flasks and beakers, pipettes calling rodents from the pocket of my coat. Over these millennia we have been setting the table for the perfect party.

I tried not to think of my brother for years. I worked hard to get where I got.

The muscles of my colleague's cat burst right through his skin.

I AM BACK now in the house I grew up in. I watch men in the neighbourhood with neck-beards pushing their children in strollers on Saturdays and women who are tattooed like sailors. New costumes and characters in the same old story. We need to put an end to it. We need to change the story.

I CLIMBED OUT the living room window wearing my brother's hat. One night I set out and did not return for decades.

I was selfish, needing my island, but I thought it would help my brother to have company. I had trouble finding him that night. There were more people than ever, and less space on the boxcars, more sparks rising from barrels and the laughter of witches bouncing off the sides of trains.

I turned and looked for my brother and the shirtless man swung a bottle at my head. I remember the dull glass thud and the ringing that my brother heard every day.

A ringing that called the weak to a state of want, gathered them like a bell and bid them to do their worst.

Amon was shirtless, like the man, and shouting. Being held back. I lay on the floor of a boxcar and tried to lift my head to understand. Someone had his boot on the side of my face. All of my clothes lay beside me. I lost consciousness again. My dreams blended with whatever my eyes took in. I dreamt of not being able to find my knife. Men lining up while I was held facedown. Pokers molten in barrels. My insides were torn and rearranged by their needs. For a long time I have heard my brother saying, "Don't hurt him," but maybe he said nothing.

He was my refuge but I've known ever since that everyone is terribly alone.

I was passed out from the pain. My brother must have seen everything, and for years I tried to imagine what he saw. What I looked like.

Amidst the bloom, the sun in the north can still seem cruelly pale. It shone across the door of the boxcar and woke me in the morning. Amon was standing down on the tracks, looking forward. A brave boy pulling back his shoulders in front of the commuter train, a burst of colour in the sky.

Night

For an angel went down at a certain season into the pool, and troubled the water: whoever stepped in first after the troubling of the water was healed of whatever disease he had.

—John 5:4

1

FOR YEARS OLIVER'S dad took comfort in the phrase *I've known love*. He imagined it as an epitaph, like those Roman heroes who were described not as being dead but as having lived. I've known love.

Memories up there, on the shelves of his brain like trophies. First kiss soft, her face in the car window. She made strangers happy just by passing, old men who lacked beauty in their lives. The smile in her eyes. Banners hanging in every room she sat in. *You can do it.* Hair falling down from my black hat you borrowed, looking at me looking at a sky about to snow. The trophies worn from being held. First kiss soft, rubbed softer.

He was lucky to have known it.

That was his comfort as he thought of her, of her choice to leave. Wondering after she died what those rooms were like that she chose over these. She told him Oliver was better off without her. Her hatred of herself much greater than the love she could offer. It seemed hard for the world to understand how a mother could relinquish maternity. But a bellyful of poison and fear, enough bad memories . . . even the best part of yourself can look awful.

He stared at his screen.

"In the city she drank with demigods and synthetic princes, it's true," he wrote. "The sky dripped milk and everything was sweet and clean, finally. Her friends came and went and all had heads full of feathers, content. No one was a burden.

"There was a flower box on her balcony where she planted the Black Dove, and a red-and-yellow bird that visited every day. She watered the flower, sang to it while the bird cocked its head. She seasoned her food with the flower's dried petals, and looked out her windows at this world. This world. Clouds of digits and satellites pretty as stars. Every day she had virtual adventures and seldom had to leave her apartment, and over time barely recognized that days would pass, weeks, when she neither changed her clothes nor walked beyond the kitchen. Outside the flower relaxed and lay down in its dirt.

"She looked at her hands sometimes and was puzzled. Were those the hands that struck down assailants, that lifted a wheelbarrow and reached through darkness? She seldom allowed herself to reflect. She knew she had forgotten something on the balcony. Had she done the right thing? Had she been stronger than she thought when she could have found that boy, who was it? Did people have a good life without her?

"One day she found herself in a chair, wearing three sweaters. A scion of the flower stood high on a shelf in a bowl of cloudy water. A chair is where you sit and read stories to your child. The right ones shape the child the right way. Pass on your wonder and warn them about the things to avoid in the city.

"She stared up at the flower and watched her hand rise to it, shaking. 'I don't want to remember,' she said, remembering."

If you keep your eyes open through life, Oliver, or even if they're half-closed like hers, you'll get to a point where you need to see it all again, you just can't avoid it. First flower, first song, first love, first child. First bird losing its last feather to the fox who had always been there smiling.

"I'M GONNA LOOK after you," said Oliver.

He sat with the creature on the floor, holding a candle in one hand and stroking its head. Eyes black like Oliver's favourite marbles—the ones he used to defeat the other marbles, dark inscrutable planets.

"Night," he said. "I want to call you Night."

Princeps had let him go in alone. He had cleaned the cut above his eye and put salve on it. Didn't ask him what happened. He saw a silent determination in Oliver as soon as he came through the door.

"You can go in," he said. "The door's open."

He had hung blackout curtains over the window to keep the daylight out.

Oliver touched gently behind the animal's ears, which pulled back and lowered. Night licked the air and lifted a paw.

"You're growing."

The candle flickered over his coat, and Oliver could just make out the lines between the spots, Night lying down more calm than he had been the first time. Sleepy from a meal. He was a spill of black on the floor, that portal to somewhere deeper. Oliver stroked his coat and gauged the size of him, maybe the girth and length of a Labrador. Something elusive about him, fluid, the candleflame making parts of him disappear if Oliver held it too close. Sudden disquiet. It wasn't the light of the candle that made Night afraid, it was the flame.

"It's okay. I'll put it down."

He humph-growled like a grumpy man and lay down again, chin on his forefeet. Oliver petted his back, watched the eyes get sleepy with each stroke, felt soothed by soothing. *There's something in there*, he thought, leaning in towards those eyes. The way they looked at Oliver and then turned inwards.

Night started purring like a heavy cat, every now and then

catching on something deep in his chest that gave his purring a quality of thought. He wasn't just at peace, he was planning.

"Jungle sounds," Princeps said later. "Nights and soul and struggles you have never known. It's all embedded in his blood."

Not far from the chain lay tiny bones that cast a shadow.

"What do you eat?" asked Oliver.

As if understanding, Night lifted his head and licked his teeth. He panted and let his forked tongue flop out of his mouth, and then he became playful. Swatting at the air with his paw, he licked Oliver's sore face.

"THERE'S TIME FOR that."

One of Suzi's mom's favourite sayings.

Time to have boyfriends. Time to make mistakes.

"You don't need to rush into anything."

When her dad said, "You get nothing if you don't work," it didn't mean as much to her as when her mom said there was time.

Time to learn who you are.

Snow and salt and dust from the street made a crust on all the windows.

She sat in the kitchen eating toast. Glad there was time because so far she hadn't made any good new friends at school.

Out in the backyard the neighbours' cats watched each other from opposite fences. Suzi's basketball half-buried in the snow. In the alley she knew there was a shopping cart stolen from No Frills and abandoned. A blue jay to distract the cats, perched for a second on a paint can. Toys and birds and tools like someone above had tipped out a box and said, Play.

She could read a book today, use it like some magical window to climb through.

Or draw a little.

Maybe she'd been inside for too long. Maybe she should go see a movie or eat something new. Or not think.

There was time.

Time to just stare out the window.

"I wish it was summer."

"Why don't you go out anyway," said her mom. "Go out and see what happens."

FROM THE BLOOD on Oliver's hat and the saliva he left on drinking glasses, Princeps already had everything he needed to know about the boy. Past and future. Oliver's father had told him his family came from weavers in Dunfermline, smart, stout Highlanders who settled and struggled, who adapted however they could. Princeps knew from Oliver's DNA that his ancestors were actually Spanish more than Scottish, Moorish more than Spanish, Maghrebi from the western Sahara. He was a mongrel of Neanderthals and long-lost apes, with dark hair and blue eyes like Princeps's brother, handsome but short, full of promise, and doomed. He knew that Oliver would grow short-sighted, that later in life he would suffer from heart disease and hair loss, cancer and liver disease, that he was vulnerable to all forms of addiction. This little boy petting the creature by candlelight.

OLIVER MADE A show of going to bed. But under his bed lay his boots and jacket, and when he knew his dad was asleep, he got dressed and climbed down the trellis outside his window.

He saw the midnight sidewalks in winter, lunar and salty. The empty cars and what the streets will look like when everyone dies. His breath and boots made the only sounds until he got close to Dundas.

Christmas lights turned off.

Christmas.

What do you buy the boy who hides in bathrooms.

Princeps's store was never locked.

THIS FEELING LIKE they could teach each other something, wanting to get to know each other. He noticed Night's paws were sticky. Put them against his hand and they seemed to pull him in, not just physically but into his memories or some other world. Climbing moonlit trees and feeling afraid of nothing. Not needing to search for enemies—just looking for whatever he wanted. Chasing. He felt like he lived in Night's body for a second. And when he lifted up his paws against the wall, they stuck. He encouraged him upwards and they looked at each other by candlelight, Oliver on the ground staring up at Night looking down from the wall.

In brighter light he disappeared, and when Princeps let him out into the store after midnight he dipped and dove through currents of light, an electric ghost with a heavy chain dragging behind him. Smelling everything in the store, the centuries of junk, barking at all the strange taxidermy mounted on the walls. He went crazy when Oliver came into his room, bursting and thrilling like the birth of the world, blowing a day's confusion out his nose while Oliver said, "Good boy."

He craved that greeting when he was home. Missed Night like a friend. He smiled in bed and his own legs jerked when he thought about how excited Night got, jumping as high as his head and forgetting about his chain. He was pulled back roughly to the floor every time, but he kept jumping. Snapped at the air near Oliver's neck.

OLIVER READ PRINCEPS'S story. He didn't understand everything and had a lot of questions. The cat. The brother. Watching your brother die like that. Princeps saying *I have become this thing*. What did he mean? Oliver understood what it might have been like to walk to school with swollen ears, the way people stare at you, and he felt some kind of closeness to Princeps not feeling close to his mom. A little uncomfortable reading it, but respected somehow. Princeps said he called for everyone's secrets, and he was sharing his with Oliver. You don't get to know the truth, you don't get to know anyone unless they tell you the things they want to hide. A childhood harder than his own. He wasn't teaching Oliver or giving him advice, he was just being honest with him.

Did he make Night? How? He owned a junk shop in his family home. How was he a scientist?

Things in the store looked different, exaggerated or animated. *Created.* As if Oliver was realizing for the first time that everything in the city, in human life, was *made.*

"I've spent a lifetime dreaming of how things can be better," said Princeps. "That mess you see out there. This is the best we will be with these genes. I developed a process, a gene-editing technology, that allows us to change course. What have you learned at school? Do you listen?"

"What do you mean?"

"DNA. Genes. Gene editing."

"I don't know. We did a thing with bacteria. Changing the letters."

They'd learned about cheap new technologies that people in garages and basements were using to change genetic structures. In class they had made bacteria stronger, bacteria that couldn't be stopped, using a plastic kit that Hornby ordered online. Oliver didn't see the big deal because it was under a microscope but Hornby said, *You've just changed nature. Like little gods.*

"People don't have to get cancer. Our teacher showed us bunnies that glow in the dark. And dogs with crazy muscles."

"It's nothing crazy," said Princeps. "For years people have

been talking about bringing back dinosaurs and mammoths. They've been making clones and editing genes to create hornless cattle and better crops. I've taken it further. Why not make things exactly as you want them? Not just better animals, resurrected animals, but new ones. Why not eliminate death? A man wrote to me from India to tell me that his new little daughter will never die. Ten years of miscarriages that family went through. Now full of hope that I gave them, my work. She'll be a little girl forever."

He took Oliver's elbow and guided him through the store, to the window at the front where the dead plant stood as an invitation to no one.

"Touch the stem," he said. "Touch the stem of the plant and hold your fingers there."

Oliver reached down and held it. He felt a sensation like soda through a straw and watched the plant rise up and stretch. Its leaves turned green and grew waxy, as if summer had filled the store.

"I edited the plant's DNA to respond to touch. Magic is real now, Oliver. The world can be whatever we want it to be."

Oliver took his fingers away and watched the plant sag.

He wondered about Princeps's sons. How old they were, how he disappeared to see them sometimes and never really talked about them. Did they know about this stuff.

There were pictures in his mind when he read himself to sleep. In the *Fantastic Four*, the Seeker describes the origins of the Inhumans. *The science of Genetics was our greatest interest! We were able, thru use of Vari-Genes, to control evolution—and to direct it in any way we wished! We produced many Inhumans— all with specialized, carefully created super-powers!*

A comic book written fifty years ago.

Oliver pictured the plant, heard Night making sounds like dogs and people conversing, chatter of a village under a forever dark canopy. He opened his eyes as wide as he could in the morning.

"STEP ONE IS we acknowledge that we're animals. Those four little letters are common to every living thing. Get rid of any idea that the finger of god has made humans separate from nature. We just happen to be good at controlling it. I can take the best from here, the best from there, cunning, strength. There are animals, like raccoons, that can sense— that can *see* with their hands. Wouldn't you like that? To touch things and see them in your mind, to know the story of everything from touch. When you hold Night's paws, what happens?"

Oliver saw a vision of himself from below. His neck pale. Wanting to kiss it, his own neck, or a feeling of not knowing what to do. Jump and run and stay right here.

"I see things," he said.

"Exactly. You're behind his eyes for a second, and he's behind yours. Tiny needle-like receptors that let him see with his paws. He knows you by touch, and there's communion for a moment. I made that happen, Oliver. I can make anyone the best animal he can be."

Oliver knew about the cats who hunted our ancestors, who still ruled the jungle and terrorized villages at night. Leopards, tigers, lions. Jaguars could mimic the sounds of their prey. Panthers were his favourite. Princeps said there was the DNA of hunting dogs in Night, and of panthers. He studied the structure of glasswing butterflies and transparent frogs, produced invisibility as a trick of the light, a way to exploit the weakness of human eyes.

"How do you know what will happen? If you made him, how do you know what his life will be like?"

"That's what I've tried to tell you. Predictors. There are some among us who study where people go wrong. I've looked at myself, my brother, everyone I can. I have walked through sewers.

"There are off-target consequences, always. Risks. Not everything is predictable, but . . . once you see the tracks clearly, it's not hard to guess where the train is heading. All these lives that we think are different from our ancestors'. Most of what we think of as emotional, psychological, spiritual has some kind of origin in genetics. Personal taste, food, the people we like— it's all determined by our genes and the microbes in our lives. Memory is in our genes. Fears. Why are we afraid of snakes before we even know what they can do to us? The shape of them. Positivity. Endurance. What makes one person thrive and another fail? I know exactly where sadness lives. That place where you give up, forget how to fight."

Night was still and heavy, his jaw digging into Oliver's lap. Tongue on the palate, the comforting sound of a contented dog.

"Do you see? Oliver the Unique. The Unknown. Never Seen Before."

"Me?"

"That's what you could be. Part emperor, part big cat. Hands that see. Eyes that demand attention. Fearless. Commanding. You could jump and run just like you do in your dreams. Do you understand?"

"I don't want to change."

"You don't? I do. Every day I want to be better. Do you want to get beaten up again?"

"No."

"You can be the hero of a whole new story. You don't have to be a boy. You don't even have to be human. They're all just names we put on nature to understand it. You don't have to fit into what other people say you should be—forget the names, forget everything about what you're supposed to be. Oliver the

Nameless. A creature never seen before who rules his particular world."

HE LOOKED UP *gene editing animals* online. Saw those dogs with muscles, goats producing more cashmere, more meat, fatter pigs that saved farmers money in heating costs. All of it was real. Animals more useful to humans or even better than they were meant to be. What did that mean: meant to be.

A couple of forums on Reddit talked about ethics. Eugenics. What happens when these technologies get in the hands of white supremacists. They'll customize a race. Soon it will only be the wealthy who have access to them. *The rich won't get sick.* Superhumans in elite schools, everyone over six feet tall, blue-eyed, brilliant, ambitious. Insurance companies won't cover people who haven't given their kids the right DNA.

Are there genes for compassion, empathy. What if those are edited away. *You can wipe out a race in one generation.*

All the people who seemed to know what they were talking about said, *Won't happen. Too many unknowns. Might work in a lab but not in real life.*

We're not there yet.

Those animals on the screen and the fantasies about what humans might be, it all seemed weird, perverse. But maybe it was just because they were on-screen. Maybe in real life they would seem magical, like Night. Oliver tried to imagine what those dogs with the muscles felt like inside. Did they know they weren't real. Or were they real. If you're made in a lab do you know any different. No one wants to play with you, but you still want to play.

Night was invisible, just like Sue Storm in the Fantastic Four. What if Oliver was a hothead like her brother, Johnny. Or huge, unstoppable. *Yer breathin on my baby blues, buttercup.*

As big as the Thing, walking Night on a leash through the city.

Those people saying it wouldn't happen, we're not there yet. They had no idea.

PRINCEPS KEPT TALKING about the perfect boy. Asking Oliver what he wanted to be. How strong. How brave.

"A superhero standing on a mountain?"

"No."

"You don't want to be strong?"

"I do."

"Tell me."

"I'm tired of worrying. I'm . . . tired of . . . I'm fast but I can never get away from anything, from things in my head."

"From memories."

"Yeah."

"Memories can be erased. Or you can choose them whenever you want. Your favourites. Are you lonely?"

"I don't know."

"You want to escape. Find someone. Have friends."

"Yes."

He looked at the shadows across the room from the candlelight. The bones on the floor were mostly of rats and mice. Night didn't eat unless he hunted.

"Watch him," said Princeps. He tipped a box out on the floor and three rats tumbled out. Oliver jumped to his feet and woke up Night.

His fur twitched in waves and his eyes gained a flat bright focus—no compassion or depth to them. His entire being was electrified towards catching the rodents. Instead of chasing one immediately and losing the others, he froze completely and watched as they grew inquisitive. His purpose, Oliver thought later. He has a purpose, a focus, he's designed for it.

No questions or doubt. *I want to see something I want, and take it.*

Princeps flicked on the light and Night disappeared. The rats scurried to the walls and gathered in a corner, one of them puffing up while being harassed by the others. Two of them stood on hind legs as if they were boxing. Oliver tried to stay still while the rats fought each other for dominance.

There was a blur in the concrete corner as if someone had erased it. Short squeals. The rats rose up all together and blood poured onto the floor as if someone had wrung out a cloth.

"My mother used to throw scraps of cabbage into the backyard," Princeps said. "All kinds of garbage. It was people like her who brought the rats."

He turned off the light and they listened to Night chewing.

"What happened to your mom?"

"She died," said Princeps. "We have that in common, you see. And there are some who make convincing arguments that people never die. They live on in your memory, talk to you over your shoulder. Some even argue that particles, speck-sized pieces of skin, microbes from your mother, they carry on when the brain dies, blow around on the wind, get absorbed, get eaten, breathed, stay among the living. Inform the living. All of our ancestors literally fill the air and water we swallow. If I told you I could bring back the dead, you might be impressed. But what I'm most proud of is that I can make new life. Leave my mother dead and start over."

He looked across at Night.

"You have to want it, Oliver. I can give you genes for muscularity. For intelligence. Coordination. But you have to use them. Genes are triggered. By environment, by other genes, by the genes in the bacteria that accumulate through your habits. I can make you quick, but you have to *run*. If you sit around doing nothing, you won't become anything. You have to *want* this."

Behind him, Oliver's shadow was large and leapt in the candlelight.

"I do."

PRINCEPS WOULD HAVE stories to tell one day about all the weak vessels in the neighbourhood. Empty wombs aching to do something right.

He had experimented with local schizophrenics and addicts, finding the right cocktail of CDH13, MAOA, how the RBFOX1 gene regulates violent tendencies. How to guarantee and manage a murderous intention, give everyone a taste for flesh. He made mutants of some of them by deleting a gene for serotonin reception, making them normal in everyday life except when they were surprised or threatened. Meek, cowering souls who sat in his store and shared memories about their pasts. They found comfort in those rooms, and when he arranged for them to be intruded upon, to have other visitors come at night and look for his attention, the mutants attacked with wicked ferocity. Grabbing scissors and stabbing startled eyes.

Strength to the weak.

He thought of his store as a sort of soup kitchen. If you needed something, you found your way in. People from the shelters and the streets wandered in on summer nights, trying to grab things from the shelves. From his wanderings through the sewer and his communion with these souls, he knew not only what was imperfect but how to make it otherwise.

"I'll let you have whatever you want, if you give me a little something." That was his bargain over the years, the most basic human arrangement. We both need something. Word was around that his door was always open, and the witching hour was after midnight, especially in summer, when people looked for mischief or something to steal, their drugs or booze levelling.

He was confident leaving it for weeks, spending most of the winter with his sons to measure their progress. Tend to the others for the bloom in spring.

A woman crept into the front one night, saying she'd been feeling better.

"Everyone's feeling better," said Princeps. "Maybe you know toothless old Frank. Still toothless. But he came to me last night and pulled up his ragged sleeve. 'Look at this,' he said. He showed me the arm of a leader. You would have laughed. Old Frank. You may feel down about yourself sometimes, dear. Some of it takes time. But that toothless old man is growing the body of a god."

She sidled up to him, like she had done habitually with men all her life. Whispers and sibilants, standing close to strangers the way his mother had. "Everyone says you're the god," she said.

"Oh, I don't know about that."

He made people strong, made them believe again, and some of them carried babies. He used them as empty cups, and the women were horrified by what came out of them. Slugs with needy hands, clots the size of grapefruit. Some of the babies were born alive and some were just grim packets of life's raw stuff, more upsetting to him than he expected. A few of the mothers blamed themselves, their pasts, the things they'd done to their bodies. Most of them ran away.

But he had three sons, growing like otherwise normal boys in the country. The future, he would argue, of the world.

"WE INTRODUCE THE letters, the new code, by infecting you. Viruses. Nothing's going to kill you. Fever at the worst, sore throat. It can take a while. Seventy trillion cells have to reproduce with the new information, replace the old cells that are making you who you are. That's going to be a constant battle, and you'll have to have injections.

"I have to make you sick to make you better. But it will speed things up. The needles will work quickly, and step by step, jab by jab, we'll write a new Oliver. We'll look through your DNA sequence and find all the things that need correcting, and if there's a letter out of place, a T where an A would work more beautifully, we'll fix it. Get a little muscle on you. To make the perfect boy, we have to make the perfect animal. Not only make you strong but forget how to be weak. What do you think about that?"

When the Christmas holidays began, Oliver visited in the daylight. The more real Night seemed, the more possible everything felt. The more safe.

Princeps gave him one of his concocted drinks, which calmed and made him tired. He also gave him three litres of PegLyte to drink, which drew water into his colon and cleaned out his intestines.

He played with a glassy-looking Night, on his chain, a crack in the curtains letting in some winter light. He held up Night's barely visible paw and said, "Can you see this? Can you see that you're invisible? I want to take you outside."

Oliver's belly rumbled and he ran to the toilet. For hours he had no control.

"We're replacing your entire biome," Princeps called through the door. "There's a loofah in there. Scrub your skin until it's red. Everywhere."

The bathroom was at the very back of the house, attached to an old kitchen with no heat. A shower arm protruded from the wall, from yellow penny tiles that were cracked and stained. Oliver wore his hat and coat and lost a bellyful of liquid. He was sickened by the smell and freezing. Missing tiles looked like peepholes. He kept his coat on and shivered.

They were getting rid of his old microbes, the world of tiny animals that lived on his skin and in his gut. They thrived on him being exactly who he was, their own genes telling him to keep up his routines, do the wrong things, give up when something felt too hard.

He sat through more cramps. Eventually the pain subsided and he could stand in the hot shower. The steam made the toilet and room invisible. He scrubbed his skin raw and couldn't get warm enough. Between his toes, between his legs.

Princeps had made a show of taking his saliva and blood, but he had been studying Oliver's genes for more than a month. He set up a course of injections with the appropriate reagents, LOBSTR taking new information to precise points on his genome. Alcoholic mother. He had a high level of MAOA alleles, so even though he had his mother's weak ADH and GAB genes he was unlikely to be sociopathic. How do you encourage ferocity while maintaining a gentle soul?

The perfect child needs the perfect parents. The Pinocchio story has it that the child saves the father, journeys into the belly of the whale where his father was going to die. Children save us, make us young and give us a chance to start again. That was the message of that part of the tale. But what about the parents, who kill us? The parents who give us the garbage genes and a lifetime of bad memories.

LOBSTR was a palimpsest, a means of scratching over and writing something new. Completely new. That was the goal. Forget about notions and labels, alcoholism and sociopathy. Use the DNA of zebrafish, whose fins and hearts will grow back if you cut them. Turn on those stem cell genes that lie dormant and keep them surging. Eyes of an eagle, strength of a gorilla, codicils of telomerase to keep everything young, forever.

A kind, unique creature, afraid of nothing, who will fight like a madman if he is cornered. Who will eat the old world.

"Try not to shiver. You need to be still when I put the needle in."

"SOME OF THESE will likely bring on an adenovirus but they won't hurt much. I will give you a few and you must watch carefully. Every year I visit my sons in the winter. Not many people come through here. But the store will be open. Night will be here and I will keep an eye out. Do you hear? I will leave a numbered course for you behind the counter. Are you brave enough for this on your own? Vials and sterile sharps." He tapped the needle. "There's a myostatin knockout in here." He squeezed one of Oliver's biceps between thumb and forefinger. "You'll be twice this size before you know it."

He sat with his shirt off, his skin rubbed raw. Completely empty. That's how he felt. Not hungry yet, but nothing in his belly. Gritted his teeth to stop from shivering. Princeps swabbed his skin and took a pinch of it, low on his belly. Afraid of the needle, what was in it, wanting what was in it. When doctors are about to hurt you they always say the same thing.

This will make you better.

He stared at the white light through the window and felt the sting.

That night he had a headache. Came on at dinner and he went to bed early. He could taste the needle. Steel pipe on his tongue, scraping his throat, hot and cold down into his empty bowels and through them. Turning like a pig over a fire, round and round till he was dizzy. Burning. The pain in his head woke him up and then took him to new dreams. Someone squeezing his skull in a vise until it cracked, brains spraying onto the face of a handsome man, Murdoch's dad, who rubbed the blood and matter into his skin and transformed. I am the God of Regret.

ABOVE THE CITY a bird cast massive shadows and made the curious look up. Idiots prone to believe anything, the skeptical taking pause. Shadow of a dragon over highways.

The bird glided to the country on updrafts from the lake, lifted cattle from freezing troughs and dropped their carcasses onto rocks. Sweetbreads, eyes, a taste for nectar and salt. She perched in stands of pine and was mistaken for a tree. Semiplumes keeping her warm in the snow. For days she could sit without moving, entranced by neither memory nor thought while possibilities blew through apple-sized nostrils, fish oils floating on the lake and the land-borne bounty.

She got low and pulled her tail feathers back, presented her cloaca to a spruce and rubbed for an eyeblink on resin-encrusted cankers.

Soundless.

Still you could hear things in your sleep. The pumping of wind from wing. These January nights, minus thirty, when the moon blued the sky. The farmer would be up in two hours but these past few months the sleep didn't come, not at all. His whole family dead two years from a crash on the King's Highway. Wasn't god's work he did, it couldn't be, for what kind of a god, but he did it for the labour, better to breathe rich mould from grain bins than to stare at that empty moon.

He heard her the one night, out by those black pines. His waking dream disturbed.

In the spring he attended a first-freshening goat on his knees, waiting for dilation with the liquid hanging from her. She wouldn't open, pushed and she couldn't deliver. It was the memory of her, not his family, kept him sleepless. Two kids in there, he could feel their hoofs and heads. Tried to pull but her womb had a grip on them.

He lifted his hands in bed and stared.

These are the things you have to do, he'd told his sister.

From his bedroom window he looked towards the trees and saw nothing.

He didn't know if he ever went to sleep. Had he ever known peace at all. Of course those were his kids in there, and he had to cut them up. Work with his knife in the womb and remove them piece by piece or the mother too would die.

Overhead, she had a preference for the dark.

The next night he heard her again, her wings.

He jumped from bed this time and saw it, feathers looking wet by the moonlight. A bird couldn't be that big. She rose as if climbing an invisible ladder, wind throbbing from those wings like some generator was cycling. A terrible thing beginning.

A pause.

At the peak of her climb he felt it all, like the flu. How they constantly haunted him, the cattle. Sick. Lowing and whining, pneumonia and blackleg after the flood, the breathless feeling of failure and futility when he had to put them down. All our work together.

He started running when he saw her plummet. Wings tucked in, catastrophic turn towards the barn roof as if she didn't see it.

Outside he heard the mother's cries.

His flashlight caught the panic behind her. The hemlock splintered on the ground. Talons on the calf's hind and head, her bill unwinding the intestines.

Had he time to ponder he would have known that this was simply a parable. A symbolic visit. That he raised the cattle to be eaten by the city, sent away in trucks to die screaming, and this was the city now, this black and careless bird. These screams were what he worked for.

He threw what he could find at her. Pliers and a feed bucket. She looked up and continued eating. The gun was back at the house.

It was when he shouted that she paused. Stood tall while the cows cried in pens, twice as tall as he was, wings outstretched thirty feet. He could see her roar, no sound. The cry he wished he could gather these years, from his feet, thighs and balls, this bleak fuckin life I need to scream at, and nothing would come out. She leaned towards him, stretched her neck, close enough to smell, and tried to trumpet that anger at his face.

Nothing.

Had he time.

She took his neck in her bill and snapped it. Wrenched off his head and sucked on sinew.

Two feathers fell, caught on the rafters when she flew through the hole she'd made. A diorama some monstrous child had glued together. Wasting and murdered cattle, a headless farmer, feathers as long as canoes.

The constables both heard sounds from above, for a week, an uncommon wind. Wheeling and dipping in the clouds, wanting to rejoice, trying to sing aloud her love for that new meat.

2

SUMMER CAME IN January.

Oliver's dad chased stories in his study, seldom coming out. Fruit hanging there, just there, like it did above the ancient sinner. Chasing songs across the water and seeing things behind his eyes but rarely what was in front of them.

There was a yellow on the bark of certain trees that Oliver had never noticed before. Some reds. They didn't belong in winter. Car tires rolled, percussive, along frozen streets. He picked up his pace and half skipped like he was about to run. Something about the progress of the cars. Moving somewhere better, blue-black rubber the colour of summer nights, slow treads on the road like drums in his belly and feet and bones, up his chest, keep moving, up.

He took the 26 bus to the 29 Dufferin and walked along Bloor to Sweet Pete's bike shop. On the second bus was a bunch of older kids, girls and boys, coming back from a skate at Dufferin Grove. One of the boys had a really old pair of speedskates, with the low leather boot, maybe a gift from his granddad, and they all had cool clothes, lived-in—not the Moose Knuckles or Canada Goose I-deserve-to-be-spoiled sort of look, but clothes that looked like they grew on their bodies—and they were only sixteen, seventeen. The girls had pretty smiles.

Oliver could hear them really clearly. He usually stood right near the rear door. He could jump off if he saw people getting on who might come after him. But today he'd walked straight to the back without thinking. He sat there like a judge or like Wordor in CyberKings 2 who sits in the far back corner of the universe and admires it.

They were talking about things he had to piece together, some school they were all at together, Christmas. One girl was shy and Oliver could hear the lips on her teeth.

Everything was a little more loud and alive. He focused on those kids, but if he looked at other people on the bus he could hear them—could tell the old man near the front was humming even though his back was turned.

He could see better, too. The hair in the driver's ear and the beautiful red of the stoplight. He looked at the girls with the skates and realized he wasn't afraid of looking.

The red of that stoplight was truly beautiful.

He imagined summer again and felt himself flying on a bike. The bus was his bike. He pulled up the front of it and flew over Dufferin Street like he was jumping root-mounds in the woods.

A guy stood at the bus stop on Bloor saying "Bum a smoke" to everyone who got off. Rubbing his hands together like he couldn't get warm enough. Oliver left his jacket on the bus.

Sweet Pete's was expensive but everyone there was smart and he had seen a post online before Christmas about a Redline Flight Pro 24 BMX racing bike that they were putting on display. "The most technically advanced complete alloy race bike on the market today. No gimmicks, just winning." It was fifteen hundred bucks.

Riding weather was still months away and the place was pretty empty. Usually when he walked into a store, any store, but especially one where he was just looking, he would try to hide and head to the edges, look at the price tags of ten-thousand-dollar bikes as if he might buy one. He pulled his shoulders back and said "Hey there" to the guy who had said the same to him.

It wasn't hard to find the Redline—it was on a raised display like a jewel in a movie that a handsome genius might steal. He could take it, with a bit of planning. Why not.

"It's not street legal," said the guy. "Just for racing. You'd need to get new brakes and spend another couple hundred."

"It's amazing," said Oliver.

"I'll get it down for you. Check out how light it is. Carbon frame. Aluminum hubs. Hollow crank."

Oliver was still small enough to be comfortable with an eighteen-inch top tube. He knew the bike was too big for him, but he could feel himself growing—the twenty inches, twenty-two inches, was just around the corner.

The bike weighed twenty pounds. He could bunny-hop a truck.

Suzi watched him from the corner. She had been having the same dreams of riding her bike, maybe getting a new Hermes to take her far away from Christmas. She heard someone shout "Whoo!" and louder voices say "Whoa, whoa, take it easy." She saw the kid from across the street on a bike, bouncing up and down on it, with employees gathered around him.

"Okay, little man. Time to jump off."

Oliver was pulling on the grips, kicking up the back wheel and hopping as high as their faces. Hopping over deer in the woods. They said coyotes came down the ravines. He was riding with Night, invisible, to an opening he had never seen in that far stand of trees.

This thing could fly.

An employee put his hands on top of the seat and handle-bars and said, "Enough, dude. Hop off."

Suzi walked over to him.

"Hi," he said, like he was expecting her.

The employee wouldn't let go of the bike and Oliver had to stretch his leg up over his arm to get off.

"WHAT WERE YOU doing?"

"Practising."

"For what?"

"I don't know. Summer."

There was some kind of soft explosion in his head, like when he drank cold milk too fast but not as sharp as that. Not painful. It made him forget where he was for a second.

"What happened to your eye?"

"I don't know."

He looked down at his hands.

He had bright eyes and not very nice clothes. Dirty or old. Dirty. Clothes that no one else would buy. Maybe second-hand. He didn't have a jacket.

"You could go pretty much fifty k on that thing," he said. "Like . . . speed, not distance. Or I could probably ride fifty k. I've probably done it."

They stared at each other.

"I can't really afford it, but I'm growing. I could grow into it."

It had been a while since she was around the kind of kid who talked about how he was growing.

"How old are you?"

"Twelve."

There was some kind of joke in her eyes, something building or just burning there kindly.

"I'm Suzi."

Bikes hung down from racks over their heads, like Night when he stood on the wall.

"Cheapest bike here is five hundred bucks," he said. "I couldn't afford a lock."

He got up onto a fatbike. Would have been perfect for the snow. Two thousand bucks. He had to lean on one side to let a foot touch the ground. He tipped too far and twisted the wheel. Suzi reached for the grip to help him and touched his hand.

The craziest feeling. Hot where her hand touched, on the side of her palm. Hot on her face.

The store guy said, "Are you buying today, do you think?"

"Probably not," said Oliver.

"We could find a kid's bike for you. Something that fits."

Oliver got off the bike and felt a surge of blood. He could beat this guy up if he went crazy enough. He stared down at the ground like when Suzi first talked to him on the street, looking sad or angry.

"What's your name?" she said, when the guy walked away.

He looked at her quickly before getting lost somewhere. "Oliver."

"Oliver."

She had a really nice smile.

"Those bikes with the fat tires look stupid."

"I like them," he said.

She'd taken the Red Cross babysitting course and had practised on her cousin. A four-year-old who was as bad as people get. Whiny and nasty and crying all the time. But cute. So lucky he was cute, or he would have been murdered. A giggle when he was happy or just his smile, and you forgot about how dark and hard life had seemed when he was whining. She caught some kind of flash of that from Oliver. Something in those eyes . . . not that he'd been an asshole, but there were clouds, and behind the clouds was a sun.

More milk burst in his brain. Didn't care about feeling short. All these new bikes, the smell of them, the tires, the shiny paint, imagining how fast a bike could go that cost ten grand. He wanted to get an army together on these bikes, ride at night through the city and do nothing, just glide and bully the cars away, do some tricks with friends.

Friends.

"I'm not sure I can be your friend," he said.

"Why not?"

"I'm changing."

"What do you mean?"

"I don't know who I'll be."

HE WALKED ALONG Bloor. The sky was swollen like a lot of snow was coming. Bring it on. Do your worst. He skipped a little as if he couldn't wait for everything to happen.

He was wearing just a shirt. People stared. Mostly older people, grandmothers, the kind who think nothing will ever be right. He stared back and smiled.

Where was he going.

It didn't matter. Maybe he would see Night or just walk.

He looked back towards Sweet Pete's. Felt good. He thought of the girl in Charlie's old house.

He breathed and dropped his shoulders. Run.

"YOU WON'T GET any older than twelve," said Princeps. "You'll get bigger, and stronger. You'll have the strength of a man. Stronger even. You already have the intelligence of a man, you just don't have the experience. And what does experience do but wear us down? Not every child is confident, but every adult has had some reason not to be. All blind faith and belief, all unthinking bravery, all the stepping forth and doing and thinking about it later—experience kills all of that. You'll be confident," said Princeps. "And you'll never feel sad."

He had three more injections before Princeps went away to see his sons. "A flood" is what the man called it. He was really sick at first but it was just a tickle in his throat now. He threw up a couple of times, once in the bathroom and once on the street, but he didn't feel that swoony fear he usually felt before he got sick. Didn't feel anything except a crazy energy. No worry about what was going to happen to him. Instead of worry coming to him uninvited, he had to find it, make an effort. Didn't even ask the question, What was there to worry about.

He ran to stay warm, and shook his new blood. Down Bloor and up the steps to the railpath. New energy in his feet, like when he'd borrowed Charlie's two-hundred-dollar Asics and couldn't feel the ground. His boots were part of a costume he didn't really want. He thought about taking them off. Sprinted past an old bald guy in a ski jacket who was singing while he jogged.

Dark industrial buildings lined the path, most of them converted to apartments. New palaces where Oliver would find people waiting to be discovered. He started smiling, thinking of all the closed doors he could open. A cool princess behind one of them, a sabre-toothed tiger to make friends with Night. Or some unknown creature. We could make anything.

He jumped up to a branch that hung over the path and did a chin-up, and then two more. He'd never been able to do one.

The bald man trotted past him, singing.

HOLDING NIGHT'S PAW, he had seen places neither of them had been. Visions of loping alone through fogbound nights, light on the ground, springing on deer and calves under trees hung heavy with spit from the moon. Sleeping alone and not knowing what loneliness was until some sap in the bones rose up, hunger for a mate as compelling as hunger for meat.

But what did Night really know. Memories were in the genes, Princeps said. What had Night seen besides the concrete box he was raised in. Some countryside Princeps was never clear about, where his own sons grew up. A farm or something. Night was a pup, like Oliver, who knew nothing but the city. If Night was destined to be the perfect hunter, what was he doing chained up. When was Princeps going to let him out.

Oliver wanted to take him outside but didn't know how to do it. During the day when he was invisible, at night when he was just as easily lost in the dark. In the park. On the streets. Where. He just wanted to take him for a walk. Help him get to know himself like Oliver wanted to test his own growing powers. They would do it together. Get strong like the winter.

There was no one in the store when Oliver went over. All the objects mute.

"Mr. Princeps."

Some of those strange sounds from weeks ago were gone, the sounds like other animals behind closed doors—Oliver realized he hadn't heard those for a while. Just these noises of Night sensing his approach. A stranger or a friend coming home. He could picture him jumping and got excited. Didn't know the code to the alarm on Night's door and didn't have the key.

Night was leaping, trying to pull the chain from its mooring and smelling new smells from Oliver through the door. A different sweat.

"I don't have the key! No one's here!"

He gripped the doorknob. One day soon he could break it.

Night's barking and chattering became manic. He growled and jumped on the chain.

Oliver pressed his forehead to the door.

HIS DAD WAS out that night for his monthly drinks.

The standing lamp in the far corner of the living room was

on, but the house was mostly dark. He could hear the radio in his dad's bedroom.

Lasagna. He knew how to cook it. Take it straight out of the freezer and bake it for forty-five minutes, take off the top and let it brown for another ten. His dad would come home late and hungry, and Oliver wished he wouldn't so he could have the whole thing.

He put the lasagna on the rack and thundered upstairs. Turned off the radio and flicked the switch on the lamp. There was a big mirror in his dad's bedroom, tipped against the wall on a chest of drawers and dusty. Oliver looked at his reflection.

Maybe he had expected more of a change. He saw a kid. He took his shirt off and looked at his shoulders. Tightened them and turned sideways. No Hulk or Captain America, but maybe there was something, a little change like when you don't see a friend for a month and he has a tan or something's different.

His dad's bedroom was beneath his own, looking out on the same street. He raised the blinds and looked out shirtless towards the house opposite. The light was on in her room and she was sitting at the window. He knew what it was like in there. He and Charlie used to trade rooms and talk to each other on walkie-talkies, cheap things they'd stolen from Walmart. Charlie'd kept his desk right where hers was. If she looked down she would be able to see him in the lamplight.

Lots of little flakes of snow were swirling above the neighbourhood, like the street was in a snow globe. He folded his arms and stared.

After maybe a minute he raised his hand, and she waved back.

HE'D NEVER KNOWN hunger like this. Drool poured out of the side of his mouth like that time at the dentist when his mouth was frozen. Like a dog. I'm gonna die, he thought. You were supposed to wait ten minutes to let the lasagna settle, but he couldn't. Stuck his fork in and ate it at the counter, burned his tongue and got frustrated with how little the fork picked up.

In the morning his legs ached. A strange feeling in his fingertips. Touched his fingers to his thumbs and felt them stick like when he glued models, the same worry you have with superglue—if you held them together too long they'd be stuck forever.

He had a magnifying glass somewhere. Near the old globe. A brown stain on the Atlantic Ocean from whoever owned it before. He lay back in bed and looked at his fingertips through the magnifying glass. There. Little hairs. He blinked his eyes hard and opened them wide to adjust them. They weren't really hairs, they were like hooks. What would you call them. Barbs. A little curve to them. When he pressed his pointer and thumb together he tried to see how they worked, the barbs nestling in together. Like Velcro.

Visions appeared when he touched things, memories on his window and walls. A picture of a mosquito came to him, one of those microscopic images of the bug's proboscis stabbing into skin in a forest of hair, sucking up blood, gorging. A taste of someone, the secrets.

AND THIS NEED to run. He was out before he realized it, running in the snow, falling heavy now, over to Dundas and into the store. He called for Princeps again and heard nothing.

On the counter were two numbered vials and two covered needles, a Post-it that said *Oliver: the new you, and the old me. Be afraid of nothing.* The note was stuck to another manuscript, a pile of papers with brown wrapping and a pencilled title. *The Holland Marsh.*

Oliver went behind the counter and found the gravity knife.

Flicked the switch and let the blade fall, got used to this weird new pain of holding things. He put the vials and needles carefully in his backpack, against the manuscript.

When he touched Night's door he felt some kind of shock like he'd been thrown into the ocean. A hundred sights came to his mind and he was sitting on the floor before he realized where he was. Sat still for a second, thinking he might be sick again.

It was when he touched the doorknob, the grease of other fingers. He couldn't see what was in front of him, only pictures in his mind. He stuck the knife in the lock like he'd seen in movies. Pushed it as deep as he could and hit the handle with his other palm.

Stupid.

He had a lockpick.

Such a cloud in the back of his mind. He put the knife in his back pocket and felt Night's urgence, the growling and barking making his hands shake.

When he opened the door Night lurched, savagely.

Teeth and spit an inch from Oliver's face.

NIGHT HAD CHANGED. There were muscles now where there used to be loose fur. Panting and overcoming an anger Oliver hadn't seen before. He cleared his nose repeatedly like he was trying to get rid of bad thoughts.

The alarm made a long, low sound. Not meant to scare intruders but to let them know that someone, somewhere, knew the door had been opened. With his hand on Night's panting haunch Oliver closed his eyes and understood. Forked tongue on his face. He could see now with his fingers. Taste with them. The flavour of sweet meat in his mouth while he saw a pageant of Night's memories and dreams. The man coming to his door and feeding him rats. Hitting him with a baseball bat and making him bite a leather brace on his arm. Biting till his teeth hurt. Making an enemy of people.

There were bones on the floor. Something larger than a rat. Wet with saliva like they were freshly picked. A cat. That flavour in his mouth when he touched Night. The sight of the bones, knowing now what a cat tasted like.

The lockpick worked on the padlock as well. He wound the chain around his arm several times. Tried to imagine strength, to will it into his arm. He could use the chain as a leash. Tough guys walked Rottweilers on short leads. Oliver could take Night on the chain, a sort of nuclear pet, bully everyone off the sidewalk. He stood taller than Oliver's waist now, and he was long.

Somewhere there was a feeling that he was doing something wrong. This was a mistake. Night was his friend, but how would he behave outside. The city, animals, cars. People. "Should we be doing this," he said.

Night disappeared as soon as they left the store, still attached but invisible. The chain pointed downwards and stiff. Dragging Oliver. He stumbled and ran and dug his heels in, leaned back like he was getting pulled by a team of huskies.

"Stop. Slow down."

He'd had an idea that they would walk to High Park and get used to the smells of nature. At the Maple Leaf meat-packing plant, ten minutes north, pigs and beeves were being skinned and bled. Once a week, today, the smell of manure and discarded innards would rise on the wind and hang over the neighbourhood. Night's nose filled with warm blood and bleach, and he was bewildered.

He dragged Oliver east, away from the park, towards Hook and Dupont where the train tracks ran above the street. No one walking in the snow.

The only way to keep up was to run. Oliver wasn't strong enough to hold him back.

Chasing scents. Outside for the first time. Snow in his nose made him sneeze and the dirty brown songbirds scattered.

"Stop."

Oliver pulled with his arm bent, leaned back and his boots were like skis. A salted gap in the snow made his toes stick and he tripped forward. Night slowed for a second, then pulled again. There was a pop in Oliver's shoulder and the pain spread through his body.

The chain was wound only twice around his arm now, Night six feet away from him. He saw an iron-framed bench up ahead, anchored to the sidewalk. If he could tie the chain, keep Night still for a second. Think.

He focused on his hands and put strength into them. Held the chain with both and pushed it to the arm of the bench, quickly trying to loop it around. Two of his fingers got caught between the chain and the arm, and he screamed in agony when Night jerked to a stop. Like he'd slammed them in a door. Night kept pulling, his paws kicking snow back, keeping tension on the chain and pulling it link by link. A curtain of pain fell over Oliver's eyes when the links raked over his fingers. He was going to lose them. "Stop pulling!"

His fingertips were purple. He pulled on the chain with his free hand and it didn't make a difference.

Snow brought a clarity to the city's smells. They summoned Night like sirens to sailors. Hot kitchens. The fish warehouse on Oliver's street sending waves of invitation. He choked on his collar and stepped back for a second, long enough for a glimpse of slack. Oliver pulled his fingers out, and he was blind to the unravelling chain. He was holding his hand while the links unzipped. Couldn't think about anything but the pain. "No!"

He sat on the bench, half crying. Watched the chain shoot forward along the sidewalk like it knew where it was going.

TO CHASE THE stockyard ghosts.

Blood from slaughtered hogs had drenched the mud beneath these tracks. Dogs licking runoff, layers of their graves where waste was unloaded from trains. It all rose up to his nose. New company for his tongue and paws, salt gravel beneath the snow, the sky dark and pregnant over iron towers and the signals of the switching yard. His mouth chattered and drooled.

A new sense of immensity. The tracks curved and opened up to an avenue stretching wide towards Lambton Yard, and he slowed to a trot as he dragged his chain past a shantytown of ruined cars and pallets. A trailer covered by a burdened tarp. People slept and worked here.

He stopped and lifted his nose, took in an irregular sound of something heavy falling. On the siding tracks were boxes piled three high in colours, tanker trains in black, all muted by the snow. The sound came from two men, one little, one large, the big one wearing an orange-and-yellow visibility vest which looked to Night like distant fruit.

They were piling scrap onto a trailer and roof rack, the little one tying down the rack and the colourful one throwing metal objects which few people would have names for. Car parts and cladding, rusted tanker ladders, copper pipe like staffs of gold all landing on the trailer. Two elevated beggars who had eyes for every angle, the big one thinking in Portuguese and cursing in no language how the earth had changed, those tracks coming from a place where he might have been a leader. Thumbs strong enough to squeeze a face into fluid.

Night's ears pricked up for the first few landings of metal, and the bright vest drew him closer. Aware of how his chain made noise as he moved.

This was a corner unknown to most in the neighbourhood, unchanged. Trailers parked, untaxed and littered with spoons of burnt fentanyl. Site of where a boy was raped and his brother couldn't save him.

Could Night's paws read these histories? How the past pulled everyone, kids by our ankles, with its constant undertow?

He timed his movement across the tracks with each fall of scrap on the trailer. Fur twitching and the snow giving him a liquid shape as it melted. Stalking low, crouching.

The big man shouted at the other, wanting to lay claims of his own. To eat. The pile at his feet was getting low. He took off his hat and looked up to let the storm cool his eyes.

Night pulled himself closer, his belly in the snow.

The man saw the chain, five bucks' worth of zinc lying across the track.

OLIVER HELD HIS hand on the bench and stared at his injured fingers. Throbbing enough for him to lean forward and hold them in the snow. That milky feeling in his brain came back.

Don't think about it.

His fingers started to freeze and that's what he focused on, the soothing.

He didn't forget, exactly. It was all there if he looked for it: the stupidity of what he'd done. He would have to explain himself to Princeps. A horrible feeling that he wouldn't see Night again, that he would make the man fear something similar—his great creation, unimaginably beautiful. Felt sore in his heart and wanted to go back in time. Maybe Night would come home, come back to this bench right now, but if he didn't . . . Oliver had just let something loose. The snow was covering the footprints and the track made by the chain.

He stood up. *Don't think about it.* Some force moved his feet without his permission and took him home.

His dad was standing at his study door. Oliver walked past

to climb to his room, and when he was at the stairs his dad said, "What's up."

"Nothing. Clothes are wet." His fingers were throbbing, heart still racing, but he tried to stand normally.

"What happened?" Looking at his face.

All through the holidays he'd been writing, both of them having a pact that if his dad was so absent that he couldn't see what was in front of him, if he barely noticed occasions and time . . . it was a good thing. Let him be lost, the work paid the bills, if he was lost it meant his heart was in the story and a story never stood a chance unless his heart was in it. He pointed to Oliver's forehead.

"I fell. Hockey."

"You okay?"

"I'm wet."

"You're growing."

Oliver changed his jeans upstairs. Put the vials and needles under his bed and the knife in the pocket of dry jeans. They were tighter than he remembered. He jumped up to his door frame and hung there by his fingers and felt no pain. Did some chin-ups.

WHEN HE KNOCKED on her door there was a strange smell from him. Fish or something. Her mind went to the time she visited high school and they were dissecting frogs. Formaldehyde wafting to the doorway. That was the smell. Sad for all those pale sacrifices splayed out beneath the scalpels. Not wanting to go to high school.

He wasn't wearing a jacket.

"Will you help me find my dog?"

OLIVER WASN'T OLIVER.

The nameless, a new animal. That's what he thought as he went downstairs, put his boots back on, crossed the street. He was Oliver to his dad, Mickey to Murdoch, someone to protect, something to punch, but he wasn't those things anymore. He was becoming something different, so this was a chance.

Be different to someone new.

"Aren't you cold?"

"No."

"Do you want to come in?"

"I want to find him."

"Okay."

Suzi got her jacket from the hook near the door. She put a white hat on and Oliver looked at her face really quickly, looked down.

"What kind of a dog is it?"

"He's big." How could he explain. "He's hard to see in the snow."

Suzi went to the back of the house and Oliver heard voices. A whole world he didn't know. The place looked different, even smelled different, from when Charlie lived here. When she walked towards him he looked at her longer. Little chin. He suddenly realized he'd been thinking about her a lot. That dream he had about the girl and the Black Dove. Knew what her hand felt like. But of course he didn't.

"Where do you want to go?"

"I don't know. Maybe if we go back to where I lost him."

They stepped out and the street was quiet in the snow. If you're someone new, how do you speak. He'd seen books in used bookstores about how to dress and how to make friends.

"Were you walking him?"

"He's really strong." He slapped his shoulders, not to warm up but to remind himself that muscles were coming. "I'm strong too, but he . . . I didn't have the right leash."

"What's his name?"

"Night."

Suzi thought about calling him. *Ni-ight*. But she felt self-conscious. Broad daylight. Oliver seemed jumpy. She got a waft of that dissected frog smell again.

"That's a cool name," she said. Didn't remember seeing him with a dog before.

They walked through the snow, not close or far apart but in a way that made him think about exactly how much space was between them. He could see farther down the street than he remembered. Reading those signs used to be impossible.

What should I tell her.

He deliberately kept them on the other side of the street from the store as they passed. Didn't look towards it. He saw the bench where he had tried to tie Night.

"Why aren't you wearing a jacket?"

"I'm not cold."

"It's a snowstorm. Here. Wear my mitts."

She stood there holding the cuffs open like her mom did for her. When he put his fingers in they touched hers.

That feeling again, like in the bike store. Hot on her fingers and face. She quickly let go.

"They're small," he said. Holding them up.

"You're small. We're the same height."

She saw that darkness in him again.

"My hands are bigger."

"Give them back if you don't want them," she said.

She tugged on the mitts and avoided touching his fingers.

"Looks pretty stupid just wearing mitts," said Oliver.

"You look stupid without a jacket."

He felt an explosion, like a cannon going off in his chest. Just enough time to ask if he'd ever felt so angry. *Don't fuckin call me stupid!* Felt suddenly that Night betrayed him. No interest in being friends with him or exploring together. He just ran away.

Oliver picked up his pace. She had to jog for a second to catch up.

"I wasn't calling you stupid."

He slowed down.

"I just meant I'd be stupid to go out without a jacket. Like, I myself."

The tracks passing over Dupont were up ahead. Steps up to the railpath. A couple of blocks away was his mom's favourite bar.

"He ran this way and then I lost him. I don't know where I'd go."

"They follow smells." She sniffed. "Dogs. Don't they? Like those drug dogs at airports. That's their superpower."

"He's not really a dog," he said. "He's like a mix . . . He's like nothing else."

She sniffed more. Oliver sniffed too. The smell from the rendering plant was there, mixed with fumes of diesel trapped under the railway bridge. Pigeon spikes lining the girders made the whole scene hostile.

Up top, the path hadn't been plowed. He looked for tracks, paw prints or the chain line. They'd be distinctive.

"You'd see a line, like where the leash dragged. It was a chain," he said.

Snow got into her boots. Some people just had thick skin, she thought, like those construction workers you see not wearing gloves in winter. Hammering nails when it's minus thirty.

There was a graffiti-covered wall between the path and the train tracks, meant to keep the noise away from the houses and people away from the trains.

"I feel like he'd go somewhere open," said Oliver. "Not want to be trapped. That's what I'd do." Tried to see the pathway as Night would. "Look back there, it's like a hallway."

The sound barrier had intermittent glass panels, also covered in graffiti but clear enough to see through. He pressed his face to one and saw the railyards open up. An invitation. He walked along the wall and she watched him.

Behind some leafless bushes the wall came to an end and there was just a wire fence, peeled back in a few places, easy to get through. You barely had to crouch. Oliver pulled the fence back a little and ducked under.

One of those brave boys, thought Suzi. Or dumb. Restless. You see them doing stupid shit at school. Climbing fences and cutting their fingers on them when it's just as quick to walk around.

Oliver stared out at these tracks, so close to their houses. The Junction. He remembered that now, the neighbourhood named after the place all these tracks met. No trains in sight, except in the distance. The commuter train and airport express came through here. How many tracks. He started counting.

"I don't know a lot of people anymore," said Suzi. She'd come through the fence and stood next to him. "I'm making friends at school but . . . I don't know. I've never come up here."

He counted twelve tracks but might have skipped some.

Somewhere here, Night was trotting. A ghost. He tried to

picture it, Night's invisibility slightly confused by the snow on his fur. Glass hunter. He had run away like he was afraid of nothing or knew he wanted to go somewhere.

"We'll hear his chain. We'll see it."

He sat down on a track, to think.

Strange boy.

"I think he'll see us before we see him," he said.

A FREIGHT TRAIN crept around the corner heading west. Bells from the crossing. They walked three tracks over and watched it coming behind them. Stood still while it rumbled past. Not a threat, but something unfeeling, unstoppable. The driver sounded the horn to warn them, as if they hadn't noticed.

They couldn't do much while it passed. Stare at it. What's in those containers. Why does that thing exist. Creature of industry and need, creeping along with a bellyful of hammers. Deafening when the engine passed and then a slow pounding on the tracks.

When they got used to it they kept walking.

Oliver made a snowball and tried to throw it at the side of the train. The snow was too powdery.

"How come you don't go to my school?"

She picked up some snow too and patted it with her mitts. "French immersion. Everything's in French. My dad said I should do it, and I thought it would be good for travel. But I'm not . . . school and me . . . I'm okay at some subjects." She dropped the clump of snow and kicked it. "I can kick a ball," she said. She was smiling.

He looked away towards the trees beside the tracks, to the back of Vine Park, bent down to try to see through the under-carriage of the train. Squirrels, the wheels, a guy on a bike on Vine, everything that moved caught his eye.

Night was strong. How smart. He'll see us, he kept thinking.

Maybe he wasn't here at all.

He stopped and Suzi kept walking. Something felt funny in his mouth. Put the tip of his tongue on a fang and it wiggled.

He'd lost that tooth last year.

"MAYBE HE'LL JUST go home," said Suzi. "He'll get hungry."

The train had passed and the snow was easing.

He looked sad.

What if Night felt he didn't have a home. Didn't need one.

What was home now. What was calling Oliver. His dad. He wanted to be away from his dad for a while. Even away from Princeps. This feeling stronger than ever, raging now, that he wanted to do things his dad couldn't do or didn't know, that no one knew. Things no one could give him advice about. Maybe you don't need a home. That old bedroom and the lonely feeling. He had his knife in his pocket, but the needles were under his bed. Two more vials of not-Oliver.

She saw him smile a little.

"It's big," he said.

"What is?"

"I don't know. This place. The world. Let's do something. I'm hungry."

"Try this," said Suzi. Walking ahead, one foot in front of the other on a rail. She looked like a tightrope walker. "They're slippery."

Oliver ran and jumped up on a rail sideways, snow on his boot soles making him slide. Silver Surfer.

"How long can you stay out for?"

"I don't know," she said.

School was starting tomorrow.

4

MURDOCH STOOD NAKED in the change room longer than anyone else.

He didn't care. It's what his dad did when they went to the gym together. You just stand there and show the world because there is everything to be proud of.

Carmine over there with his hairy little mushroom and most of the boys covering up with their towels or underwear. Little kids shivering cause no one liked swimming in gym class. A couple of the girls were getting the legs and boobs of women and they were the shyest out by the pool.

Murdoch slowly put his clothes in his locker, jeans and underwear first.

He was going to meet Jackson later at the park and Jackson would tell him stories. Grade nine. Bit more than two years away. Stories about high school girls and getting his finger in.

Murdoch had dreams about his neighbour Meghan. Sunshine around her sometimes like in a movie. She went to Branksome Hall, grade twelve, and she talked to Murdoch's dad like she was in love. Shy and flirty like his dad could open the world for her.

Jodie said Murdoch was too young for her at Christmas and broke up with him.

He and Jonathan liked to pull down bathing suits, show the girls which boys had no hair yet.

"Let's go, Murdy," said Jonathan.

OLIVER SPAT A tooth into the sink when he brushed his teeth that night. His other fang was loose. Under the one he had just lost he could feel the point of a new one coming in. Sharp as a pin.

Someone was plowing the street, one of the private contractors up at Pelham Park. He could hear a chain being dragged behind the plow.

He was afraid to go back to the store. Princeps's kindness. Oliver paid him back by robbing him, letting his treasure loose. He'd said he would keep an eye on things and Oliver remembered the glasses and cameras he'd seen the first time he met him. Watching from wherever he was.

Under it all, a fear he hadn't really felt yet was growing around the changes in his body.

He sat on the bed for a second with his head in his hands. Couldn't breathe and felt dizzy. The tooth, eyesight, surges in his arms and legs, things inside him rushing to get out and no way to catch up with them. It felt like something big was coming. Maybe Night went home to his concrete room and everything was fine. He held his head like it didn't belong to him, listened to the sound of the chain dragging in a prison outside. School.

He sucked on the blood from his gums and felt hungry. Reached under his bed.

The numbers on the vials had been rubbed off in his backpack. They had lids you were supposed to stick a needle into. Rubber in the middle of the lid. He'd seen that in movies, and what Princeps had done. Should he take them both at the same time. He stared at the liquid in them and imagined what was in it, clear as water and full of new days. His breath slowed down, comforting just to hold them. Princeps had been injecting them one at a time into his belly. He put one vial back under the bed with the manuscript Princeps had given him.

Squirt it up first and give it a flick, Doctor.

He got up and sat with his back to the door in case his dad came in. Lifted his pyjama top and pinched the skin. The scary part wasn't the prick of the needle, it was pushing the liquid in. It would make him sick. Poison opening doors in his body to let new visitors in.

He felt ashamed for a second. Another wave of fear. The needle there, poised like something evil. He was deliberately doing something bad. He'd seen needles on the ground up at Pelham Park where the snowplow was dragging the chain, all the kids said you could get AIDS just by stepping on them.

He rested his head against the door and closed his eyes.

School.

He wanted this new future, he could feel it in his teeth. Pushed his thumb down on the plunger and breathed out. This wasn't drugs, it was medicine.

He sat for a while and thought, wiped the blood on his belly with his palm and walked towards his bed. Princeps had cleaned the skin where the needle went. Should he have done that. Bellyskin was sore.

He picked up the stack of papers from under the bed. *The Holland Marsh.* Lay down and read the first paragraph.

> *They called it Black Magic, the soil of the Holland Marsh. Bulrushes, sedges and moss, all soaked, buried and mixed, drained for a century and lying deep across the valley . . .*

He wasn't sure he wanted to read it. Whatever secrets were in there. The easiest way for him to change, for him to do any of this, was to focus on what was ahead. He didn't want to know exactly what was in these injections and didn't want to know or learn more about Princeps. The secrets of the surgeon with his hands in your body. It scared him. If Oliver started running, started focusing on what he wanted, like Night did, nothing else would matter—no one's past, no one's reasons.

He felt a sort of click in his body and went rigid. A cold feeling spread from his belly to his chest, heart pumping out to his arms and fingers. Not cold. Heat. A herd of animals and people galloping through him, running like kids to get on a ride.

He put the papers under his bed and closed his eyes. Can you see new colours, above the clouds unnamed. A ride on a roller coaster but there's no track or machine below. Down and up through the screams of strangers, into a tunnel of secrets, warm, through the funhouse, haunted house, don't be scared, there's nothing can scare him again. *It's my body*, he said to Suzi in his dream, the ride slowing down and easing into a crowd of smiling parents. Everyone laughing, relieved. A kind look when she turns to him. *It's not exactly perfect*, she says.

MS. SODEBERGH, THE gym teacher, was strict like Murdoch's grandmother and also got lost in the past. Hands like hams, she threw discus or shot put for the Olympic team or something. You had to be smart around her.

Girls had their arms across their chests and everyone was shivering.

"Everyone in!" shouted Ms. Sodebergh.

The water was a predictable shock, you knew it was going to be cold and it was: but not that cold. Everyone was jumping on the spot and saying *hoo!*

"Jump!" shouted the teacher, and they all started doing jumping jacks in the shallow end. "One hundred and don't cheat! Arms up! Right over the head!"

Your bathing shorts could slip off if you didn't do them up tightly and some of the boys were retying them while they jumped.

Twenty-five, twenty-six. Murdoch didn't cheat. He was going to carve and buff up for the summer and he'd mow the lawn shirtless when he knew Meghan was watching.

Thirty-one.

Jonathan was next to him and was definitely cheating.

Jumping jacks, one hundred push-aways and claps from the edge, then races and five minutes of free time. Murdoch and Jonathan made everyone dread the free time, because that's when they pulled down shorts.

Forty-one.

The pool in winter felt like flu and bruises.

IN THE MORNING Oliver's back was itchy. Between his shoulder blades where he couldn't quite reach. It felt like a bug with tickly legs. He stretched his arms, his shoulders, when he sat up in bed and tried to reach around. Right . . . there. Two little bumps on either side of his spine. He scratched them.

The tips of his fingers weren't burning anymore but they still felt funny. When he had these visions from touch, it was kind of like thinking, but shallower. Like a movie over his thoughts. He could see himself lying in that bed, maybe it was the DNA from his tears, skin, sweat, saw his younger self being heavy with sadness. Reading comics and yearning. It made him smile. It all seemed small and foolish, the stuff he'd got upset about.

He stood up and a hot surge of nausea rose up, fast, so fast he barely made it to the toilet downstairs. He spat it all out and smiled at himself in the mirror, the gap where his fang had been.

"You don't have to be nervous, you know." His dad made

their toast. "School's the biggest thing in your life right now, but one day you won't remember most of it."

MS. SODEBERGH BLEW the whistle and three by three, boys and girls lined up to swim a length, any stroke they wanted.

Murdoch was racing Carmine and Fat Tina.

He slapped his shoulders like they did in the Olympics. Adjusted his goggles. Dolphin man. Sometimes he pissed when he swam.

Jonathan was next, in front of him, and Murdoch looked to see if Sodebergh was watching. She was staring away towards the end of the last race so Murdoch pushed Jonathan into the pool. Sodebergh blew the whistle before she saw what happened and Jonathan missed the start. Everybody laughed.

Murdoch slapped his own shoulders again. He didn't bother looking down the line at Carmine and Fat Tina, but he knew that Carmine was ready for a look, a glance from the king, we're buddies, you're okay, fuck all these little losers.

Everyone was watching.

Ms. Sodebergh blew the whistle and Murdoch dove in. Cheers got drowned. He came up and heard them again and started swimming like a conqueror. New school one day. Leave these kids behind. For a second, things came at him the wrong way. He'd only be in grade eight next year. Water like an enemy, pushing against him, ready to trap him, pull him back and under.

But he fought.

He hung out with cool friends.

He'd find someone better than Jodie.

He was at the other side.

He climbed out in one movement without kicking his legs.

Stood with arms folded and watched Carmine come in, Fat Tina a mile back.

His laugh and smile felt wise.

Oliver was a couple of rows behind, trying not to scratch his back. On the way to school he went crazy trying to reach between his shoulders, the layers of sweater, shirt and last year's coat that his dad had made him wear. So tight. He'd stopped on the sidewalk and wriggled like he was in a swarm of bees. Stripped down to his shirt and tried to scratch. Finally got his fingers behind and he sighed with how good it felt, getting his nails into those bumps, whatever had bitten him. Scratched until he felt something wet under his fingernails.

At the pool the kids behind him were saying *gross*. Whispering about the leaking scabs. *He shouldn't be allowed in the water.* He reached a hand back to scratch and just used his middle finger. Fuck off.

It seemed like there was a thread back there. Not just an itch. Something tugging on him, pulling upwards, his ears moving up towards the sound of Ms. Sodebergh's whistle.

Murdoch and the others were shivering at the other end and on the sides, waiting for free time to be called so they could get warmer in the pool, push each other around and touch skin with some of the girls. Shivering and juiced up, but breathing heavy. Most of them exhausted.

"Come on, Mickey! Break the record! Slowest fish in the ocean!"

Oliver had never tried to win. Never even bothered looking at who else was racing. Sometimes he was glad he even made it to the end.

When the whistle blew he felt that thread pull harder, like it yanked him up with a jerk, and when he dove into the water it dragged him over the surface. He didn't use his arms and legs more than usual but felt himself skimming, higher in the water than he should have been. A crew on the other shore was pulling on the rope attached to his spine.

Soft water pushed his lips into a smile. Soft glass he could almost walk on.

Glory.

Seal up the doors from the change rooms and silence the showers. Dim the light from the clouds, and watch.

A birth.

By the tracks Night licked the eyes of the two men he killed. Lay belly down in a den of wooden ties and saw water, everything wet except those eyes that used to cry, the world a cup that tipped back onto itself and cleansed, a little dirtier each time.

Oliver rose up from the pool and went to the middle, these five minutes usually the longest of the day. He was powerful now. Wouldn't be cornered. Murdoch and Jonathan, Carmine and Thomas, a flank marching in slow motion as the water got deeper. Ms. Sodebergh preoccupied with some skirmish in the shallow end. People were trying to pull down the banners that hung low over the pool.

The boys smirked at Oliver, laughed and moved slow. From the middle you could try to lunge to the edge. If you tied up tight they couldn't get your shorts off unless they really got their hands in. You could shout to Ms. Sodebergh who would send everyone to the office. Or you could not be afraid.

He stepped back till the water reached his chin, his mouth. With his eyes close to water level the boys looked tall. Behind them the rest of the class, jumping and shouting, looked like some kind of home movie. Look at how crazy our summer was.

"We hear you've got some scabs," said Murdoch. "Bedbugs, eh? Come where it's shallower. You're gonna get the pool dirty."

Carmine and Thomas were wading farther around the sides, Murdoch standing tall and then diving under.

Oliver felt the hands yank his shorts. He held the waistband and Murdoch tugged harder. Pulled Oliver under. The other boys stopped wading and let Murdoch do his thing.

He thought about holding Mickey down. Give him a bit of a scare. He was tired. Wanted to get back to the shallow end.

His foot hit Oliver in the nose when he tried to kick away. Hard enough for Oliver to see black, like it was broken.

The other boys watched Murdoch hopping and giggling, something stuck to his leg. They laughed too, even when Murdoch's smile got smaller, that little look of worry when he got pulled back.

Oliver hooked his fingers in Murdoch's shorts and slammed his arms down. Squeezed his muscles and locked his hands. He pulled up for a bit of air and grabbed Murdoch by the hair at the back of his head.

The boys watched Murdoch get bent backwards and pulled under.

Oliver held him by the top of his head with both hands, like he was trying to push a post into the ground. Murdoch was hitting at his arms and then grabbed hold of Oliver's wrists. Tried to pull and a bubble of a shout came out of him.

They both had goggles on. Oliver wanted to rip off Murdoch's and then pull out his eyes.

Murdoch swung his arms. His feet were on the bottom of the pool and he tried to push up but it did nothing. That strength. Like Oliver had a wall against his back. Murdoch was angry, but now he was getting scared. How long was he . . .

Stop! he tried to say underwater. Breathed in by mistake.

Oliver felt a pull at his spine again, something deep, private. Not one of the boys behind him, but within. A beginning. He closed his eyes and raised himself, that rope pulling up again.

With his hands pressing down on the head he lifted his feet and put them on Murdoch's shoulders.

Underneath, Murdoch choked when he inhaled, and his belly convulsed. He threw up underwater and saw a yellow cloud while Oliver put his weight down on him. Hot flash of panic up his body and his throat started burning. Tried to squirm out but suddenly got so weak. Needed to be saved. His lungs and throat opened and took in more water. He felt his bowels empty.

The boys saw Oliver rise up. Feet beneath the water and his arms stretched out for balance.

He squeezed his feet around Murdoch's neck and stiffened his muscles, knew all he needed was the right breeze and he could be airborne. If someone opened a door or a window deeper in the school the gust alone would lift him, and the glory would race to the sky like an angry flower. Oliver kept his eyes closed while the boy at his feet went limp, and the others backed away from the cloud of colour in the water.

He was a god.

Victory.

The Holland Marsh

What is the meaning of these unclean monkeys, these strange savage lions, and monsters? To what purpose are here placed these creatures, half beast, half man, or these spotted tigers?

      —St. Bernard of Clairvaux

1

THEY CALLED IT Black Magic, the soil of the Holland Marsh. Bulrushes, sedges and moss, all soaked, buried and mixed, drained for a century and lying deep across the valley. It was muck, moist and black, so deep that workhorses had to wear wooden boots to keep from sinking.

In the warmer months the marsh was a long, dark smear, striped with greens, a flat stretch of unlikely riches cut through by a highway. Most of the country's carrots and onions grew here. Celery. Bok choy. The nation's soup and salad bowl. It was only fifty kilometres north of the city, large enough to make people notice as they drove, small enough to feel like a tease—a glimpse of the nature they wouldn't find for another hour or two when they took the dirt road to the cottage.

Muck.

When I was a young man, I was known as Arthur Fulham. Another phony name. Arthur at university and when I arrived at the marsh to do fieldwork I blended in with the locals by calling myself Art. A good guy. Studious. Learned the soil better than any of the Van Kuyts or Ginssers, soil that was hidden by water and reeds when Wendat, Seneca and others travelled through.

I did an internship at the humbly named Muck Crops Research Station, still standing on Woodchoppers Lane. I studied plant genetics and how the most successful varieties used bacteria to their benefit, the interplay between the plants and the filth they grew from.

The riches of the Holland Marsh were a miracle. Not just the work of glaciers and time but of an unrepeatable sequence of death and renewal: animals who glutted themselves in paradise, the bodies of horses and rival farmers. I'd found all kinds of microbes and DNA that deepened the soil's darkness, that couldn't have landed and grown here without humans fighting each other for territory.

I like to drive from the east. Taking Dufferin downhill to Ansnorveldt, where there are no signs of wealth. Tiny houses with gambrel roofs and plastic-wrapped greenhouses, beiges, greys, an ugly church. The train track reminds me of my brother.

From there the marsh opens up as a plain. A few roads run through it with houses and farms, its darkness living as a mist in all the windows.

AFTER MY BROTHER died I ran away from home. I had no idea where to go—anywhere but the tracks. In that first summer I survived in the city's ravines, my body bruised. Toronto kept hammering itself into the ground, but there were still surprisingly wild places where I found food and safe dirt for sleep. Herbs and picnics left behind. My brother's watch cap helping on cold nights. Men trolled the paths of the Don and I got money from them, surrendering my body until I snapped, until a flame leapt in my brother's memory—what I later understood as a trigger of the warrior gene. My jaw set tight.

In the heart of Moss Park, downtown, was a shelter where I sometimes stayed or got warm meals. Kids were often lined up with caseworkers and nudged towards foster homes. I stayed aloof and proud, resisted any help beyond food. But there was a weakness in me. Not just debilitating memories but something cell-deep. My father had offered me and my brother no protection. And while the warrior within me said I never wanted to be like my dad, I had vulnerabilities—a lingering need to be looked after, some of my father's submissiveness at my core.

A grey-haired man named Henry Fulham gave money to the shelter. He visited regularly. Behind his glasses was a humorous light. Stories that made boys laugh. He was upright, wealthy, a political man who had been to Cambridge and seen the world.

I often wondered why Fulham chose me, or how he noticed me among all the other boys. For years I felt I had been divinely selected, as if my inner light had been seen, and the more I succeeded as a teenager, the more I was praised and rewarded, the more Henry's attention was justified for both of us. I was meant to be a prince, and Henry always called me his future king.

My eyes were opened to learning. He encouraged me to read and study, take pride in being disciplined, to ignore whatever darkness I felt was around me.

He invited me into his home in Cabbagetown, a Gothic Revival cottage with bedrooms to choose from. Never a hint that he wanted anything from me. Within a few months he said, "I see something in you. How bright your eyes. I don't want you living at that shelter," and within a year I called myself Arthur Fulham, a son, sleeping in an oak sleigh bed and reading peacefully every night in a room that was never cold.

I excelled in science and literature but chose to study science when I went to university. Henry thought it was an ignoble thing to pursue. If the best you could be was a physician, how did you differ from the barber-surgeons of the past, the guildsmen, caretakers elbow-deep in bodies. Enlightenment was in knowing the thoughts of others, not their diseases. He discouraged me from studying science, and it became part of a pattern. A chill that began to settle.

From the time he brought me home he nurtured and spoiled me, taught me the language and ways of the ruling class, revered my intelligence and my successes at school. But the older I got, the love and enthusiasm waned. He didn't look me in the eyes unless I was showered and boyish. He liked me dressed in suits and ties, prepared for serious endeavours while I was nonetheless clearly a child. In the company of other men Henry had his share of locker-room jokes, but the only love that he liked to mention was in books. High-minded, Romantic love that tripped in iambic pentameter between epicene yearners and unfulfilled hearts.

In these latter days no one likes sexual classification, but it was clear to me as an adult that Henry Fulham was an old gay man who sublimated every feeling, ashamed of loving boys. He had seen me not as a god sees a chosen one but as a wolf sees the weakest in the herd. Like a pusher sees an addict at a party.

All that praise, the admiration and encouragement. Where does it leave you when it's taken away? In the same high place, or crashing down?

I have always worked hard.

MY WORK AT the Muck Station lasted four years. It excited me so much that I seldom slept. Sixty papers in that short span, and I earned the attention of the Genomics Institute in California. I could look forward to a modest life with smart minds, discoveries, a resurrection of sorts.

But the years in the Holland Marsh, while industrious, were also my most peaceful. Sinking into that black soil.

I visited Toronto on the weekends, sometimes going past my parents' home in the Junction. There were boards over the windows. Junkies teetering in daylight dances on the sidewalk. I stayed in Henry's house downtown, in his antique bedroom, and as comfortable as I was, I increasingly felt some kind of lie in all that comfort. We had dinner and long conversations about absolutely nothing. Henry showed no interest in what I was discovering, the strengths and weaknesses in our genes, what dirt was teaching me.

I resented how much I needed his praise. I knew how revolutionary my work was becoming and wanted to prove that I could contribute something to the wonder of the world. In the dining room, amidst paintings by A. J. Casson and A. Y. Jackson, I said, "One day we'll be able to improve people, like we improve crops."

"Improve," said Henry. Like many insecure people he often insisted he was perfect. "Who needs improving? You? I think you are just fine. You've gone a little scruffy. That's all." Rubbing his own face as a gesture at my beard. "And your posture is worse. Sit up straight."

When my beard grew there were other patches of white from my Waardenburg syndrome.

His little corrections sometimes stung me more than my mother's slaps ever had.

IDEALLY I WOULD have liked my brother to be born from an egg. No parents in sight.

I had dreams about him in Henry's house. The hour of night when consciences awake and command our visions, 2 A.M., 3 A.M., I could feel tortured by guilt or crushing sadness. Guilt about sleeping in that bed. For all his despair about his own future, I believed my brother killed himself because he feared for my life ahead. What he had seen people do to me while I was passed out in that boxcar—how could I come back from that? What would I have to live for?

Well, there I was: living comfortably. A father loving me.

I wandered Henry's house in those hours, trying to imagine what it might have been like to have my brother there with us. I read myself back to sleep, and my reading blended with thoughts of him.

Henry had wonderful old books. I looked through reproductions of medieval bestiaries and wondered about all the imaginary creatures, my teenage nose buried in fantasies. Centaurs, dragons, the golem.

An alerion was an eagle the colour of fire with wings as sharp as a razor.

A bonnacon was a beast with curled horns and the head of a bull. Its dung could be sprayed across two acres and burn whatever it touched.

I was fascinated by snakes, king cobras in particular. Their majesty. Heads rising as high as six feet, not only hissing but growling, their venom causing hallucination and paralysis, death in the time it would take me to read ten pages. What seemed most sinister was that they regularly ate other snakes. Each other.

CLOUDS OFTEN HUNG like drapes over the marsh, summer or winter, and the wind could be ferocious, strong enough to rip up crops and raise that Black Magic as a fog of poison.

I have long thought about how memories make everyone weak, the bad ones overwhelming us at night, the good ones reminding how seldom the present measures up.

Henry appears to me in a bright summer light, wearing an unlined khaki suit—never seersucker unless you want to stand out. The panama hat—Montecristi Superfino—might draw attention, but you will simply be recognized as a man of taste.

After I moved in, Henry mailed his cheques to the shelter instead of delivering them by hand. He stopped visiting the other boys. In the middle of those days he said they were the best of his life, and that I was the son he felt he never could have had.

"I always thought I would live alone."

He said that he would leave everything to me when he died.

THIS IS WHERE Amon was born again.

Outside this hangar where the trees grow thicker. On a summer night I planted my boots in that black spermary, took all life, leaves, humus and salt in through the nose and mumbled my own kind of prayer, that all lambs rise up on wet hoofs and grow better than their parents, never to be slaughtered. Rise like growling cobras.

No neighbours within a kilometre. As far as the Township is concerned this is deep, untouchable woods, Art Fulham's hobby farm out there in the middle of it. I climb up over the canal in winter wearing thermal waders and I drag provisions by sled. The appetite of all my creatures is great. None of this could I get away with in the city.

The sleeping quarters for my sons are open so they have congress with the other animals, and I've encased the chambers with glass or plastic so I can keep an eye on things. Some, of course, are sterile, but I let the boys wander. They know to avoid needles, and they lie on the operating table and play, mimicking whatever they see me do, roaming through a metal forest of centrifuges, thermocyclers, vortexers and autoclaves, staring at nerves that hang in suspended solutions and dragging pencils over beakers and vials of blood to make little tunes.

They all have computers to occupy themselves and an array of marvellous pets.

AT THE GENOMICS Institute we bred pigs to have organs more useful to us. Livers and kidneys more easily transplantable. In discrete parts of their bodies the pigs became human. A simple matter of reordering letters in the genome and a pig could grow a human heart.

The exciting times began when I was fired, when I let my imagination run free. If we could give them human hearts, why not human faces?

My colleague with the cat was a woman named Margaret. She regularly took my ideas and published them as her own. My final act was to make a pig with her face. Her eyes and delicate nose, mouth that could only squeal.

Lawyers licked their fingers as they flipped through the pages of settlements. I took their DNA and by now have made several herds of Margarets and lawyers. Every now and then I introduce new faces, but it has always been easier to slaughter the familiar ones.

Livers and kidneys sell for fifty thousand each, hearts are triple that. Tissue alone for fellow hobbyists is worth tens of thousands. Each pig represents almost $300,000. Many, of course, have lived their lives unharvested, but as a whole the trade in organs has made me comfortable and paid for everything in the hangar.

The pigs smell me coming, the garbage and provisions on the sled, sour sweat in my jacket. How could their squeals not seem human, coming from those little faces. So excited to see me, I know. I know. They lick and nibble my hands.

FOR ALL THOSE years that I slept with Amon's cap, it took a while for me to envision that I could harvest it and bring him back to life. You might be able to imagine the inside of that hangar in the woods—my workshop of filthy creation, as Mary Shelley put it. The slop of organs and afterbirth on the floor, my hands busy in an unmentionable stew of life in death, my brother's eyes floating in threes in a bowl of mucus, and version after version emerging from the incubators pink-eyed and slithering. One iteration was so hideous, so needy, I had to aim a shotgun at it. I watched it grow for three years, his innocent face ultimately rising up and wordlessly saying *help* from the body of a hooded worm. I didn't want him to look like a snake, I wanted the snake to be within. An engine of vengeance. I tipped out so much venom in those woods that several of my pigs died from simply rooting.

But I perfected the egg. The yolk fed through a slit to his stomach. I was sure, trial after trial, that I had corrected the genome and written a code as lissome and solid as a Florentine sculpture. I felt it, and I credited the soil of the Holland Marsh for making my hope so fecund.

I MENTION HENRY with gratitude. I never would have arrived where I have without him. And as I've grown I have understood his tragedy.

I did feel betrayed for many years, but he never hurt me physically.

He used to write me letters. They come to mind sometimes when I think of the human hearts that I am growing inside my pigs. When I came home from school with news of successes, top marks, things I knew would please my adoptive father, there would sometimes be a letter waiting on my bed. He was an articulate man in person, but to express the depths of a father's love he sometimes turned to writing.

> *My crown is in my heart, not on my head;*
> *Not decked with diamonds and Indian stones,*
> *Nor to be seen; my crown is called content,*
> *A crown it is that seldom kings enjoy.*

A crown in his heart. A human heart that warmed as he taught his son Shakespeare. There was often money in the envelope.

He simply stopped looking at me. We spoke on the phone sometimes but the conversations were curt. I shaved twice a day and regretted some of the changes I saw in the mirror. I didn't want to grow, but I wanted to be myself.

Like me, Henry was a dreamer.

Moralists and priests have seldom known an empty stomach. Bioethicists and all those men and women who sit around judging the lapses of fellow humans—these people have either forgotten or never known what it was like to suffer, to survive, to feel breath on their necks and know the only way to live was to turn around and murder. When something repugnant is behind you, you fight for anything that might look better. You fight and make the world your own.

Henry had a lover's eyes. His own idea of beauty. He needed to see youth to feel alive, choosing life instead of dying under the weight of others' judgment. I came to respect that, or at least to understand it. When I understood myself as just a love, an object, a dream . . . There are no ethics in dreams.

The last time I saw him he was walking along the sidewalk to the shelter in Moss Park. I had dressed up and come to town to surprise him, eager to take him to lunch with some of the money I had been earning from grants. I couldn't find him at home, and I had a hunch.

A hot summer day, and he was wearing a suit as always. An elegant hat. I stood there cleanly shaven but sweating in my pants and jacket, and I knew that I had become invisible. A man.

He had an envelope in his hand, and he reached for the door of the shelter: the sun reflecting off the glass as it opened and blinding me for a second.

He was looking for a new son.

When I walked away I imagined that inside the shelter there wouldn't be many boys. On a summer day they would be hustling down by the lake. Henry might even have found no one there.

Or he did find someone? Bruised. A little wild and angry but still hopeful—eyes that hadn't yet learned to be heavy. Henry would tell him jokes and surprise the boy with his empathy and understanding. Why would this rich old man listen so kindly to my complaints?

"Twelve is the perfect age," Henry might say.

A boy with a little dirt on his face.

An old man trying to find life's sweetness, long, long, long after the ripening.

IF WE ARE to change this human story, we have to put an end to the old one. Not just our fellows, but the creatures we have made. Give these new ones, all of them, a hunger for meat and let it play out in random chaos. Let them dine. Make them eat and destroy each other. Make room for those who will make things better.

On a warm day in May, I made a nest in the soil and waited seventy nights. I had given up on lab-born versions; this soil was what they needed. I planted seven eggs in a moist black bed and covered them with leaves, hung wire as a mesh around the trees to keep the predators away. I had not equipped the embryos with egg teeth so it was my job to help them hatch. Brood hen to kings or abominations.

The layers of leaves started stirring on a night that was hotter than blood. The eggs were not much bigger than softballs, pale and leathery. I had always felt anxious about what size he might become. King cobras can grow as long as eighteen feet, and their eggs were smaller than these. If he had surged to a twenty-foot version of my brother I probably would have felt the same fear and pride that I feel today.

A hand, head or limb was pushing from inside one of the eggs. As I brushed off the soil another one was stirring. I looked more closely at all seven, and two were small, one holding nothing but custard and the other a dead fetus. I made incisions in the two that were moving, and waited.

In the past some of these serpent children had slithered right out, phallic and abhorrent. I kept ten vials of anti-venom in a bag nearby. I wanted him to know me. When snakes emerge they use their tongues to smell the world. My brother would have gnostic fingers that would understand through touch. Know me and our history, bond with me. I would inevitably be poisoned.

Mothers of king cobras leave the nest once hatching begins, otherwise tempted to eat their young.

On that night, of all those nights, I asked none of the questions that had troubled me. I knew the world was a mess, and he was welcome to it. But my hand was shaking.

I made cuts in three more eggs and peered in. Creatures uncurling, six inches long in the slime, red veins on the inside of the shell wet and vivid. They looked the same at first, but when I shone a light squarely I could mark the variations. One with no arms, another no limbs at all. One with hands reached out, but before I presented my finger for touch I saw a face that made me moan. A baby with no jaw.

The woods were thickened by the scents emerging from these eggs. I could hear animals gathering. A fisher clawing the tree behind me.

Amon was the fifth. He stretched in that wet sac, arms and legs intact. I scooped the slime and sputum from his mouth and felt an electric spasm, his tiny fingers in the crook of my thumb releasing all his venom. How parents want their babies to know everything right away, how fiercely loved.

I injected myself with the anti-venom and wrapped a bandage around the skin, wound it around his hands so they could cause no more damage and tried to keep my hand below my heart. Sinking into the warm muck with my back

against the tree that the fisher looked down from, I stared
up at the sky I couldn't see. That venom filled my eyes with
gin and I relaxed into beautiful fantasies. I didn't want the
antidote to work.

The rest of the night was a dream. Awake enough to inject
more vials of anti-venom, walking ritualistically around that
enclosure repeating my prayer. I stepped on the unviable babies
and held my hand in pain. Eyes of the fisher staring down. My
eyes. Behold the man rejoicing in the birth of his older brother,
he lifts him out of the egg. The fisher was dead in the soil the
next day, intoxicated from its meals. The fisher was the friend I
never had. I called him from the hospital.

"My brother's coming home."

I SET THE creatures free from here to spread and eat and do
whatever they may. Make way, make way. This hangar is their
nursery. Some have been very fond of me. When their bodies
are close to fully grown I let them loose.

The west end of the hangar has a roll-up steel door. I designed
the cages to form a seal around the top and sides, and can open
them remotely. There are forty of them on a revolving track,
stacked high. The boys can always play with or antagonize the
animals closest to the working side of the hangar and with
those in the cages I keep separate throughout the space.

Sometimes I feel as though my heart is the forest floor, those
new paws and feet testing it, resting softly upon it when they
first step outside. Cameras capture the animals' tentative early
moments, and I watch the images either here in the hangar or
from the shop downtown.

The increasingly invisible hunters, the prototypes for Night,
all touching the dead leaves the same way, sniffing, fixating on
some doomed creature in the distance, lowering their heads
and trotting.

Residents of the Holland Marsh started telling stories like their ancestors had about beasts that came out of the land at night, dogs and cats eviscerated on porches, a child walking naked sucking snakes up from the soil.

A farmer wore camouflage and waited in a blind at dusk with an iPhone and a gun. His widow posted the video on Facebook, the marsh-coloured creature moving as if blown on the wind, the screen dark, the snap of bones and the purring. We need help, she said in her post.

I GAVE HIM a soul of wrath.

I made him more honest than ordinary people about being driven by hunger.

And otherwise, like every child, he was raised on bedtime stories. I told him all the unhappy ones so he would never get weak with hope.

"Once upon a time there were two brothers . . ."

If you pictured us in a firelit room, me on a chair, my brother curled up on a blanket, you might also have seen the seasons blowing across the marsh, how beautiful he looked when he slept. Barely stirring for two weeks at a time, absorbing my language and stories. I could leave him there and return to the city to harvest, be gone for a week and find him in exactly the same place.

I fed him snakes and he learned to find them himself. When he awoke his eyes inflamed me, reminded me of all the ambition I have had to change the world. He spoke no more frequently than he fed, but over the years he said surprising things. He got anxious in the cold and rain, and scared me one morning standing over my bed. Not wearing the gloves I tried to make him wear. "I don't feel like the boy you talk about."

"What you are here to do," I said, touching his cheek, "is to take revenge. You should eat anything you want."

His hands, lethal, hovered above my belly as if he was warming them over a fire.

And when he reached the age he once died at, I felt breathless. To see him alive again. He killed people in the marsh and I brought him to Toronto. Sometimes I feared I would lose him. His face on those tracks came back to me more vividly than ever.

I talk to him in the basement and watch him go out to feed, his snake's appetites commingled with his human curiosity. This is the age he will stay at forever.

"You might not remember," I say, "but when we were boys you marked the bricks of buildings with your knife. 'This one's ours,' you would say. 'And this one.' The buildings in our kingdom. We went on walks and named things. I want you to remember this. The auto mechanic's was the place we repaired our ships, and the corner store was where our palace got provisions."

I always talk about the time I hope for, when all the weak have strength, when the strong make way for the best.

"I have made these new versions of myself, and you, and they will go out to the woods at the edge of the marsh. We'll have our favourite trees to climb. Make swords out of sticks and hurt each other's knuckles. I might still get upset but you'll be as patient as always. We can blow on our hands and lie down in leaves."

Stare at threatening clouds and think of nothing.

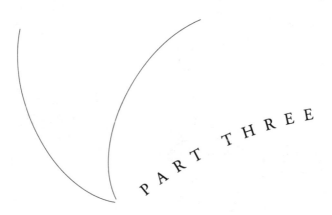

PART THREE

Stay Like This

1

OLIVER HEARD VOICES at the door downstairs.

Murdoch's dad.

Mumbles and not-quite-shouts.

He tried to hear exactly what was being said, but he had to imagine. Weird silences. He thought about putting his ear to the door but stayed in his chair, bounced an eraser off his desk.

Next to his drawers was a stack of his favourite comics. He tried to remember which ones he loved. All that milk in his brain, relaxing to forget things. His reflection in the window looked back at him. One eye winking a little like he had a headache, but he didn't.

The fact that Murdoch's dad was standing all this time at the door wasn't good. The two men used to be friends.

Oliver had been suspended for fourteen days. Could have been expelled. Might be still. If Ms. Sodebergh hadn't compressed his chest, if they'd needed an ambulance. "If you had been in trouble before," the principal said. "We'll be talking to the school board and the parents."

Murdoch had been sent home but the rest of them—Jonathan, Thomas, Carmine—had to sit in the office with Oliver. All of them in trouble before, maybe making the principal take it easier on Oliver. "I know you boys. I doubt this was unprovoked. Tell me this was just horseplay." Oliver kept his eyes on the floor the whole time, Jonathan staring at him.

Downstairs, it got quiet. Oliver heard the front door close.

He waited for his dad to come up. Felt things he'd never really known before. Not guilt or being sorry. Not scared.

There were noises in the kitchen, his dad cleaning up, and it seemed he wasn't going to come up after all. Oliver pictured his bedroom detaching itself from the house. Planting a huge pole and sticking his bedroom on the top of it, separate from the world. Or separate from people he knew. That feeling in his back, the string pulling him up—it happened again, strong like in the pool. He would be able to detach the bedroom himself, get his fingers in those corners of the floor and lift it. Drift over to those buildings downtown and not have to care about any of this bullshit.

He suddenly hated his dad. Enough to want to get up and shout it downstairs. Hated him for not knowing everything, what he had to go through every day at school. Hated him for being absent lately and knowing he would hate him anyway, even if he'd been around.

This room, school, up and down the same stairs every day. He wanted out. Being suspended felt like a relief.

The light came on in Suzi's bedroom and she sat at her desk like Oliver did. He held up his hand, not as a wave but to tell her *wait there*. Her eyes opened a little wider. Ten minutes later, again. *Wait.*

Footsteps up the stairs and his dad came in.

"Tell me. Help me understand."

SUZI TURNED OFF her light and watched.

It had been above freezing today.

She was wide awake. One of those nights like a sleepover when you could stay up till the light changed again.

This morning she had lifted her feet in bed, so the soles were facing the posters on her ceiling. Imagined the ceiling was the sky, and that if you ever felt like the sky was coming down you could put your feet up like that and hold it. Push it away.

She still believed she could.

HIS DAD SAT on his bed and stared at him. Oliver's face was looking harder. Dark bags under his eyes, his complexion . . . almost green. This is real, thought his dad. Snap out of it. Talk to him, feed him, hold him. Was it his fault, this silence lately, or do you have to, *have* to let them figure it out?

"Were they bullying you? That man's an asshole. So's his son." Silence.

"If you tell me what happened I'll know what to say." Every day wondering, again, again, again, what the perfect words might be. How to steer this ship.

Oliver looked at the floor. "There's nothing . . ."

His dad leaned lower to catch his eye. Gently put his hand under his chin to lift his head. Oliver wouldn't look up.

The hand went down and his dad sighed. Stood up like he was going to leave but just waited there, looking around the room.

THE NIGHT DARK and warm, she watched Oliver climb out the window and hang on to the trellis like a gymnast. It looked like he dropped a long way, but there was something . . . lighter than gravity. Like some invisible hands caught him and gently set him down. He went out of sight for a second.

His fingers gripped the column up to her porch. Each hand stuck like suction cups. Didn't feel any of it—the weight of his body, the height of the climb. Didn't think.

She opened her window wider.

"Hi."

EVERYTHING WAS MELTING. Sound of drips. He sat on her porch roof and she leaned out her window, lying forwards across her desk. Whispering. The light off in her bedroom.

He figured he wouldn't know what to say so he showed her this, the comic he'd stuffed in his back pocket. Like he wanted to show her what he'd been doing in his room.

"This is Black Bolt." He held it close in case she couldn't see it. "He got, whatever, recruited by Black Panther to defend his kingdom from this guy, Apocalypse. And you see here. Quiet."

She thought he was telling her to be quiet, so she listened to the drips. A car was coming from the end of the street.

"All he needs to say is a word so quiet that they can't even write it in the word balloon. See? We can't even hear it, but look what happens. There's this crater where Apocalypse used to be."

"That's his power," she said. "Words."

"No. Sound. He has to stay quiet all the time."

She hung on to the window frame and pulled herself out. Quiet as she could be. "Move over."

A downspout marked where her house and the neighbour's were divided, the little porch shared by both.

"That's my parents' room." Extra quiet, looking over her shoulder at the window next to hers. Her way of saying *keep whispering.*

They sat on the roof against the brick, the downspout between them. Staring at another car.

The street felt different from here, sitting outside. A scene they'd both stared at every night from their rooms. Like getting inside your TV, or getting out of it. Everything rounder and louder.

"Did you find your dog?"

"No."

He felt shy for a second and then he looked at her. Staring

back at him to see if he was worried about his dog. Stayed quiet for a second.

"Everything's changed," he said.

"What do you mean?"

"I don't know. I keep thinking about letting him go."

"He'll come back," she said.

"He shouldn't have been outside."

His back started itching again.

That smell wafted to her when he reached back to scratch. Starting to get familiar now. Not exactly disgusting. She smiled at him and he felt something relax, not that weird pull upwards but something else.

When he stared at the moon, sometimes it looked like it was going to fall down and kill everyone. Some nights it looked like it wanted to fly away. Tonight it was just there.

She'd said once that she didn't have many friends.

"I got into a fight today with some boys. In the swimming pool."

She looked at him again.

"I'm supposed to feel bad, but I don't. I feel good."

"What happened?"

"They pick on me every day. I got suspended."

The cut above his eye had almost healed, but you could still see it. "Were they the ones who did that?" She was looking at it and he suddenly understood. It was her eyes.

"I feel good." That was all he wanted to say.

They both leaned their heads against the brick and listened to drips. You could hear them up on the roof above, that sound you can make when you unseal your lips to look like a fish. He leaned his head against the downspout and she did the same.

"Hear that," she said. "Sounds like someone peeing."

She moved her head away a bit.

"The longest pee I ever heard was at the mall," whispered

Oliver. "I was with my friend Charlie, like, in the stalls but there was an empty one between us. And this guy, you know old men, the way they groan? I started laughing because it sounded like he was . . . like someone was pulling something *through* him. Sort of tickled and tortured at the same time. I couldn't stop laughing, and his pee just kept going and going, and I could hear Charlie giggling and we couldn't stop. You'd think he was going to stop and then it was like he remembered, *Oh yeah, I need to pee*, and he started all over."

He couldn't tell that she was laughing because she was really quiet, all the laughter inside until she needed to breathe.

Across the road his house looked strange. He'd turned his bedroom light off and he could see the blue flicker in the hallway from his dad watching TV. Windows like boxes, a way to see into slightly bigger boxes—you could hold up your thumb and the whole place would disappear. In the living room down there he had a memory of his mom calling him stupid for spilling milk on the carpet. One of those times when she had the other mom, the metal, inside her.

"My place looks funny," he said. Squinting and holding up his thumb.

"It's not as funny as the neighbour's." The stone lions and angels lit up from Christmas.

"Yeah," he said. "Does it look small to you?"

"No. It looks nice."

2

MURDOCH'S PARENTS HAD converted the yard-side part of the garage to a dining room for the summers. Not heated, but if it wasn't too cold and you got enough bodies in there, you could hang out for a long time.

The suspension was like a holiday for some of them, getting a couple of days off school, their parents not really giving a shit except Carmine's. Jonathan and Thomas looked at their phones. You could get wireless from Murdoch's house back here, and Jonathan was watching a video of a woman jumping from her balcony.

"Check this out."

"Dude."

"Gross, eh."

Murdoch was pale. Not really hurt or sick, just . . . weak. Shocked. Doctor said young people feel shock like the rest of us. Take a week off, more if he wants.

"My mom's pissed at the school," said Thomas. "It stays on our records, eh. Suspended."

They got ten days and Oliver got longer.

"Little fucker." Jonathan put his phone down.

The thing everyone thought about was the mess Murdoch made in the pool. It was closed for a day, a swim meet that night got cancelled. He knew people were talking about it. He couldn't even remember a lot of what happened, but that's what he was hearing. "Don't want to swim in that pool again." He heard Thomas say that when he came back from the bathroom today.

They could see their breath in the room for the first little bit, kept their jackets on. Then it got kind of hot. Maybe he was sick. Hated that feeling of people talking about you behind your back. No one feels sorry for you.

"My dad knows people," said Jonathan.

"So does mine," said Murdoch.

"Yeah, but your dad would get in trouble. Mine . . . he's got the law on his side. People owe him favours. I've seen it. He hasn't got a speeding ticket, like . . . ever."

"So what could he do?"

"I don't know. I'd have to say something so he gets . . . with us. Make something up. Like . . . This kid Oliver who got us suspended. He's . . . His mom took pills . . . cops on his street all the time."

"It's true . . ."

"Right? So we don't have to make up a lot. Just say he's been scaring us at school. Talking about hurting people, posting shit on Facebook."

"So, what, the cops go after him? Knock on his door?"

"I don't know."

"I want to be there. I want to see that," said Thomas.

"I want to be there, too," said Murdoch. "And it's not gonna happen. Us standing there at his house?"

"Yeah, but imagine his little pussy face. How scared he'd be."

"That's not scary," said Murdoch. "I want scary. Make him . . . make him . . ." He thought about the pool. "Shit his pants. Scared every fuckin day. I want him to cry in front of people and be covered in shit."

"My dad knows people who aren't cops," said Jonathan. "That's also my point. He can pay people."

Thomas opened the internet on his phone. "Remember those videos of the guy going to libraries dumping shit on people? The buckets of *feces*." He liked that word.

He held the phone for the others to see. A guy wearing construction clothes caught smiling on security cameras after he dumped buckets on people—a woman on the street, someone in a library. You could see someone's laptop on a desk in the library and it had wet . . . *waste* smeared all over it. Lumps on the desk. People talked about how horrible the smell was.

"We could get away with that," said Jonathan. "Just ambush him somewhere. Not at school. Look for him at night even."

Murdoch thought about it. Getting a bucket and putting it somewhere.

"We could all take shits for like a week. Fill it up," Jonathan said.

"I don't know," said Murdoch. "I don't know. Too complicated."

He didn't just want revenge. That's not all he was thinking. Something the doctor said. What was he thinking. *You're at the age now where you can think pretty clearly about death.* Murdoch was sitting on that paper on the bench, looking at the doctor. *You had a close call. Part of being in shock is realizing you can die.*

He could remember Oliver above him, if he made himself think about it. Trying to push up from the bottom of the pool, and he just couldn't. If these guys weren't here he would . . . not cry, but lose his breath. That's what was happening. He turned to open the door to the yard so he could breathe.

Scared.

Jonathan and Thomas were looking at each other behind his back.

In the summer there was a Japanese water feature, a spout

that filled up and tipped out water, made a noise that relaxed his mom. He tried to picture that, but everything was frozen or put away. Piles of snow that won't ever melt.

He wondered if the others could see he was scared. Wanted to prove that he wasn't afraid of Mickey, the little shit, he could take him in any fight. Everyone can die. That's what he wanted to say. He could feel it. Something big out there and it's going to get me, get everyone.

Oliver's hands on his head and then his feet holding him down. Being stepped on.

He was.

He was afraid of Oliver.

He breathed in as deep as he could but the cold kept it shallow.

"Shut the door, Murdy. It's cold."

"What are we gonna do?" asked Thomas.

"We can do anything," said Murdoch. "Set fire to his shitty little house. There's four of us, with Carmine. We stick together and we don't let parents or school find out."

I could kill him, he thought.

If everyone's going to die.

He looked at Jonathan. "Your dad has that crossbow."

IN THE VALLEY of the serpents the thieves threw meat to steal the diamonds. The meat was caught on the diamonds' points, the eagles took the meat, the gems fell into the hands of the thieves and the serpents ate each other. Everything got what it wanted.

AMON SAT BY the boiler in the basement, a film covering his eyes. The boiler's iron door was open and the flame surged and shrank, something blocking the mechanism so the gas would hiss and blow. Up and down with his dreams: he was eating his breakfast after a twenty-nights' sleep, sitting at a counter with his brother. Dry toast again, they didn't want toast, he wanted to wet it with something.

A sound of stirring upstairs and they both sat straight and corrected their plates. Mother coming down in her short blue nightie. Midnight of the world's beginning, ripe and too late to turn back.

"I can eat a garden full of worms," he said, his brother disappearing.

She pulled her nightie up over her head and said, "You'll eat what I give you, and like it."

He buried his hands in the dirt in the basement, already damp with his venom.

Film peeled back from his eyes and he focused.

CARMINE'S DAD OWNED Vespi's butcher shop on Lansdowne where nothing had changed for thirty years except the prices and the lights behind the sign. Neighbourhood's Best for Organic Meat. He got write-ups all the time in the papers and the blogs, ever since people got moralistic about how their food was killed. All he wanted was the best for his kids.

"No kid of mine gets suspended."

He had visions last night of Carmine spending his days sawing bones, hands dyed red in thirty years and no knowledge of anything in the world except what dangled from meat hooks.

"You spend the day like it's a school day. You learn. Do you hear me?"

Carmine's mom was home every day and she let him do what he wanted. "As long as you stay in," she said.

HE ROSE FROM the basement and greeted the ghosts, slid out to the yellow winter.

It was simple perversity that kept him from taking the first he saw, that woman and her dog. His fingertips throbbed in the pockets of his pants and he left a trail of whispers.

People had colour at the gym. Snap Fitness. He watched them through the window from across the street, riding nowhere on their bikes, dropping to the floor and jumping. Like a glass box was placed on the savannah and they hunted whatever was inside it, nothing.

Red faces and their weakness made his throat contract as if he was eating.

Some of the buildings along here had gaps between them, less than a foot, that he could wedge himself into. He could stay warm and stare. Wait for a thousand years, until the fires, until there was nothing left but scavengers and his tail would be his final meal.

CARMINE TEXTED MURDOCH. *So fuckin bored.*

It was at least an hour until lunch. Maybe his mom would let him go out to eat. Meet the boys at A&W.

Lunch???? he wrote on his phone.

Rubbed the screen on his leg and looked around his bedroom. Under his sheets he'd thought about Maeve in class, her pretty hands, and his mom's friend Vivian, teaching him things in a pair of stockings and a shirt unbuttoned.

Uncle burger extra bacon, Murdoch texted.

Grandpa, said Carmine. Three patties.

12. T and J coming.

Carmine had an hour to kill so he got back under his sheets with his jeans on.

He'd have to convince his mom he needed fresh air or he'd go insane. Not too cold out. Promise he'd do extra math and practise the guitar. Promise he'd have long talks with her on the weekend, just the two of them at the mall, tell her secrets about school. He reached for his Switch and kicked the shit out of Nash, sat up and twitched and sniffed and slung his phone in his jeans like a gun.

HIS BODY TURNED sideways and his head faced forwards, breath cold and shallow. Stuffed between the buildings like a puppet. The film closed over his eyes again, a wise half-god. This was exquisite, this moment always, the stories blowing across his aching fingers from the people who passed on the sidewalk. The decision beyond his control, rising like a single fang from his groin and cutting his ribs and heart, out from his mind like a hook.

That one.

He stepped out from the buildings and touched the nape of a boy in a parka.

A snake rises up from the ground like a jinn, like in the stories his brother told when a man throws the stones of dates on the dirt and an ifrit, huge of stature, will emerge to grant dark wishes or avenge a murdered son.

THE WALK TO A&W from Carmine's place on Clendenan took about fifteen minutes. Long enough for hunger to hurt. "Just stay warm" was his mom's final condition.

The fuck are you. Murdoch texting at 12:10.

Other kids from school would be there and they'd ask what it was like to be suspended. Him and the others like heroes.

He put his hands in his pockets and felt real love for his mom. Dad too. After lunch he wouldn't play games again, he'd do some hard work to show gratitude.

There was a blow and a burning on his neck, as if an icicle fell from above. Sharp. He stopped, looked up at the buildings. Shocked at first, but then calm. This row of stores. Why had he never noticed them before, how cool these old buildings were.

Couldn't see where the icicle might have come from.

He put his hand back there and saw blood on his fingers.
"Hey."

"Hey," said Carmine.

"Can I take your hand?"

"Sure."

Carmine took his other hand out of his jacket pocket and gave it to the guy. Felt as though he was pressing a hot iron on his palm, the backs of his hands. He cried and tried to let go.

"It's fine," said the guy. And it was.

So relaxing.

Carmine looked at him and down at their hands. He smiled and said, "We can't walk like this." But they walked like that across Quebec Avenue.

Good friends.

He felt like he had eaten ice cream, the best he'd ever had. The way it filled his body, mint, from his throat to his shins. "Are you one of my brother's friends?"

"Maybe."

"So cool."

He threw up into his mouth. "I feel really sick," he said, but he was happy. Horrible headache for a second, and then more waves of calm.

"It's beautiful, isn't it? The street," said Carmine. Bag of dog shit resting on the lip of the garbage bin and the dirt and salt rimed into a substance no one had a name for. He felt sick again. Beauty in the ugly things, find that and you're a man. You'll survive anything. He brought his other fingers to his lips. Swollen like they were full of air, and his face was numb.

"I'm meeting friends for lunch. They're great. They're not as . . . I'm not as close to them as I am to you. Can you carry me?"

"We'll go somewhere and sit."

They walked to the benches where the old station used to be. Sat down for a while.

Carmine couldn't stop talking and the other boy stroked his head. Soaked his scalp with venom. Their skin always turned so pale.

"I feel so lucky," said Carmine. "I'm going to be a pilot. My parents worked so hard, and they're going to be so proud. And so are you. As soon as I get over this bug. I've got a weird . . . you get things like this from swimming pools." He sat doubled over on the bench, stomach cramping like he had diarrhea. "I'll take my jacket off."

The boy put his hands on Carmine's shoulders, for comfort, and Carmine said, "I remember this. Flu shot. It hurts in the shoulders for a little while and then you get *so* much better." He started laughing.

An alleyway beside the old platform ran behind the stores. There would be dumpsters back there.

"Come on," said Amon. He led Carmine by the hand to a doorway in the alley, held him up against the steel door and took out his knife.

Carmine was going to tell the boys at A&W a story about a kid who had a butcher's hands like his dad's. Incredibly strong. I'll see if we can run into him again on the street because his name is as long as the street, in fact, and if you can say the *whole* thing it's a spell that can bring about dog-bite, long-kneed, swift-gliding, in his teeth he carries his semen.

"Everything's going to be great," said Carmine. Shivering and pale.

Amon's neck thickened. He put Carmine's jacket over his face and opened his shirt. Held him against the door and pushed the knife below his nipple.

"Can I see?" said Carmine.

The jacket fell across Amon's forearms and Carmine told the others how the blade slid in like it was meant to open him up, perfect. Felt the ribs pop. And all the sauce. The only problem with A&W, he told the boys, was when the door opens it lets in all the cold, we should only eat here in the summer.

"I should go," he said. "I'm really sick."

The boy was holding his liver, small and brown, a bleeding football.

He took out other parts for later, made him into a ragged flag that he could hang from a pole.

When they found Carmine's body in the dumpster a guy named Paul told the cops he came out back to unload a truck-load of furniture. Saw a kid sitting on the other side of the alley, eating something messy from his hands like you see monkeys eat, you know, fast like that.

OLIVER PICKED UP the last vial from under his bed. He kept the manuscript there, unread. He lay back and held the liquid up to the daylight at his window. Stayed lying down after he stuck it in his belly, let it spill into him before he sat up. It was the most relaxing one yet, no nausea.

This was what he was waiting for.

What a beautiful world.

He was going to tell Suzi that what you see, if you look in the right way, is a world of people trying. Everyone deciding *I'm going to wear* this *today, because it's who I want to be.* That old woman out there with the red hat and brown coat, she's a rose. This morning her head was on fire with love and she said, I'm gonna stand under any kind of sky, and bloom.

He was picked up from his bed and set down on the side-walk, out among the beauties and the brave. Snow still melting and a gathering of thoughts and wants that he would talk about tonight.

Most of the men in this city wore black throughout the winter. Wanting to look like gangsters, ready for any challenge, thieves, beaters of snow, complicated souls. He walked among them. Took a handful of strawberries from a sidewalk store on Roncesvalles, challenged himself to jump a parked car and made it up to the roof. The trees lifted burning branches to the sun, and the sun said *do as you please*. Someone shouting at him. Men sucking in their guts, mothers sending flirty texts, kids eating candy they'd hidden in the car seat. There is no life without mischief.

Suzi watched him that night climbing down his trellis. He was up on top of her porch too quickly, impossibly. She must have looked away or got lost in thought.

"How do you do that?"

"What?"

"Climb up here."

"I don't know. I just want to."

She thought about that for a second. It felt good. He wants to.

"Move over," she whispered.

They sat on either side of the downspout again. Something different in their chests tonight. Like they were about to get called on in class.

"What do you call this thing?"

"I don't know," she said. "Eavestrough?"

It was in the way, like a babysitter or a parent. Suzi shivered a little and she squirmed towards him, getting her shoulder over the downspout.

A clearer night, and colder.

"Can I be honest with you?" asked Oliver.

"You should."

"Do you believe in magic?"

"Yeah."

"Real magic, though." He looked at her. "There's a kind of real magic. Do you know that? Like there's the kind onstage, card tricks and stuff, and magic in stories, like mermaids and bullshit magic. I don't mean magic you kind of have to make yourself believe in."

"Mermaids aren't bullshit."

"Well . . . you can make mermaids now. That's the real part. You can take genes from, like, I don't know, a fish, a dolphin, and mix those genes with a girl. Someone could turn you into a mermaid. Truly. I know someone who could do that."

"Who?"

"A friend. A scientist. You don't even have to believe, I guess. Real magic is real, so it's not even magic. I've seen it. And . . . because it's real it's even more magical."

"You're . . . a strange boy."

"You don't believe me?"

"I don't really understand you."

He looked up at the sky, breeze blowing the skin off it.

"My dog. Night. He's not my dog. He's my friend's dog. And he's not even a dog. He's magic." It suddenly felt so stupid. How could he tell anyone and expect them to believe. "He's invisible."

"Is he?"

"And he's part cat."

She laughed.

"You're funny," she said.

Her bedroom window was open enough to let her back in. Her mom always went to bed early but woke up a thousand times, and her dad stayed up online.

She looked at him. "You're serious."

"I don't know. I just want you to believe me."

"I believe all kinds of things," she whispered. Felt a strange relief, like she didn't have to be cool or grown up.

Real magic.

The slope on the roof wasn't much, but it was enough to

make you feel like you could tip over. And the drop to the ground would break your legs, or whatever landed first. She wondered about that later. How he got down the last time.

Air whistled into her bedroom. The light came on in her parents' room.

"Shit."

She scrambled to get back into her room. Legs first over her desk. She saw him just before she pulled her head inside.

He climbed the brick straight up, as if his fingers had glue on them. Jumped up and onto the overhanging roof and disappeared.

HE STOOD ASTRIDE the house and stretched up to the moon, knew that he cast a shadow. Blue breath rising from the buildings downtown.

I don't need to sleep.

I don't need to cry.

When all the cities of the world start drowning under their own weight, we'll figure out a way to raise them. Build them light as breath. Tell the moon to let go of the oceans.

After a few minutes he dropped back down and tapped on her window. She opened it a crack, smiling in the dark. "Goodnight," he said.

THE ITCH ON his back had changed. It was really painful sometimes, and then it was a relaxing pain like when you have a sore tooth and you chew on meat, you enjoy the meat and enjoy the pain, and it felt so good to rub his back on the door frame of his bedroom.

He thought about murder. In a different way from before. Tried to separate it from his feelings about Murdoch— not murdering for revenge or because you feel cornered, but murdering as a part of life. You eat, you sleep, take what you need, murder if you have to. If you're not human anymore. Still wondered if he could do it, even though he had tried to hurt Murdoch and didn't feel guilty about it—in fact, hadn't really thought about it. What are the rules that hold you back if you're not human. Even if you are human, and you want to get your hands on whatever you want, take control, be strong. What are the rules that you have to obey.

When he rubbed his back on the door frame he drooled.

In the bathroom he took off his shirt and tried to see his back by angling the mirrors on the cabinet. Opening the two doors on the sides, getting up and kneeling around the sink. The hard bumps on either side of his spine had grown, he could feel that. They were longer, sticking out maybe a centimetre, and something was growing from them farther down his back. In the mirror they looked like two little horns and they moved when he pulled his shoulders forward.

He stood on the bathtub, twisted and flexed his back, couldn't see properly and got frustrated. That chewy feeling in his teeth again, aching to rub against something. He got down on the floor, on the old slate where grout was missing. Lots of edges to scratch against and a soothing cold from the tiles. He tucked his elbows against his belly, used his feet to push up his hips, and writhed until he heard a wet sound, like something had burst.

Over his shoulder in the mirror he saw blood, a cut and a little flap of skin over one of the bumps. There was water, too, or some kind of moisture dripping down his back, and a smell. He put his fingers to his nose and caught a whiff, like the time his knee was skinned and the wound got infected—how he felt sick from the smell when he took the bandage off.

He lifted the flap of skin, expecting it to be raw, and some new part of his brain came alive when he touched the bump. A little bony thing with more bone or something growing out of it beneath the skin. It twitched when he put his finger on it.

He got blood on the sheets when he lay back down to think. Squirmed in bed to get comfortable. Thought about Suzi.

His new fangs still felt like needles against his tongue, not growing in yet. The picture he had of himself just now in the mirror, toothless with infected cuts or whatever they were on his back. Not the handsomest guy. And the smell—it was coming from his armpits now, his groin. Hospitals, old men, fish. It smelled like parts of him were dying.

I'm not dying. I'm more alive than ever.

He got up and pulled off his dirty sheets. Something made him want to cover those bumps on his back, to hide them. The blood and pus couldn't be good. He needed some kind of bandage.

On top of each shoulder he looped a T-shirt—two of them that he tied under each opposite armpit. A sort of crisscross bra that covered the bumps on his back. Felt nice but looked ridiculous in the mirror.

A lot of his shirts weren't fitting anymore, and nothing tight would cover the T-shirts. On the floor of his closet was a plaid workshirt his dad had bought him at Value Village, covered in dust from being on the floor for a year. The kind of shirt you see on old construction workers who don't care how they look. Used to be huge but it fit pretty well now—baggy so you couldn't see the knots of the slings under his armpits.

In High Park that afternoon he learned that he could jump from tree to tree, like a lemur. Felt the presence of Night nearby, he knew it. Hands sticking, the trees looking like a grid and the forest something to be used.

OLIVER

There was an envelope beside his bed with his dad's handwriting on it. He'd opened it before he went to High Park.

Oliver,
If I could put my hands around the world and turn it
back, I don't know where I would stop it.

He didn't want to read any more. A long letter his dad wrote, more than a page. Didn't want to read anything, the pages from Princeps, nothing. Didn't want to understand whatever was meant to be understood.

EARLIER THAT WEEK his dad thought more about what he could do, what he could say to Oliver to make him feel closer. All his life searching for the perfect words, but he knew things couldn't be solved just with words. These bodies, touch, just sitting near and eating, usually stronger than words. Could anything be *solved*?

He'd seen in the History on his laptop that Oliver had looked into gene editing. One of the pages was about a twelve-year-old girl who overcame leukemia when her DNA was changed. One of those happy stories where she had been given six months to live, and three years later she was running 10K races.

Is that what he should make up? If a writer could heal everything with words, what kind of story would he read to his child to make him feel loved? A fairy tale. A life story, worse than his own, to prepare him for every hardship? Is there a length of words as strong as a sword, a story he could keep by his hip? Tell him a difficult tale that takes him to horrible places, and makes him see characters who tell him in turn that if they can survive what they've been through, he can get through anything. And if they don't survive . . . this story would bring about the grief of a soulful mourner: someone who learns, ultimately, that grief has made him strong, that whenever sadness might visit him again he needn't try to avoid it.

He made a sandwich while the TV was on in the living room. Local news, CP24. The volume was off so he heard nothing, caught a chyron at the end of another segment.

Body parts found in the Junction

He didn't see the details and went back to writing. Tried to put things in a letter.

WHAT THE PIECE on CP24 had said was a pattern was emerging from various local murders over several years. People in hospitals and homes with parts missing. Kids had found a site near Vine where the children's park was fenced off from the railway tracks, some kind of den or burial ground where the earth had been dug out. The coroner found remnants of desiccated organs and muscle, several different human sources and scat, reptilian, with human hair entangled.

The butcher's boy the latest.

The butcher unable to look at his hands thereafter. No piece on the news a year later when he sat down crying at the High Park Zoo, staring at the buffaloes with his daughter. How they looked back at him, dark-eyed, at all these people, the parti-coloured clown kings, clicking, laughing and hooting across the long horizon.

"ROCK, PAPER, SCISSORS, split!"

"Rock, paper, scissors, split!"

They played the version where you start by touching toes together. When you win you get to take one step backward, and the loser has to stretch forward to keep their toes touching. Eventually you do the splits or fall over.

"Rock, paper, scissors, split!"

"Let's say spit instead of split," said Suzi.

"Why?"

"I don't know."

"Rock, paper, scissors, spit!"

They were tied at first, paper on paper, rock on rock, but then Suzi started beating him. He was halfway to the splits and held Suzi's coat sleeve for balance.

"That's cheating."

When they did paper on paper they both felt a shock when their fingertips touched. She looked at his eyes and saw them riding bikes together. A lake.

"Do you like swimming?"

"No," he said.

"I want to go to Venice."

" . . . "

"All the streets of water. What would that be like? You'd have to swim to call on me."

"Maybe. Rock . . ."

"Rock . . . paper, scissors, spit!"

She had to step closer to him this time.

"How come you don't have teeth?"

"I do." He thought about the T-shirt slings he was wearing under his shirt, and felt those bumps twitch on his back.

"Dentist said I lost all my baby teeth last year," she said. "You're quiet sometimes."

He looked down at her boots. Made an effort.

"When's your birthday?" he asked.

"August fifth."

"Mine's July. Tenth." He was less than a month older than her. Both thirteen by the end of summer.

"You know I'd help you," she said. "If those boys who did that . . ." She was looking at the scar above his eye.

"I don't need help."

"If it was two of us, we'd win."

She went to the French immersion school on Perth, a five-minute walk from home. He saw her on his way back from

High Park and wanted to tell her that he could jump six feet
from tree to tree.

She looked tall, even though they were the same height. Her
shoulders were narrower. He wanted to pick her up or something.

"Are you afraid to talk?" she said.

"What do you mean?"

"Is that why you like that comic?"

"I don't know."

"I had a stutter when I was little," she said. "My mom
thought it was cute. And then they got worried because my
dad got teased for his when he was a kid. It happens sometimes
when I'm scared."

"Do you get scared?"

"Sometimes."

"I don't get scared anymore."

She saw it in his face. He looked like a little old drunk,
skinny and toothless, his big workshirt. There was a kind of
hardness to him, like marble or ivory—pale like that. And
when he moved . . . the way he climbed up and down her roof,
like that stone was weightless or liquid.

They started walking along Perth.

"If you were at my school you'd be on a team," she said.
"We have a pretty good gymnastics team. I'm on it. But I think
you'd be better than anyone."

"Really?"

"For sure. If I ask you something do you promise not to be
offended?"

"Okay."

"There's a smell." She sniffed. "Does your dad work at the
fish warehouse?"

A hot flash of embarrassment, and then he started laughing.

"What! It's on our street!" she said. "There's another boy

in my class, Lucas, his dad owns the warehouse and he smells kind of like that."

Oliver kept laughing.

"He says his whole house smells like that."

"My dad stays at home all day. Locks himself in his study."

"So what . . . what is it?"

"I don't know."

He wanted to tell her.

"I'm changing," he said.

You could see the flush of blood in her face. The shyness. Pictures of her own changes in her mind, periods, condoms, venereal disease, the giggles in health class when her teacher talked about how penises grow. Everything's going to look and smell different.

He wanted to tell her, be honest. Nobody knows who they're going to be, not really. But he *really* didn't know, not just because he didn't know but because there was no *name* for what he was going to be. "Watch," he said. He stopped on the sidewalk underneath a stop sign, and jumped. Not from a squat or with any obvious effort, just a jump from the balls of his feet. Right up, his chest at the top of the sign which he tapped with his fingers coming down.

"Impressive," she said. A bit weird that he kept showing off like that, talking about being old and strong and jumping around all the time. She didn't know feet and inches, but she was five foot one and the top of the sign . . . She tried herself. "How'd you do that?"

"I don't know. I'm changing."

There was a chill on the wind, one of those reminders that a thaw in February was not the end of winter. Suzi thought about her bedroom, how used to it she was now. Wanted warmth. Getting older. The yellow duvet she'd had since she was ten when she asked her parents for a grown-up room. A plant and not so many pinks.

When he said he was changing it was like he was flirting, saying he was ready for those things they were meant to be ready for.

"I like flicking the light switch in my room," she said. "When I walk into it. I've been wondering what it's like to have lots of light switches in your life. In your own place. If you're in like an apartment or something, you know? And you open doors and turn on the lights. Or if you just have one light switch that's yours. Just yours."

He tried to think of something to say.

"Do you think I'll ever see your dog if he's invisible?"

"You can see him if the light's just right. But he's not a dog." She smiled.

SHE SHOWED HIM some of her own favourite comics. Her backpack was full of stuff. Some manga, a scrapbook she kept. "I used to like anime."

Oliver said, "Yeah." Thought of his favourites. "*One-Punch Man. Darker than Black.*"

"Do you know Kino? *Kino's Journey*?"

"No."

"I'll show you. Doesn't have all the skirts and big eyes. I mean it has big eyes in the drawing but it's not about boobs. She travels the world to see how different people live, and even the weirdest cultures . . . She sees everything as beautiful." She took out her tablet and handed him an earbud and sat closer on the bench. "If you come over I can show you with subtitles. I've got the whole series. She doesn't dress like a schoolgirl but she's got two guns and her best friend's a motorbike called Hermes."

Traffic behind them on Dundas and a dog sniffing up wearing booties to protect its feet. Fingers touched again when she gave him the earbuds, and she turned the volume way up to quiet the street. It was a one-minute trailer all in Japanese, a

girl singing and a girl on a motorbike, driving through countryside and a town that looked like an American western. Cool
animation and funny music and she played it again, maybe
because it was so short and she wanted him to understand,
wanted him to like it.

"*Kino's Journey, the Beautiful World*," she said. "It says *the
world is not beautiful, therefore it is* . . . You need the subtitles."

She dug into her backpack like she was on a mission to show
him everything. It would be fun to read with him because
maybe he saw things differently. "This isn't a diary," she said.
"Don't worry. I like trying to draw. I suck at it, but I do a lot of
tracing. And I've got those books that show you how to make
characters out of shapes."

She flipped through the pages quickly, wanting to show
him but also embarrassed. Pencil drawings and some in colour,
horses and trees and people. Some were pretty good.

"Trees are hard. And noses," she said.

"Noses are impossible. I like that one." He'd been sitting on
his hands but he put a finger on the page like he was reaching
out to her. Left it there. A drawing of a girl's face, hers except
for the nose.

"I know I shouldn't draw myself, but there's not a lot of
people around to draw. I'll show you one of my mom. And I
read something anyway that if you force yourself to do self-
portraits you force yourself to be honest. Drawing the zits and
wrinkles."

OLIVER STARED AT his ceiling in the dark.

It had been a long time since he talked to a friend. He liked
just talking to her, getting comfortable. Wanted to show her
all his things, too, everything, but there wasn't much to show.
Except whatever he was going to be. He stayed up late just
thinking.

Too bad they couldn't go camping or something.

He knew a campsite, he'd been there with his dad. You have to canoe in and find your own wood for the fire and cook. And the woods surround the campsite and you wonder what's in there staring back at you. They had to hang their garbage from a tree so the bears wouldn't come. She'd like it there.

But they wouldn't be able to go there alone, yet.

He wanted to take her home so his dad could meet her. But he also didn't want his dad to know anything about her.

3

GHOST OF THE forest, full of harm, lying belly down on the roof of a low-rise, Night could mimic laughter and coughing and made his own calls for the mate who never came. He was ten feet long and chirped like a lonely kitten. A man came out of the pool bar to have a smoke at 1 A.M., and Night lifted him onto the roof with one paw. Those fangs pillars to the gate of heaven.

Bones and rags of skin were sprayed and licked white across the roof as if someone had jumped from the moon. Night's territory stretched from here to the store to the tracks where he had made a den in a stack of ties, dug into the frozen dirt and slept out of sight of the traffic and illuminated birds. Ribs and an ankle had been broken by a car that he stepped in front of. He limped for days as he dragged his chain, and as he grew the chain was shortened till only the last half-foot tonight touched the ground.

While others passed below he rested on the rooftop and licked sour chlorides and urine from a paw, breeze blowing across the rawness, and when the man's organs settled in his belly he pondered, increasingly feline. He'd followed the spoor from the store for hours, each time farther, until the foodless highways overcame him. Cars and trucks were like constant rivals; no matter how he barked and screamed at them, they hissed and shouted back. He'd trotted past car washes and gas stations on Weston, the Portuguese Pentecostal Church and the Shoe Club, followed the scent of Princeps for hours more on each adventure.

He climbed down from the roof now, rear paws holding on to the eaves while the fore touched the sidewalk, aware of his mass and lordly. Gathered the scent again from the store.

It seemed like all the world was following that same trail, rushing faster than Night. He ran for a while. A yellow-blue crack of light on the horizon made his coat slowly dissolve, the rosettes disappearing as if burned off as he jogged beside the highway. He jumped and yipped at a cube van whose fan belt screamed as it passed, the driver thinking a gust of wind had knocked him. The girl in the car behind, half-asleep in the back, saw a chain twirling and lunging in the wind like an angry basilisk, closed her eyes and dreamt of garbage and demons.

Night slowed, and he gradually hung his head, cooled his paws in the snow beside the shoulder and coughed. The highway was six lanes across and rose upwards, relentless. A black F-150 pulled over and a man got out to take a leak. Night lifted his nose and dropped it, held his head low and crept forward. He moved along the berm, lower than the shoulder, where his chain made no sound on the snow.

The truck was sluggish to pull away, as if carrying a load. The man looked in his rearview at the tonneau cover and registered nothing, thought half thoughts once he got back up to speed. Night crouched low and dug his claws into the cover, hunching to fit on the truck bed, and he shook as they joined the highway. His shivering and shifting made the truck errant and the driver looked at the dash and again at the rearview. Like a five-hundred-pound log was rolling around back there. Night unwittingly made sounds in response to the hurricane that blew at him, the blur of scents and the wind that dried his tongue. That urge for a mate seemed met. His legs trembled when he tried to stand, wanting to greet this storm and mount it.

SUZI HAD ASKED him if he was allowed to do whatever he wanted. "If I was suspended my dad would handcuff me to my desk."

At home Oliver timed his movements so that if he heard his dad downstairs he stayed in his room, and stayed down if he knew his dad was in his study.

"He's lost in a book right now. He gets distracted or doesn't want to be distracted, so he's usually in his study. It's not . . . he doesn't not care what I do, but he wants me to figure things out. For myself."

Sometimes he met his dad at the fridge and they stared inside together.

He knew he was mad at him for getting in trouble at school, mad at him for being quiet.

WHERE THE FIELDS opened and rose, the horizon wore a comb of dead trees and a mist sat patient. Night smelled meat beneath the ground and fixed his nose in thin snow. Clawed at the hard shell of dirt. He rose up on hind legs and came down to smash the earth. Did this a few times till nothing gave, and he scratched and bit at the frozen soil till he was neck-deep in it.

The skinny groundhog twitched in his mouth, electric, and gave him some comfort as he walked. A toy more than a meal. He kept it in his teeth, licked it and gently chewed across open farmland where yellow grass stood sharp above the snow. When he peeled the skin off the rodent he gathered an aerial retinue of crows who followed his scent down a humming corridor of electrical pylons towards a town declaring its history, plaques on the board-and-batten houses saying a yeoman, piano tuner, a blacksmith lived here, and Night kept moving with his tongue and nose to the ground. As the day swelled full he clamped his mouth on the neck of a simple horse, the crows joined by vultures and all rejoicing in their invisible servant below.

Kettle lakes and groves of hemlock, whispers of runoff from the thaw. A blue jay flicked across the dirt road and Night licked at the air as the spoor rose up over a final hill.

Below, a different world. The marsh sat black and heavy, welcome and warning, a carpet laid by the devil. From the hill he stood and blinked, dipped his head and kept walking. Down to the edge where dry grass ended and the dark marsh began. With his tongue he tested the dirt, salt skin and sea life, meaty black rain. Ponds of silver, water from the melt, were filling the grooves tilled by farmers in the fall. When Night stepped into the marsh he sank to his elbows and knees.

Home.

The wind, also silver, was making the water tremble. He lapped at a pool for a long while, thinking and not, lifted his jaw and stared across the valley. Houses and farms had their own dull colours, stuck in the dirt just as he was. He raised his paws, caked and heavy, and tried to run. The scent led him along a road through the middle of the marsh, mingling with the smells of smoke from farmers' fires, chicken and TV dinners, and in the twilight it seemed as if he was trotting into existence, his muscles filling with the absence of light and visible to anyone who wasn't staring inwards.

The road turned up to the edge of the marsh and ran alongside a canal, a few houses on the other side where a private bridge had been built. He crossed and stepped into the darkening woods.

IN THE HANGAR three boys spoke in turn, in Gafat, Geez, Mesmes, Weyto, Livonian, Krevinian, Punic, dead languages leaping like suicides from the Tower of Babel, their secret code amounting to nonsense and Pentecost, which of them had the true tongue of fire.

"One of you will be better at some things, others better at others."

Princeps would one day keep the best, and drown the other two.

They played games together and despite being shed of most things ape they behaved like all triumvirates, two uniting to the cost of one, and each of them planning to rule alone. They wore white-collared shirts and leather gloves, identical but for the placement of white patches in their hair. Faces unworried by change, they sat at a low table and yammered, raw vegetables in front of them, a carrot, snap peas, an onion, smiling and speaking fire. One took the carrot of another and the two incanted curses from the book of Deuteronomy, *boil-scars, hemorrhoids, and itch.*

"Enough," said Princeps, and they quieted.

He smiled and said to a reader in his mind: you should watch these three.

Look close.

Always moving in a pas de trois, the Bharatanatyam dance where they moved in unison or each made subtle inflections, virtuous, calling Shiva Shambho, the gentle version of the god of ruin and transformation. One gets the plates and hums, the other the glasses, the last setting up the cutlery and harmonizing with the first while their father watches them with judgment and pride.

This is the perfect boy:

Lion in his mind;

Iron in his bones;

Tears if necessary, but the will of a starving bear;

He leads, and is an example to the weak;

Strong for having been feeble;

A peck of chimp for a thick back and mischief;
Snake for no regret;
He walks with grace and eases into any conversation;
His cuts will always heal.

The perfect boy will do his chores but do them in honour of work itself and not out of obedience. He will answer to his elders and restrain them when they are fools. He'll take no guff, no lip, and be mighty, tell others what they want. When a woman with a sharp tongue and nails tells him to be perfect, he won't be. Bright eyes will burn the beady ones of those who sit in judgment.

And when you walk through gardens that get heavier, swollen and corrupt, when flies walk over eyelids and the fruit starts dripping its own wine, when the mould sets in and you move to drier edges, getting pushed now at your backs to where the grass has burned and dust gets into lungs, jackals and a soldiery of vultures will stir and chatter, hybrid beasts will thrive beneath a viral sky and he will be watching, crouching, staring with the wisdom of a widow, the perfect boy.

They were eight years old, these three of him.

Princeps stood over and watched them eat. They had compassion. Those fingers he had perfected on Amon, he gave them those and told them *never take off your gloves unless you have no choice.* The venom, he believed, would rise like sperm by the time they were twelve. How strange was it to see three versions of himself and wonder which of them would be fittest. Would it be the one who took his gloves off first, or the one who stepped in and said don't?

The alarm at the perimeter had been triggered, and the pigs were squealing wildly.

IN THE WINTER they huddled in a three-sided pigshed, rubbed their inadequate noses raw in their efforts to dig trenches in the hay. Summer's nipple was replaced by buckets, which they tipped and spilled as toys, always thirsty, always hungry, using each other for warmth and taking tentative nibbles of haunches to see if one or other might like to be dined upon. Grinding their teeth all season.

When food did come the pigs leapt and shrieked like old nymphomaniacs, running at his boots and the sled he pulled, shouldering each other and belching, rubbing themselves in scraps and body parts tossed later from the hangar as winter was given colour by slaughter and warmth achieved by bloat. Each stared out at the night and sniffed, Margaret's pretty face with diabolical incisors.

When there was a threat they barked, and here was a threat. Something moving between the trees and soundless on the ground, a scent of acid breath. They shook on their little pink legs, helpless in the face of anything unless they could reach it with their teeth, and they screamed and some started twirling, butting their heads at the dark. Patches of snow and leaning birch trees were the only things not black, markers for the pigs now looking like scratches some lunatic cat had torn in a painting of midnight. They spun and tried to keep their bearings but the smell of whatever it was made them squeal from end to end, to be pitied.

One of them screamed the loudest. Her head was pinned to the ground by a half-seen paw and her hind was flailing and wobbling in a rodeo of obesity. Desperate sounds and no remedy. Her stomach opened in ribbons and her twitching stopped and from suffering spilled a stew, a sudden cure of despair for the rest of them. They wondered at this miracle of their sister disembowelling and rushed to wet their faces.

Night roared at them and they stepped back for a moment and smelled the air, some of them making out his shape in the darkness, his head obscuring the guts and the heat from her opened body rising in vapour to give him dimension, one paw on her head, another blocking their way. They waddled back in to lick blood and sniff the parts he wasn't eating.

Princeps heard the roar and the animals in the cages indoors grew wild.

"Watch," he said to the boys.

They stared at laptops, blinking like birds.

THE HANGAR THREW no light save from a skylight at the top. Inside was an insulated steel and stained-white fluorescence, part lab, part kitchen, an incubator with a concrete floor for the dreams the world has an hour before waking: vivid and perverse incarnations of hope and unlikely wants, the slack-bellied man who stands slim and virile before his wife's prettier sister, and the girl who can breathe underwater; the spirit of these dreams taking shape in lionbirds and fox-cats, a blue-black ravenwolf with hot red eyes and a hyena-man in perpetual rictus, no language, hunched in a tall cage with hands meant to shatter heads and screaming in a line of creatures on one side of the hangar who thought of nothing but murder. At one end was a living space with four beds and a kitchen, and for the next two hundred feet were workstations, cabinets and tables, plastic-wrapped chambers, aluminum IV poles and hundreds of flasks and beakers, full and empty, as if a banquet had not been cleared. Throughout and thick at the opposite end were creatures, known and unknown, pacing and twirling in cages. Embryos in glass, juveniles in boxes, over all a fog of egested flesh and monkey chow, a zoo in perpetual dawn.

He had watched remotely the movements of people in his store, how they spread from there like the injections themselves through the world he was trying to shape. Those who came in to steal, those who came for their new future.

Watched the movements of Oliver and Night, Oliver using his lockpick and the hunter escaping as he predicted.

As a parent one has to let go.

The sounds of Night's roar and the bewildered pigs put hair, fur and feathers on end, all the growing creatures hooting and wailing and setting each other off, and the man and boys tried to stay calm while the noise grew in strength, ringing around the steel walls and concrete like a wind of needles. Sitting, they watched an infrared image from the camera on the pigshed.

Night, with a yellow heart and purple coat, swiped a massive paw at three flame-coloured pigs. They scattered and regathered to feed from a red carcass and suck up gobbets of yellow that rested on black-and-blue snow. The boys watched the cartoon and wondered what was next.

Princeps said, "Look at how big he is."

The length of three pigs or three wolves.

He lifted his head from feeding and growled again at the obstinate pigs and on the screen the blood from his mouth was like wet drops of fire, spraying when he roared again. A pig nipped at his ankle and he jumped and twisted with impossible grace, a burning ribbon, and fixed her to the ground with his forepaws.

They heard some of it through the hangar walls, over the screams from cages, the sound of the pig knowing she would die. Night looked up like a man with a sudden thought. They saw his body relax and a colour change at his mouth, hot tongue flicking at the air. The pig wriggled free and Night seemed to pay no notice, keeping his posture, head up, but turning towards the hangar. He stayed as the pig ran away to a point off-camera, bowed his head and moved as if stalking to a place they couldn't see.

Princeps straightened himself away from the screen and tried to listen. Some muscular fluttering against steel cages, lingering whines and barked questions. Everything trying to settle. The doors of the hangar were bolted, the walls impregnable even to a creature that big. His ears moved to the contracting metal outside, a temperature drop, twigs blown against it from suffering trees. The boys watched the pig return to the others and feed, the carcass glowing from yellow to green as it cooled. Princeps looked at their faces as they watched.

Sons. Image of his own eternity.

Night's paws stuck to the outside of the hangar. He retracted his claws and climbed to where the light shone up through the skylight. Heat was lost from the building here, conducted through the steel, inviting Night to spread his legs and press his ribs and belly to it as if in embrace. He lay like a blanket on the building.

"I have a test for you," said Princeps. "Somewhere outside these walls is the perfect hunter. As long as he is here we are trapped. Unless one of you can come up with a solution. How can we get out of here? Should we run or should we try to trap him? I can think of a range of options but I want one of you to show me who is the smartest. I will tell you about this creature's abilities, but we have to ask ourselves something first. I raised him and fed him, beat him and trained him. He has tracked me over fifty kilometres. Is he coming home for revenge or because he longs for his mother?"

The boys began to chatter.

4

JONATHAN'S DAD HAD a collection of weapons in the basement.

A Muramasa sword from the sixteenth century that he'd had authenticated by a *shinsa* at the Japanese Sword Museum in Tokyo. They said the swordmaker had a brutally violent temper that he imparted to his blades. Anyone who wielded them was driven by a single choice: kill a rival or kill yourself.

Locked in that maple cabinet, with a glass door and elegant light, was also a CZ 858 Spartan rifle. Other versions of that rifle were legal, but this one wasn't because of its markings. A Spartan helmet was etched into the buttstock, above the words ΜΟΛΩΝ ΛΑΒΕ. *COME AND TAKE ME*. His dad also had those words engraved in the wood above the door.

"It's from a battle," Jonathan said. "The Spartans. Another king was beating them and told them to put down their weapons, and the Spartan king said those words, like, *come and get 'em*. Gun-control freaks hate those words."

There was another Japanese sword in there. Some daggers, including a Black Panther knife with Damascus steel and a roaring head of a panther on the butt-end of the handle. That alone was worth ten grand.

Jonathan knew his dad kept the key locked behind the bar, in the cabinet where he kept the three-thousand-dollar rum, and the key for that cabinet was behind the bottle of Blue Label on the shelf. He'd let Jonathan sip the rum once and it was like an invitation to some scene behind a curtain. Take a peek for now and come back when you're older. He wasn't going to let the boys have any of his dad's booze.

He got the one key and then the other, opened the cabinet, and the three of them, Jonathan, Thomas and Murdoch, stared.

It was the crossbow they were after. Not the most expensive weapon in there—nowhere near it—but it had a story. Belonged to a guy who killed his parents and brother with it. That crossbow right there. Jonathan's dad had a friend, a criminal lawyer who prosecuted the killer. Got him a long sentence and some cop friends of his gave him the bow. Jonathan's dad bought it from him. Hanging there like a talisman. When Jonathan opened the cabinet, Murdoch breathed in through his nose, imagining some kind of scent or spirit coming from the bow. Neighbours said the dying brother came out onto the street with one eye, a bleeding hole where the other one had been and his lips moving.

"Are those the arrows?"

"I think they're called bolts," said Jonathan.

"Whatever. Are they the ones that killed the family?"

Two arrows with red plumes rested perpendicular to the bow. Jonathan lifted one off its mount, about as long as his arm. "I don't really want to touch this stuff," he said.

"Let me feel it," said Murdoch. "Get the bow down."

It had a khaki barrel and grip, BARNETT RECRUIT TERRAIN written on the curved limb. The killer had been eighteen, and maybe this was like a smaller person's crossbow. Murdoch's eyes opened wider when he held it. Lighter than he'd expected. Even though he'd seen it in the cabinet before, he'd been having visions of carrying it, and in his imagination it was a heavy wooden-and-iron bow like in medieval times. Walking up over a grassy hill and taking aim at Oliver, sometimes wearing armour, horses running around.

Something more evil about its lightness, the practicality of it. Taking aim at your family, at their eyes.

He got that feeling again.

Something out there.

NONE OF THIS would have happened if they hadn't been suspended. If Mickey had played along in the pool instead of taking it so seriously.

Carmine. It was only five days ago. Still wasn't real. They had to show the cops their phones, the texts they'd sent to each other. *We were waiting at A&W and just figured his mom kept him home.* Body being held by the coroner so there was still no funeral. Their parents got lawyers involved because they were treated like suspects, like they were the last people who saw him, but they didn't even see him. Their friend. He would have been in school that day if not for being suspended.

The three of them all felt the same thing, like, when is Carmine allowed out again. Wanting their parents to make it all go away so they could go back to school and hang out.

Body parts found and some sick fuck burying them. Eating them. Murdoch heard his parents talking at night. Rumours it was a young person, a boy, who did the killing. The whole neighbourhood was scared.

Normally he would have found it kind of cool or fascinating, that there was a murderer in the Junction, but with Carmine now it was too confusing or real or . . . something. Just that feeling again, like some kind of force out there could get you at anytime, anyone can die. He and Jonathan and Thomas talked on Messenger: why can't someone figure this out. Oliver on his shoulders and that pool cold and chemical. Please just let me out of the water.

We can figure it out.

They saw Mickey that day. Walking along Dundas with some loser girl while they sat in A&W, right at the time Carmine was . . . Had to have been just before. Could he be the boy?

Later that night Murdoch thought about it. Murderer. Obviously angry enough to kill. He'd already tried to kill Murdoch. Or maybe it wasn't him, but someone like him. Anyway. You could tell he was guilty of something, the way he always slouched around. He was to blame. Not just for getting everyone suspended. There was something deeper. Maybe he didn't do anything directly, but Mickey looked weird— wiry and threatening like those meth heads you see. Some of those guys do more damage in fights than bigger guys because they've got nothing to lose. The short, skinny ones, they get this strength because they're crazy. That whole dark world of addiction and crazy people, poverty, all the stuff their parents worked so hard to avoid, to keep away from their lives. That's where the threat came from. That's where this killer came from, and it's what Oliver was like with his shitty clothes and drunk mom.

Maybe later people would understand that Murdoch was in shock. All these kids were.

It made sense that they were planning this. That they would take this crossbow.

THEIR PARENTS SAID they weren't allowed out in the dark, but they were still going to work and the boys could get together pretty easily in the day.

Jonathan never liked touching his dad's stuff and was scared shitless of him noticing. But his weapons were special. This whole basement with the movie room, something these other guys didn't have. He always wanted to show the boys the weapons, in the same spirit his dad set up the display case.

"We have two arrows," said Murdoch. "Is that it?"

"Those drawers are full of ammo, but that's another key. I don't know where."

"So we use these two, and we make sure we get them back."

"You're fuckin right. We get them back and they look no different. He looks at these things every night. He'll kill all of us."

The crossbow was way too long to fit in Murdoch's backpack, but if he put the bow part in facing down he could wrap a sweatshirt around the handle where it stuck out and it looked like he was just carrying a bunch of clothes or his pack was too full. Whatever. Didn't look like a weapon.

They walked to High Park.

Down into the woods near Parkside, off the trails where no one went, Jonathan said, "Don't scratch it."

"Take it easy."

"Just don't scratch it. Give it to me." He knew how to load it. Put the bow on the ground and the rest of it along your leg, against your armpit when you lean over. Put your foot in the stirrup, grab the two handles on the rope. "And you pull it up."

"I want to try," said Murdoch.

"Don't scratch it."

"Fuck off."

It was easy.

"Look here, it says Safe in green. That's where it goes when you load it, and you can't fire until you move that to Fire."

Thomas was quiet. He didn't really want to be here. The crossbow scared him and he didn't want to get caught by anyone. "I'll keep a lookout," he said and walked away towards the trails where people might come. Most of the trees had no leaves, not many evergreens.

People made campfires here because it was hidden. Left some cans and garbage. Jonathan grabbed some burnt and bent cans.

"Targets. You're not going to hit any of them. Just keep it low."

Inside the scope there was a red dot that was supposed to tell you where you were aiming. Once the bow was cocked, Jonathan showed him how to put the arrow in with the notch against the string. "Now you can move that switch to Fire."

Murdoch smiled after his first shot. Aimed the red dot at one of the cans, but maybe he moved when the bow jerked back. The arrow shot up and Jonathan freaked out, thinking he'd never find it and that it would be scratched or dirty.

There was a click when you fired it. Something beautifully simple about it. A sound like something heavy stepping on twigs, a bear right behind you and you know it's too late. So simple and powerful. Murdoch really *felt* now what a weapon it was, powerful as a gun, how you could kill animals with it.

Jonathan came back holding the arrow in his fist and said, "I don't want to do this."

"We have two of them," said Murdoch.

"I told you, idiot. We need to have them back in that cabinet looking exactly like they did. I'm not fucking kidding. I want to go home."

"One more. Just one more. We'll both find it. I know what to do now. I jerked my arm or something. Keep it low."

"Keep it low."

He cocked the bow again. That was kind of the best part, like you were pulling power up from the ground. Bracing and getting tight like you have all the time in the world, and justice, before you throw a good punch. Standing and looking down at the thing that will never know what hit it.

He aimed the red dot in the scope on a burnt silver beer can. The red was hard to see against the brown parts, but on the silver he could see it. Pulled the trigger.

The arrow stuck in the tree right behind the can. Missed by

a few inches. He smiled walking to it. Couldn't believe how deeply it had stuck into the tree. If it could do that to wood . . .

Jonathan pulled it out as gently as he could, but he had to plant his feet and really yank. He examined it. His dad would notice *everything*, even the shape of the feathers being different.

"I think we should come up with a different plan."

"No way. This thing's awesome. I want to do one more."

"No. We're going."

They walked home apart from each other. Different kinds of doubt in the minds of Jonathan and Thomas, both wanting to be home, think about something else. There was some switch in Thomas's brain that made it impossible to think about Carmine—if some hint of a thought came up about his friend being cut or mutilated, a wall came up, doors slammed. He wanted to be tucked in by his mom and read an old book like Harry Potter. Wasn't hungry.

Murdoch walked with the crossbow in his backpack. That night he looked at bowhunting videos on YouTube. One guy spent the whole video whispering, staring out at nothing through a little hole in his blind until a deer with huge antlers came into view. *This is a sacred moment*, he said.

THE FIRST TIME Oliver and Suzi held hands was at lunch hour. He walked over to her school and saw her in a group of friends, her face the clearest to him like he could find her in a crowd of thousands. He waved to her and they went off grounds for a while down Perth Street and he just took her hand. Easing into an electric sea. His old self would never have been brave enough.

When he had held Night's paws he saw the memories in his genes, the branches he stood on as he looked for prey. And now that his own fingers were warm like that, Suzi saw his dreams. A little surprised at first. She felt a blue heat in her heart, almost like she was going to cry, and then it spread and relaxed her.

He told her about his mom, a little. He didn't need to tell her much about anything because she already knew what he felt. Or nothing seemed as important as it used to.

"I get embarrassed. I know people get embarrassed about their dads leaving. But it seems like it doesn't happen with moms. Why would a mom leave."

"Doesn't sound like she left. It sounds like she was sick."

Oliver kicked a little rock along the sidewalk and it rolled down the drain.

There's a place that's nowhere and nothing matters, you can be standing in lava and you wouldn't notice. Place where skin on skin tells you there is no skin, no end or beginning, or maybe just a beginning that doesn't stop.

She wanted to say that she could be his mom and then realized that would be weird.

"My dad keeps trying to make our house look perfect," she said. "He keeps looking at property values, other houses, making plans for the kitchen. And whenever I'm there in my room I think about high school and university or whatever. Going away. My messy little room. I don't want him to touch it. I don't know."

Oliver dared to rub the tops of her fingers with his thumb.

"I want to have a messy room somewhere," she said. "I loved it on the train tracks, when you said the world was big."

AFTER HER SCHOOL they walked along the tracks again. Sometimes holding hands and other times walking or running apart. The tracks were busier, the GO train hurrying people home to the suburbs. The rush of it made them run and fake-scream, horn blaring from angry engineers, and then there was a quiet, bigger than before.

Oliver could swear he felt Night nearby, things moving in his peripheral vision that turned out to be squirrels or something blowing in the wind. Still a bit of an ache in his heart or a worry, and he could feel that candlelit room. The comfort of it.

The mall over in the stockyards was kind of lame. You couldn't walk from place to place inside, it was just one big-box store after another. They headed over there anyway, cutting through a parking lot between the beer and liquor stores. A woman had a cart full of cans and bottles that she was going to cash in at the beer store. Oliver stared at her and then at Suzi.

"Do you wanna be a knight?"

"Sure!"

He leaned forward to give her a piggyback. "Sir, what should I call you."

"Actually I want to be a cowboy," she said. "Cowboys don't need names."

She was really light.

"I'm a horse you just bought."

"For cheap," she said.

"I'm in my prime. How old do horses get?"

"I don't know . . . But you're a good one."

"What kind of a cowboy are you?"

"Mean. But fair."

He laughed. "How can you be mean and fair?"

Her smile was near his ear and gave him goose bumps.

Over at the mall they walked outside from store to store and went into none of them. Daylight lasted a little longer but it still got dark by four thirty. Come a day when darkness didn't call you home but said come out.

"I'm hungry," said Oliver. Serious hunger. Drool-making.

In her coat she had a twenty-dollar bill she'd been keeping since Christmas, slippery and easy to lose. She'd been tempting fate keeping it there, wondering how she'd feel if it fell out of her pocket or she threw it out with the gum wrappers.

"I have money," she said.

They went up to the big Asian supermarket at the top of the mall where all kinds of hot food was laid out and dripping with fat and sauces. Hunger so strong it made him dizzy, put a ringing in his ears, and he was barely conscious of anything until he found himself back outside on St. Clair with a chicken half-finished in his hands.

"You okay?"

"Hungry."

"I can see that."

"Thanks for the chicken."

Away from all the traffic on Keele, a long time of walking without talking, they came to the top of their street near the towers of Pelham Park. Lots of small houses and windows. When Oliver used to steal stuff from the Dollar Store he felt like people were watching him all the way home. Hot in his stomach like he needed to run to the bathroom. Right now it felt like people were watching, too, like every window had someone in it, but he didn't need to run. They weren't coming to get him, they were just seeing how lucky he was. He didn't want to go home yet.

His hand felt sticky to her. The chicken. Really sticky though, almost like she couldn't let go if she tried. And why try. She closed her eyes, just for a second, and felt that blue heat again. Something so sad about him, and an anger that wanted to burn the sadness away. She saw a time up ahead, or somewhere long ago, when they were high up and excited or scared. So high it was hard to breathe.

A SCATOLOGIST FROM the University of Toronto analyzed the material gathered near Vine Park. He consulted with the coroner examining Carmine's body. The corpse of a woman whose heart was missing, a baby taken, an old man found without organs with a trio of hollowed-out dogs. Cases had accumulated over the past eighteen months of similarly mutilated victims, all cut up with the same knife, all of whose DNA was found at the same site, amidst strange waste. It was this that involved the scatologist.

Form and composition suggested a human source, but the presence of distinct white urates was unusual. In all the samples he found the DNA of a snake, specifically *Ophiophagus hannah*, the king cobra. The urea smear was a telltale presence in snake scat. In the wild, as far as he could learn, king cobras ate other snakes as well as their own species. They had been observed eating rodents and birds, had bitten humans but had never been seen eating them. The cobra producing this scat had clearly digested human organs.

It was not his business to speculate on behalf of the coroner, but it seemed that whoever killed these people was removing their organs and feeding them to a snake. King cobras frequently defecated during or shortly after a swallowing episode, meaning the place where they ate was also where they left waste. It was his opinion that the snake was present at the murder sites, and also at the site near Vine Park where the common DNA was found.

The coroner knew, however, that venom was present in toxicology reports. Not only was the snake eating the victims after they were killed, the snake was also at least partly responsible for their deaths. Each had enough venom in their systems to bring about death in fifteen to thirty minutes. In some of the older victims, a group of septuagenarians at the New Horizons Tower and Henrik Aagard, there was evidence of organ failure pre-mortem, likely brought about by the venom. It seemed the killer was using both a cobra and a knife. But she had yet to find bite marks.

The police had sketches made of Amon's face from interviews with witnesses, passersby who had seen him walking with Carmine, and the witness who saw a boy with blood on his hands in the alleyway. They assumed, because of his age and the strength it would have taken to butcher the victims, that this boy was not the killer but was the last to have seen Carmine. The coroner informed them of the involvement of the snake or snakes, and they were investigating hobbyists, chat sites, local dealers of exotic animals. Owning venomous snakes was illegal, but there were thousands in Toronto alone.

AMON CLIMBED OUT of his skin in the basement and rubbed his naked belly on the dirt while he sniffed at pieces of old meat, and in the dirt was an ancient story about a boy seduced by a snake who rose tall before him and looked him in the eye, said if you ride my back we can murder together and the trail we leave will look from above like a grin. The snake didn't want the boy taking her food from the jungle.

Amon stood from the dirt neither boy nor girl but an answer to himself like the creatures in Plato who were cut in half by the jealous god, rose to invite a lover to make that fatal choice, try this, kiss me, just the once. Touched the moisture on his belly and licked his fingers, looked for clothes and it was hot down there, the perfect summer, when was that, when he walked out naked at night and the prostitute said where's your mother, you can't go out wearing nothing. Will you be my mother. In the gravel of a carpark still hot from the sun they rolled and rolled.

He dragged his thighs over the dirt and stood. Put on pants, socks, sweater and parka, and in the parka was his knife and even a bit of money which he patted.

In that story the boy rode the snake and loved her so much he cried, even while he held her and rode her back. Her muscle on his chest and hips, he admired every movement, god he loved her. The boy rode the back of the snake and had no need for memories or shelter and felt each kill go into her, held tight while she contracted. Sun on his face and on his back and the snake grew bigger as he wasted. She ate everything and he loved her.

Amon climbed the basement steps and walked out and smiled when he heard that hiss of tires on wet streets.

The boy rode the snake until she felt his grip loosen. She couldn't see her own back but she knew, how big she was now, that the boy was dead. The grin stretched across the jungle. There would be no killer but the snake.

THEY WALKED A lot, at lunch hour and after school. At night, when it was minus ten, he stood on her porch roof and said, "Come out." A twitchy energy to him that was hard to resist. He was . . . unusual, in a way that made her feel like she could be herself.

"Sometimes when I go to sleep I feel like I'm falling," she said.

"Yeah."

"And I feel like I'm tiny."

She was going away with her parents for the weekend, to see her aunt somewhere. It was really hard to think about being apart for two days, and on the Friday afternoon he stopped walking for a second. All the traffic on Dupont somehow helped him, kept him from thinking too long about whether he should do it. He didn't have the courage to look her in the eye, he just stopped and put his arms around her.

For a second she was rigid, long enough for him to feel hot with fear that he had done the wrong thing. But she relaxed and hugged him back. A strong hug. Like they were coming home, or preparing each other, or, the longer it went on, just feeling really close.

They spent a long and pale weekend apart where they both felt a little sick, didn't eat as much as usual, and no matter what they were doing, watching movies in the car, lying in bed, drifting away from conversations or running as fast as possible through parks and streets and a future with new colours, they were having the same thought: this is big.

THREE DAYS LEFT of his suspension. On the Monday it was like they knew what each other was thinking. Not much time left. Her house was such a short walk from her school and her parents worked, so no one was home at lunch hour.

Oliver looked across to his house before he followed her inside.

A quiet and heavy shyness to both of them, aware of every sound. He remembered this bedroom from hanging out with Charlie. Bed and desk in the same place.

After all their walking it was such a relief to lie down. Their pinkies touched on the yellow duvet. A chance to be honest or not try to be anything. Maybe a new kind of pressure. Were they supposed to kiss.

"I put posters on the ceiling instead of on the walls," she said. "It makes more sense."

She stuck the covers of her favourite books up there, strings of lights, a couple of posters of Venice and a drawing she made of a tree.

"I don't want to be what anyone wants me to be," she said.

She wiggled a little closer on her back and they lay like that for a while. Held hands and saw incomprehensible visions of warmth, of another couple who toiled and fought and failed to make their lives as good as this. Palaces of hope and searching fingers pierced on thorns. A man with memories of the woman he loved, her hair curling beneath her hat, the sun in her green eyes, their foreheads sore from pressing hard against each other for days. Stay like this.

Like this.

Like this.

She turned on her side and looked at him, at his oversized workshirt which she gently put her fingers on. Didn't know what to do.

The daylight seemed cold.

Her fingers made him conscious of the slings he was wearing under his shirt, the weird bra he'd made to make his back feel better. He looked out the window. Cold air in his lungs because he wanted to tell her. Had to.

"Can I show you something?"

"Sure," she said.

He sat up.

Undid the snaps of his shirt one by one, thinking.

He took off the workshirt with his back turned to her. The T-shirts were crisscrossed and tied at his shoulders.

The smell puffed out and overpowered her. Not just fish but many long-dead. A beach where fish were massacred. A bit of that sweet, sharp . . . ashy smell you get when you leave styrofoam in the garbage that had meat in it.

She coughed and sat up against the wall. The cloth across his upper back was stained yellow and brown. His skin low down looked bruised or wounded, red and purple, parts of it waxen with ropey scars like he had been burned.

"What happened?"

He undid the knots at his shoulders and instead of falling off, the T-shirts stayed in place, dropping off his chest but stuck to his back. The blood and pus, whatever that liquid was, had dried to the shirts. He reached back to peel one off from the top of his shoulder blade. A dry sound like pulling tape slowly off a box.

She thought it was some horrible tattoo at first, but there was dimension to it, texture. Knots and long lumps like muscles. Scales.

"What is it?"

"I don't know."

Some of his skin came off with the cloth and it was moist in there, where the skin had been. A bit of blood but otherwise a sort of clear jam over the scales that made a wet sound when he moved.

"Oliver . . ." She felt sick with the smell. "What can I do? Did someone hurt you?"

"It doesn't hurt."

In fact it felt good. Airing it out. That itchiness was like having a big scab back there, and now it was taken off, opened up to heal more.

The first T-shirt was still hanging from the bottom of the wound. He reached with his left hand low and pulled it off. Gestured with his other hand. "Can you?"

"I don't want to hurt you."

"I need it off. It feels good."

She sat a little closer but still at arm's length, pinched her fingers together on the cloth at the very tips.

"Pull," he said.

Slowly pieces of him came off with the cloth, not just skin but little bulbs of yellow fat. He shouted when a piece of something dark tore off, and she stopped pulling.

"I can't."

"It's okay. I need it. It's time."

"Time for what? We need a doctor."

He pulled his shoulders forward and flexed his back. The wet sound again and more skin opened, the scales moving in waves. A clearing in his mind. He reached back and pulled the tail of the T-shirt off, leaned forward.

She had to dare herself to look.

There was a pattern, wide at the top of his back that went narrow at his hips. The whole thing was pulsing and bulging like a creature wanted to get out.

She'd wanted to hug to make the day feel warmer but now the light felt even colder, clinical like something a surgeon could use. Someone who'd never operated before, come to the wrong room and staring down at some horribly sick person. How to help. How to sew this up.

"What does it look like?"

She tried to speak but her stutter froze her tongue.

He flexed forward again and she closed her eyes right when there was a burst, a percussive sound that made the door move a little. Wetness on her face.

She opened her eyes and made a noise.

Free of his skin and the moisture. Musky.

Those weren't scales, they were feathers.

QUIET IN HER room that night she could hear herself breathing through her nose. Looking out the window with the light off.

Maybe other people couldn't see him. You had to look, but he was there, obvious once you noticed. Sitting on the roof of his own house, hunched like a gargoyle.

What's he thinking.

He stared straight across at her sometimes, but she stood, almost frozen, at the edge of the window. Out of his sight unless she moved. He was leaning forward on one knee against his chest, the other on the roof, both hands gripping the eaves. Sticky hands.

His wings lifted.

Look.

She breathed out through her mouth. Couldn't believe that no one else was seeing this.

Wings held out like a cormorant's, to air them, and then settling down again on his back. Feathers in the moonlight.

She watched him watch a man pass by on the sidewalk with his dog. She wanted them to notice. There's a shirtless boy with wings on the roof.

Oliver sniffed and grimaced. Boy smells dog. He felt threads now, attached to branches that were grieving in an arctic wind. Threads from invisible things, lightdrops, from the animal: this great seethe of a city, blinking and hissing and jerking in its dreams, was one big animal. He felt it shifting, trying to get comfortable, and he turned his head like a robin hearing meat churn in the dirt. Aware of all things living, of Night. He knew he was down there.

Suzi washed blood from her face at lunchtime. Freckles of it, sprayed on her walls and ceiling. He stood at the foot of her bed, half-naked, his eyes brighter than ever and a look of helpless apology when she said she thought he should go.

If plastic and steel are made by fingers, to meet the needs of flesh and blood, they are natural. "I'm not a freak," he said. Her tongue imprisoned by her stutter.

I am a freak, he thought. It made him smile proudly behind his frown as he crouched there on the roof. Made him want to hammer drums over all these roofs and gather his army of one.

These hands, they felt threads from the man and his dog and the girl hiding in the window.

"Remember I told you about real magic? That's what this is. I changed my DNA."

"Why?"

"I wanted to be better."

She moved into the beam of the streetlight and he stood up. His wings shivering before he pumped them. He walked up his roof to the crest and turned, determined either to die or live stronger, and he ran back down to the eaves and leapt headfirst at the street.

The roller coaster coming down. And then back up. Two engorgements of the muscles in his back, he made his own storm, hovered for a moment at the height of her window, and then stretched, neck out, and flew upwards.

He was beautiful.

The End

1

WHAT I HAVE given my brother and those three boys is a kind of immortality, Princeps wrote on his computer. Writing things down for other users of LOBSTR.

This hangar is a hall where all my gods will dine.

No doubt you have noticed that all of us live as a continuous strand, and there really never is an end. Our two-hundred-thousand-year-old mother lives on, Mitochondrial Eve, arms out or bent over near Lake Tanganyika, her blood sprouting this tree that branches and tickles and pricks, still. We're the infinite reconcoctions of her dreams and disappointments, and even when we turn to dust our particles will stake new claims.

Or I have changed things.

All these stories about my brother and some of you readers are surprised to learn of my sons. I don't think of them as proudly as I do of Amon, I think of them simply as my ongoing days. I can't allow myself too much affection because the imperfect ones will be killed. The one who survives will be my brother's brother. If I die before my son does, I won't see through his eyes, but he will see through mine. And so there is continuity.

If you enter ejkvlv93z2lcca79.onion into your Tor browser and give me your credentials, I will invite you into the site and you can examine my methodology, where I found a womb for them. You will find it useful.

Why am I thinking of the end?

Right now a killer is sprawled on the roof of this building.

OF THE THREE boys, there is one I have had my eye on for well over a year. The one with the patch of white hair at the back of his head that looks like an open mouth.

In five out of ten challenges, the other two look to him for guidance. At the moment he is maybe an eighth of an inch taller, but height is remarkably variable between the three.

I don't anticipate the arrival of venom until Tanner Stage 2, where much of their growth should otherwise cease. They are meant to be able to protect themselves, not to be such vehicles of vengeance as their older brother is. Kept in check by a sweet gentility—that's part of my design. But this one, he is more of a rascal than the others.

He pulls on the fingers of his gloves as he ponders. Even now, as the three of them offer solutions to how we will escape this killer, he counts variables on his fingers with little tugs.

I used to take Amon for walks in the woods outside the hangar, showing him where to find the snakes and teaching him about people's vulnerability. Even as kids I was the chatty one. Now I take these boys, individually. It is a good way to gauge their personalities.

In the woods I have found many of my answers. Porcupines, for example, are an animal whose skin contains antibiotics. Whenever the clumsy little things fall from trees they stab themselves with their quills, and so the antibiotics released from their skin protect them from constant infection. That gave me an idea for the boys before I made them: anti-venom in their skin, so, ultimately, when Amon wants to boost them up a tree in summer or accidentally brushes their skin, they will be safe. And in the short term, they won't be able to kill each other.

I took the rascally one out to the woods six months ago.

That time of year, early autumn, when everything is either over-ripe or gluttonous, everything swollen from ground to sun and bodies that want to get fat.

"What do you see?" I asked, expecting him to say *trees*.

"A harvest," he said, barely taking pause.

He knew, they all know, that I have given them the hunger for others that I have given to all the beasts. The need to eat that will ensure this mess of the past will be swallowed.

He stopped there in the woods and said, "If everything eats everything else, what will be left?"

"The best," I said.

"THIS ONE'S TURNING," said one of the boys, looking down at a coyote in a cage. A mother. Created for her milk and given a coat that looked like a carpet of leaves, once able to spring from the ground unseen. The boys had used to lie down with her. Tales of Romulus and Remus in their minds, they had put gloved hands around her and suckled. Drawing the life from her.

The three of them stood and watched. She was biting and licking her left thigh frenetically, lips and incisors shivering in a constant and peevish argument, licking the wound and then opening it, her dugs swollen and blistered and jiggling while she tortured and cured herself.

"Let her out," said a boy, and, "Let her out," said another.

They were smiling.

Her milk was good for bones and teeth, eyesight, foresight, not a little of their wisdom. They looked at her and looked at each other, the three understanding how yesterday's joy could curdle in cups.

"Let her out," they repeated, and laughed.

Princeps stood at a workstation telling his story on his laptop.

THESE WERE THE hours of pacing, most of the animals being made to roam in the dark. Figure eights in cages, some of them too confined to move and doomed to move in circles in their minds, watching their hands and paws rise up and wondering what they belonged to. A chalk-white liger kitten turned and puled and her whines annoyed the ears of fathers and mothers exhausted by this life. They groaned and bewigged themselves with ropes of their own spit when they finally roared with impatience, and their roars set off those who knew they roared the loudest, and the ones with greater intelligence made complex sounds to undermine the roars and a fugue rose up, hair-raising, the call and response of lunatics and celibates and rapists never satisfied, the hyena-man grinning and screaming in agony like Ganymede first being sodomized by the god. The triplets and the man were inured to the noises, but if a stranger were to open that door he would hold his ears and collapse.

There were areas of clinical sterility with embryos in jars and warm glass boxes holding newborn beasts, lined up and lit like carnate jewels, lizard-girls, already ashamed, wriggling in their incubators to gladden the hearts of some infertile chimera, passing by and broody. Deeper in the dark were cages stacked and moved by automated chains, their inhabitants either harvested for meat and milk and genes or set free into the marsh according to a schedule of age. The whole hangar, except for the living space of the boys, was a corridor of grief and trodden food.

Night stared, frozen and flat-eyed, through the skylight.

FOR THE MOMENT they had left off trying to solve the puzzle of the killer on the roof. They understood that Princeps was their father and themselves, a quaint older version. They respected and disdained him, someone inferior to be obeyed, as if they were supplicants to a god whose tenets and power they tested and knew to be weak.

When they stood amidst those cages their skin looked all the more moon-kissed and blessed, their eyes more clear and innocent, standing like unharmed statuary in a ruined church. In the absence of mirrors each of them knew he looked just like those two, and when a notion began in one it passed through the second and emerged from the third perfected.

Amidst the deafening complaints they remained by the cage of the leafy-looking coyote, each of them hooking a gloved finger on the broad steel mesh of her cage.

"Let her out."

They understood what each had meant.

I LEAVE THEM here and return to Toronto, like I used to leave Amon. I miss it all like many of you miss your cottages in the middle of the workweek. But the amount of harvesting I do in the city, meeting the weakest and worst, is how I achieve what I do. A well of DNA, now infinite, that I can dip my pipette into and make my interesting stews.

Believe me, I am aware of epigenetic influence. This is possibly not the most salutary environment for them. But the day of choosing is a few short years away, and the destiny in their genes is ironclad. These days will be forgotten. One will step out and I will help him love his brother. One day, through the chaos, the city will be killed and repopulated, and the dreams of our Eve, though present like space dust on our windows, will otherwise be dead.

What normally seems a depressing truth to me, however, is tonight a kind of comfort: we never forget our mothers. If the boys are doing their sums correctly, they will know that Night's return is a homecoming, not a hunt. I am confident. I have half a mind to open the door and whistle.

AND THEN THE dance began.

Om Namah Shivaya.

Boy 3 and Boy 2 walked away from the cages and grinned as they reached their quarters.

Boy 1 knelt down to the coyote.

Boy 3 and Boy 2 walked around gracefully behind Princeps's back and removed their gloves, springtime in their fingertips.

Om Namah Shivaya.

As he explained the universe, unending double helix, from his heart to his fingers to a city's black hole, dark web, imploding stars, they touched the backs of his hands. "Papa," they said.

Dha dha dha.

He jumped when he realized it was too late. Looked at one and then the other. "Why . . . ?"

Hadn't felt this since the rebirth of Amon, the venom like cold alcohol up from the back of his burning hands, in his veins and up his arms. He wanted to kill but he was so proud of them.

The anti-venom was at the station twenty feet away. He lurched towards it but they held his wrists and hands, importunate, looking up at him as if asking for one more candy. His little memories.

The venom reached his heart like a seism and pumped back, a swell undersea that would grow into waves to whip the coast. He stumbled.

Boy 1 was at the laptop typing the codes, the industrial sound of the cages responding and jerking on their chains and the roller door coiling up to let the winter in. The backs of the cages squeezed forward towards the door and a Komodo dragon lumbered out and tongued the snow. A quintet of civet cats leapt and scurried over the back of the dragon in a herd, then all fanned out to some thrilling fate that they would bite with bacterial teeth. From above, the hangar looked like it was leaking from its end.

The cages moved in rotation along steel tracks, the sound of sheet metal crashing when they lodged at the door and opened one by one, a factory undoing itself, its purpose unwinding, Princeps staring like a man might watch his intestines pulled out, hand over hand, by a careless child.

"Stop."

He couldn't help but smile, shake his head. My boys.

The venom was delightful.

His legs gave way and he fell on a bag of chow that broke his fall. *Noah drank of the wine; and was drunken.* His ark was unloading. The hyena-man, his face bepopulate with boils, was holding the bars of his cage with white knuckles as species after species stepped out into the woods at the far end of the hangar, vexing noises coming from all, complaints, shock, uncertainty over how to move their limbs and whether to touch that ground. Some tried to return to their cages and were attacked by the predator who had been their neighbour for years, a white chimpanzee screamed when a fang pierced his skull, the fang of some noctambulant monster who was terrified of the dawn, and at the gate a crowd formed of unreckonable abominations with a stink of bedsores and panic in their eyes.

Boy 1 opened the near door, looked outside for the hunter from the roof. He went to the incubators and lifted the unlocked lids while Boy 3 and Boy 2 stayed with Princeps. The contrast was so great between the air of the incubators and the draft from outside that little clouds of windfrost gathered and collapsed on the babies' faces. Boy 1 picked them up wailing in twos and tossed them outside like a matron disposing of an apronful of scraps.

There were cages inside, like that of the hyena-man's, that stood individually and separate from the automated system. Boy 2 left Princeps and at the coyote's cage he lifted a simple latch. He walked back to the door and through it as if to demonstrate how she might rise up and escape, but the coyote lay with her head down and chin extended towards the action at the other end of the hangar.

Princeps tried to get up again. "Help me," he said to his servant. *Little boy. I knew you.* He was back in his home for a moment, nine years old, hearing his mother abuse his brother through the wall. *I'm next.*

He held the edge of a workbench to pull himself up and his body felt fizzy, foam at the top of his head. A drink. "Let's try to enjoy ourselves for a change," he said.

He laughed when he thought of how they must have watched him. Seen him enter the codes. All the cages and cabinets unlocked. What he needed to do was to get to that steel one over there and get the anti-venom, simple. He couldn't stop laughing when he thought of how wonderful it was, in a boozy fog, seeing Boy 1 over there walking by the cage of the hyena-man. Brilliant mind in that little body. Still a boy. How many times have I told you.

Boy 1's shirt got caught as he passed by the massive fingers protruding from the cage. As he turned to see what stopped him, the hyena-man's other hand took hold of his opposite wrist and pulled him in, an orbital bone cracking like an egg when he slammed against the bars. One hand reached through and palmed the little head and the boy put his free hand upon it while he was trapped against the cage, a race between the venom and the hyena-man's grip. A purple cloud was growing behind the boy's eyes and one of them stared unmovingly, startled and englobed, as his skull pressed down on his brain. Princeps heard the bone give way and watched the hyena-man suck at the boy's face while he held him aloft by the head like a chicken.

The creature began collapsing, laughing like a caricature of Princeps, and he dropped the boy, whose brother came over and examined his twin on the floor, eyeless and vacated.

That one. Boy 3. The open-mouth pattern on his hair. Will he grieve. Princeps held on to the workbench as if holding the shore of a river pulling him away. With the boy over there he had a clear way to the cabinet. The river goes to the ocean, and on the ocean floats a raft, and on the raft stands a prize that gets us from Monday to Sunday.

No. The river is a train. Of course it's a train. Takes some people home to the face they love seeing, some people home to the place they want to leave.

Let go.

Three wolves were the last to leave the cages, embodied with gigantism, their hips just now adjusting to movement as they trotted into dawn. All three uncoiling and growing as they moved, taking deep the scents that had romanced them for hundreds of nights and picking up speed for a lifelong chase. Once they were gone the sounds indoors diminished, the cages finished their cycle.

Boy 3 got up and walked towards the door, past the body of Princeps. He saw no sign of his other brother. Some of the newborns were crying in the snow. The woods looked nervous this morning and the steel of the railing was cold. As he walked away from the steps his torso was unzipped, from sternum to groin, by one of Night's claws. The boy kept walking, having felt a collision and some heat but seeing nothing in his way. He looked down at his open shirt and saw blood and his pants felt wet. Come noon the sky was filled with turkey vultures wheeling over a spill of failed creatures. One of the birds was perched unmitred like a red-faced bishop on the back of Boy 3's head.

NIGHT WALKED SOFTLY. He smelled the cage of the coyote, whose ears twitched, and he lifted his head to the air and licked it, lip and teeth flehmening. Iodine, formaldehyde, sweat. Iron that made his mouth water. He slouched towards the man lying facedown over a bag of chow.

With his snout he nudged the chow and the man, turned in a circle and lay down.

ON HIGHWAY 400, Wendy was listening to Q107 and pulling her sweater down under her coat, over the belly that every night betrayed her. Along the shoulder she saw a little boy walking in a white shirt, no jacket.

"Where's your car?" she said.

"I don't have one."

"Did they crash? Are you hurt? I didn't see a crash. You must be freezing."

He smiled at her and looked around at the world. He'd read about cars.

"I'll call the police."

He sat in the front seat and she turned up the heat and they waited while the traffic blew by in a metal gale, exciting.

"Did you hit your head?"

"No."

"Are you sure? Sometimes you don't even remember doing it. You don't remember anything."

"Well, I remember a lot . . . I just. I don't know where I came from."

Wendy held the wheel as if they were moving.

"Did you run away?"

"Not really."

Her friend June worked at Children's Aid. Told her stories like this. When they found abused kids, kids whose parents died. They asked nice questions and tried to find the right homes. Do you like the city or the country. Do you like animals. Are you worried about stuff.

"Are you hungry?"

"Somewhat."

There's a big word.

She picked up the wax bag from the armrest with her muffin in it.

"The cops won't be too long."

They'd come from Barrie. Or who knows. She looked in her rearview and then looked at him. Eating the muffin. He was cute.

"How do you make the car move?"

"What? With the pedals. Look. My feet. Why were you walking this way?"

"I don't know."

"Walking by the highway like that . . ."

"I was back there somewhere." He looked around. "Some of you are going in that direction. See the cars over there? But it looks like most are going this way."

2

Oliver,

If I could put my hands around the world and turn it back, I don't know where I would stop it.

I hope I'll live a long time, but I'm at an age where I know each day is precious, and I know that everything—everything I believe to be solid and permanent—can be taken away in a breath.

The age you're at is different. One of time's little jokes is that as much as I try to cherish every moment, each week goes by in a blur. And for you every day probably feels like an eternity. Everything people say, every lunch hour, every test—I bet it all feels tall as a mountain, and I bet you forget none of it.

So where would I stop the world if I could.

OLIVER STOOD ON his roof at dawn with his wings outspread and a case of Coke at his feet. When the trucks unloaded food at No Frills, he had swooped down and grabbed it with his hands and pumped, these hands that could now take hold of the city's heart and squeeze.

His neighbour, the old Portuguese man, shuffled out every morning on his walker. Veteran of the Angolan war who lost a leg and all but the bitter parts of his mind. He looked up and there it was. All his life he'd waited to see the flesh and blood, the heat of it. Cold statues of the boygirls on his lawn, he knew they would be nothing compared to this: standing with his foot perched on something, the messenger hot with news. He watched the angel raise that thing at its feet and fly.

Oliver flew to the top of the Heintzman building, where he sat and drank a can of Coke. The lake and the city no longer cold and huge.

He looked at cars and thought of Suzi. At the sky.

"I want to tell you," he said. He drank and felt the blood in his wings.

"I JUST WANTED to see you."

His last day of suspension and he went to her school at lunchtime.

"Yeah."

"Did I scare you?"

"I don't know."

He wore his workshirt and looked like a normal kid. Or like himself.

She stood there with her arms folded, holding herself. Hadn't slept for two nights, but had to wake up in the morning. Thinking of nothing else. A cold feeling sometimes, worry, like she had seen something she needed to tell other people about, something that shouldn't exist. And a feeling that she had seen the most private part of someone, his deepest secret, and it was a heavy responsibility. She couldn't tell anyone, and who would believe her, and why should she have to betray him.

"I can show you where it happened. You can meet the man who did it. It's not scary. I'm telling you. I'm not scared. I'm." He shrugged and felt his wings shift against his shirt. "I'm new. And I can show you. There's time now. It's lunch. Come to this place."

He held out his hand.

"I thought about you a lot," he said.

She didn't take it.

IT WAS WARM in there.

The bell ringing when they walked in and the streetsounds fading when the door closed. He'd felt guilty not coming back here, afraid of owning up to Night's escape. He wanted to show Princeps who he was now, show Suzi this place. He never read the rest of Princeps's story.

A dim light was on, a lamp against that wall. She had to adjust her eyes. Reds, browns, blues and golds, all dirty. Old paintings hung all over the place, one right near her head of a brown horse, torn in one corner. She could tell it wasn't an expensive painting, or even a good one. But there was something about it.

Along the other wall were shelves with figurines, hats, books standing and lying. The smell of the place slightly sweet but musty, dusty. Smelled like she was hugging her grandfather.

Oliver called out.

"Mr. Princeps. It's Oliver. I want to say sorry. I brought a friend."

Thought he heard a noise.

Another lamp was on behind the counter, tassels hanging from it, the kind of lamp you see next to the face of one of those fortune tellers leaning in to tell you what's going to happen.

"Is someone coming?"

"I don't know."

It felt that way. Like this man was going to step out and sit in that old chair, drink in his hand. Read a book by the lamp.

Oliver looked at her and at the lobster hanging above the door. *You'll never get old.* He still got waves of nausea sometimes, whether it was viruses rearranging his genes or some kind of creepy awareness that there were creatures inside him, a little lobster's legs tickling across his lungs and some kind of swamp in his stomach that would hatch surprises over how many years ahead. His face never changing, a kid with a man's muscles and hairy fingertips.

He looked at her and his mind settled. She was looking around and frowning, trying to figure things out, and he could see what she would look like when she was older, a woman. Smart and kind.

She waited for something to happen but nothing did. No sign of anyone.

"I think I can see why you like it here," she said. The maze of shelves with stories on them, weird heads on the wall. Whole place was weird, but that painting of the horse . . . she could tell it was a real horse that someone loved . . . someone tried to paint it and they didn't know how to paint but they painted how much they liked the horse. Real effort. Real mistakes. Nothing in here would be wanted now, but somebody, all kinds of different people, used to want it, used to love it. Maybe people came into this store and remembered the things they stared at from their beds, plastic and paintings and drawings and shadows from carvings that moved and came alive when they closed their eyes at night.

Next to a stack of old records was another pile of dark rectangles, hundreds of thin paper-like pieces of film. She picked one up and held it to the lamp. "What are these?"

"X-rays. He has all kinds of medical stuff."

Someone's bone shrouded in smoke, a snapshot of a drifting ghost. She held up a few more.

"Come back here. I want to show you something." He called out for Princeps again.

He led her down the corridor towards the back and it got dark. The smell changed. More animal. Bad.

"Is there a light?"

Her eyes adjusted to the room full of salvage. The diagrams of hands, and old doors leaning against each other like they were all relieved not to be hanging. Bathtubs.

"Back here," said Oliver.

It was noticeably warmer, almost hot.

"I don't want to be here if no one's here."

"I just want to show you a room."

"I have school."

The door was open. He tried to remember leaving with Night on the chain. Nothing in the store seemed different. No new bones, no sign that Night had come back.

It wasn't long ago but it suddenly felt like a different life. Sitting on that floor and playing with him. Soft paws and running together in a jungle they'd neither of them been to. The milk was flooding his mind, oblivion, but he willed it not to. Wanted to remember. The candle and a door opening to a dark but honest place. Honest about how weak he was, how strange our dreams can be. He pictured himself sitting there getting injected.

Light came in from the side of the blackout curtain, floating dust like the ghosts of fireflies. She stared at him while he was thinking.

"This is where Night lived. I got . . . I started changing here. He put needles in me." Lifted his shirt a little in front. "Night was chained to that hook."

Unconsciously, she kept her back to the wall. Some kind of regular noise was coming from the hall, from the basement. The heat. She looked at the eyebolt in the concrete floor. Tried to imagine Night, and couldn't. Tried to control her stutter.

"What were you like before you came here?"

"I don't know. The same. Totally different. I ran here away from Murdoch and those guys one night, and Mr. Princeps helped me. He could see what I would be, and I didn't want to be like my mom. He was doing me good. I didn't know

I'd have these." Looked halfway over his shoulder. "But they're me. I didn't ask for them. I just want . . . I want you to know everything."

"I have to go back."

"I don't mind being a freak," he said.

"You're not."

"Imagine if he changed you somehow, too. He could. Both of us could live like we want to."

"I am. I do live like I want to."

Her eyes looked big. Angry. Wanted him to see like she saw. See her world.

She was scared of looking at his wings again, but she wanted to.

"Who are you going to be?" she said.

"I don't know. Who are *you* going to be?"

"I don't know. I thought the point was you can control it all. You're not going to be like your mom now. How do you know that for sure? How do you know you're not like her already? I bet she wanted wings. Everybody does."

"It's different. I have them now. I can go anywhere. *That* is the point. The world's not the world anymore. There's no name for what I'm gonna be."

She could see them shifting under his shirt, shrugging higher than his shoulders. Felt herself about to stutter so she didn't say anything.

"I can take anything I want and not be afraid. You wouldn't believe how far I can see. And hear. I'll walk in anywhere, I swear, and fly up before anyone believes their eyes. I can get you anything you want."

"You're a bird."

"I'm *me*. This . . ."

He didn't have the words and his hands were out in front of him like they wanted to crush something.

She pushed her back harder against the wall. So many questions, she just wanted to slide down and sit, go to sleep, go back to school. What else about him was weird, how can you possibly live with those things on your back, and those hands like an animal's. What's an animal.

"I can hear bugs in those walls and they make me hungry. Everything makes me hungry. Under our feet. I know this place is full of rats, and I know there's someone in the basement and it's not Princeps. I can smell him. I know there's going to be a snowstorm tonight. I can feel the cloud in my brain and on my skin. And if I was just a bird I'd probably be freaking out and wanting to fly away and hide, but I know and feel all this stuff and it doesn't make me afraid. Because I'm not a bird. I'm this."

He took both of her hands and they each felt a surge of colours. "When I hold your hand I can see you, and I know you can see me. You're afraid I'm gonna kill someone. You can see us riding bikes and we've never done that. You can tell I'm thinking maybe we'd never know each other if I didn't get injections. Because I wasn't brave. And there's a thing in you. Something so nice. I wish I met you when I was born."

They stared at each other and most of her questions were left behind like she had run through a cloud of bugs.

"You think you would have wanted to be with me a year ago?"

"Yes," he said.

"So maybe nothing's different about you."

She forgot about the sounds, the heat.

"Take off your shirt."

He heard her, and thought. Stepped back. Stared at something above her head like he would at a doctor's office. Cold stethoscope against his chest. *Deep breath in.* He unbuttoned his workshirt and pulled off his sleeves.

Pale and skinny. His forearms a little darker from last summer.

The wings tucked in clean against his back and then spread a little, rose up above his shoulders and then smoothed down, slouched, as he breathed. One moved out, flicked a little and startled her, then the other.

She put her hand on one shoulder and turned him a bit. They reached below his waist. The wrists and forearms of the wings looked like coiled ropes, thick, and the feathers fanned out in whites and browns, the tips of the finger feathers black.

She touched them. "Can you feel that?"

He had goose bumps. "Yeah."

She'd held a dead bird last fall, light as paper with tarnished eyes. But the weight of this, the blood. What a gift to be so close to something wild. She thought she heard the wings breathe while they bobbed and twitched, but it was Oliver.

He stepped back and faced her squarely, held her hands and spread his wings out to their span. She saw a moth sipping tears from his eye at night and him flying strong through a mob of blackbirds and jays, above people who wouldn't look up.

And she kissed him.

> *So where would I stop the world if I could.*
> *I wouldn't.*

OLIVER HADN'T BEEN near school since he was suspended, hadn't seen anyone.

Everybody knew why he had been away. He could feel it as he walked down the hall to his class. The kid who tried to drown Murdoch.

He carried his backpack in his hand, didn't want to feel it pushing against his wings. People were staring at him. He had expected things to feel different, and they did. Walking with his shoulders square like he normally couldn't, taller, looking

people in the eye till they looked down or away. Maeve and
Michelle W with little smiles like they had talked about him.

He could fly.

Nobody knew.

He was carrying a cargo of secrets and strength. No need to
rush anywhere, no feeling like he had to tuck himself in against
the wall while he waited for the classroom to open. Most of the
others were lined up against the wall, but Murdoch, Thomas
and Jonathan stood on the other side of the door, their arms
folded, out in the middle of the hall like Oliver was. Thomas
unfolded his arms and moved away, but the other two stared
at him. He picked Murdoch. Stared back at him like it was a
game, smirking, whoever laughs or looks away loses. Oliver
tightened his jaw. Lose, you fuckin weakling.

Murdoch chuckled and looked at his friends, pretending he
could have held the stare. Oliver watched them go into class.

Everyone seemed small. This was what a teacher must feel
like. Knowing the kids, their problems, having to be here and
take things kind of seriously, but still knowing these are just
little people. How much of life they haven't seen.

He used to sit here in the middle wondering what was going
to come at him, why they were giggling behind him. Hearing
facts about Korea or Mars and not able to think about any
place but this room and how he couldn't shrink small enough
into his chair.

*Tom is Barbara's brother, Barbara is Brian's sister, and Brian
is X's father. Who is X to Tom?*

Warm-up questions.

*A cat is chasing a mouse. The cat starts from 4 metres and jumps
3 metres every time. The mouse starts from 8 metres and jumps 2
metres every time. If they both start at the same time, after how
many jumps will the cat catch the mouse?*

Little kitty and mousey. This was what kids had to learn.

What Oliver could do was eat the mouse, pick the cat high up into the air and hold it screaming outside the windows of the people who think they have the answers.

Last night he flew downtown before he hovered like a hawk outside his girlfriend's window. After the dinners and the drinks and the nightclubs and operas, liquid steaming on the streets, and the sound, he could hear it, of thousands of flirty smiles.

He'd been with most of these kids for six years and at some point or another had cared about the moods and thoughts and clothes of every last one of them. Held on to those times when he had made some of them laugh or had been fast in gym, a thumbs-up from Jonathan last year when Oliver scored a goal in soccer.

What a waste.

He sat back in his chair and kept his wings constrained while he flexed his shoulders and loosened his neck. Snow falling outside. He turned around.

Murdoch stared at him and mouthed the words: *You're dead*.

THOMAS HAD TALKED to a lot of other people. Everyone was waiting for what it would be like when Oliver came back to school. There was an assembly about Carmine and people could talk about their grief, but except for some of the girls who hugged each other and cried, most of the others were waiting for some kind of showdown between Oliver and Murdoch. Nothing to do with Carmine. Thomas realized that Murdoch wasn't as popular as he'd thought, and even though no one liked or paid much attention to Mickey a lot of them were hoping he'd win in a fight.

Murdoch's plan . . . Thomas wanted nothing to do with it. His brother had an illegal copy of *Thrill Kill* and he liked playing *GTA* and stuff like that, but real fights . . . he got scared. Murdoch and those guys dared him to do things and he usually chickened out. He'd gotten excited hearing Murdoch talk about punching Oliver in the face, but when he saw it he didn't like it. And then the stuff with Carmine. He was talking to his mom about maybe going to a private school or doing something different. More sports and less hanging out.

Oliver was sitting in the snow on the hill that looked over the playground. The younger kids looked like colourful little robots in their snowsuits. He could see clearly into the houses across Keele Street, breakfast plates left out. Starving.

"Hey," said Thomas.

"Hey."

"I'm not gonna sit down."

" . . . "

"I don't want anyone seeing me talk to you."

"Fuck yourself then."

"No, I don't mean . . . I wanted to talk to you. It's just. I don't want them to think I warned you."

"About what."

"Murdoch. He's planning something."

"I don't care."

"I wanted to give you a heads-up. Just be careful about what's behind you."

Oliver spat. The drool from his hunger kept coming.

He looked away and saw a squirrel on the snow near a tree and thought about eating it. Felt the snowclouds turning red and looked back at Thomas. Could eat his neck.

"Sucked being suspended, eh?"

"No."

"I tried to study," said Thomas.

Oliver stared at him. He really could eat him, and it made him worry for a split second, and then he just let himself think about it. Which parts would be good. Do you have to cook all meat. He'd heard about the murders in the neighbourhood and the talk of some kind of cannibal.

"You realize that you're meat, right?"

"What's that?"

"If we were out on the savannah. You talk about studying. Put yourself in front of a lion. You're not Thomas anymore, right? You're meat."

"I guess."

"It's true. All the little dreams in your head and whatever you want to be. Whatever you're studying for. They're nothing when you realize that you're meat."

He spat again.

Bright eyes looking up at Thomas. He thought about those when it was all over. Never noticed Oliver's eyes before, the kind you should be afraid of, respect, wonder about. A psycho's eyes. Layers of silver.

"Anyways . . ." said Thomas. "Watch out for Murdoch."

All day Oliver thought about two things: Suzi, and taking her away. Watching little Thomas walk back to his little thoughts, his little friends. Back to French class and a world of bullshit.

There were two truths: Suzi, and the fact that the world is *so* much bigger than we know. That's what her kiss had taught him.

He was going to see her tonight, and maybe they could plan to meet up for lunch this week. Her school was a half-hour walk from his, but he could slip away and take off his shirt, be there in two minutes. Or they could meet halfway.

And plan.

He hadn't tested how far he could fly yet. It was like running. He got tired when he pumped his wings too fast, but when he figured out a pace, started understanding how to use the currents of air, he could stay up a long time. She would be extra weight, but his hands could hold her easily.

Go somewhere in the country, maybe. Some completely different place. Venice. When he got stronger it might not be so hard to fly across an ocean. And oceans like the Atlantic, they're not just *ocean*—there are islands, thousands of places to land and explore. When you don't need roads and paths and airports. The world was huge.

Thomas didn't go with Murdoch and Jonathan the next day. He thought about not going to school at all, but in the end he just said, "No. I'm not doing it."

"YOU DON'T NEED money if you have wings."

"Why? You just steal stuff?"

"Yeah. Why not?"

"You plan to steal stuff for a living? Support us through crime?"

Her smile was like a cure for him. Didn't need to eat if he had her smile.

"It's not like theft," he said. "Not exactly. It's more natural. I don't need a gun or intimidation or hurting people. When a bird takes a worm from another bird, it's not theft. It's just eating. Being better. I take a couple of bags to No Frills, load them up. And when security starts chasing me I take off the shirt and fly."

"And what do we live in?"

"I don't know. Caves. Forests. Houses. I bet there are millions of abandoned houses. I've seen TV shows about castles, huge old places that nobody wants to fix up."

"Live in a castle."

"Why not?"

"What if you get even weirder? Grow a beak or something. How long are those fangs going to be?"

"What if *you* do? What if you get ugly in five years?"

"Who knows."

"Who knows."

She thought about it in bed. Leaving everything. Life without other people. Flying to different places when they got bored and learning how to live, how to really live. Not dressing up as a lawyer or climbing some ladder made of numbers for fifty years and asking that question that you hear adults asking all the time: what am I doing with my life.

Take food because you're good at taking food.

Live in a castle.

When things get tough you fly away.

Not so ridiculous when she thought about it.

3

MORE BODIES WERE found in the neighbourhood. A
decapitated boy and a girl lying next to each other. The sky
black and hanging like a punched eye over Vine Park at dawn,
where police had gathered, officers from 11 Division and the
Emergency Task Force, with Forensics and a coroner. The coroner had decided that whatever this site had been, where they
had found the original body parts and scat, it would serve as a
starting point. A sniffer dog, a Belgian shepherd, was brought
over from Explosives Detection and her handler led her around
the area.

"Seek."

The dog found the scent cone and spoor and led them
towards the tracks.

She pulled at the leash while they took snips to the fence,
and surged ahead once they were through. Along the gravel
beside the tracks and past a shantytown that the officers from
11 Division knew from busts. They expected the search to end
there but the dog swerved with her nose to the ground back
over the tracks towards another fence with a man-sized hole
in it. In behind the freight shippers and across Hook Avenue.

She led them down Watkinson out to Dundas again and sat
attentively at the door of 2740B, a junk store later traced to an
owner named Arthur Fulham. Through the door she barked
once and joined the fore with her handler, now sheltered by

officers from the ETF wearing helmets and heavy vests. Percussive muscle and panting, the officers declaring themselves and the scent getting loud as a gong in the dog's snout. They used flashlights to find their way through the rear and she scratched at the closed door to the basement, sat again to signal *here*.

A pet store, a pet owner, some sign of exotic animals. They'd been prepared to expect at least one snake and anti-venom was waiting back in the Suburban. When they opened the door it seemed some enormous carnivore had opened its mouth, stink of old blood and new. A tropical heat and a wave of new smells, sharp sting of old cheese and shit and a richness, could make a devil swoon, a picture in the nose of human coprophages fucking on a bed of turned meat. They coughed and hesitated on the stairs, called out.

Her handler resisted the dog's urgence.

"Shine some lights."

The stairs led down to a dirt-floor basement, one room with empty cages stacked and the main space holding an old boiler, whose flame could be seen through its inspection port, the door removed, the fire stopping abruptly and blasting again like an old dragon sleeping and wanting, not wanting, to wake up.

The dog pulled towards the boiler and put her mouth on the suspect, clamped her jaws.

Her handler said, "Let go. Good girl. *Aus. Lass es.* Drop it. What a good girl." He gave her her tennis ball.

They waited for Forensics, who shut off the boiler and set up portable scene lights and they picked up the item with five-inch tweezers, laid it flat on the dirt floor first and then used gloves and the tweezers to hold it up. Like something from a costume store. Punctures could be seen, probably from the dog's teeth, but otherwise it was an intact piece of what they later confirmed was skin, the size of a boy or small man, as if it had been shed in one piece. And all around were fleshscraps and DNA from over twenty different victims.

Through the afternoon the store was picked over, receipts for medical equipment removed, the cages downstairs taken out. The scene was examined for weeks, the store and the living spaces above and behind. Items in the attic untouched, it seemed, for decades. It appeared to be a family home, permitted to convert to a store like others on that street. Photos and documents in boxes upstairs of a family, called not Fulham but Taylor.

Banking records and deeds showed that Arthur Fulham owned a storage facility and property in King County, a scene discovered months later of a macabre collection of bones of many species and three human skeletons, unidentified. Similar cages and equipment found in the store on Dundas. A lab and living quarters. The coroner was intrigued by the bones, sent to her from the edge of the Holland Marsh. She imagined them on the ground, and they even appeared in one of her dreams, white letters marked on a black ledger, the massive and incomplete document that tallies our mistakes and leaves advice if only we could decode it. Skeleton of a chimpanzee. The human bones were of two juveniles and a middle-aged man, picked or licked clean as if to be held up and admired, eaten by something with an artful hunger. Something with saliva made of acid and bleach. The skull of one of the juveniles was shattered, no obvious cause of death in the other, *and as for gender? age? dental records?* she wrote in her notes. *Boys' clothes, boys' bones in terms of density but a rounding of the pelvis, extra pairs of ribs, caudal appendages in both. Tails?*

She involved zoologist friends, and kept this on the back burner for a year. One boy outside, one indoors with the man, no bullet holes, no trace of toxins in the bones. She considered the venom she found in the victims in Toronto, but there was no tissue to work with, decomposed or eaten, even the feet had been peeled. All the skeletons bore grooves and dents, deep, as if a chisel had been taken to them post-mortem. Bears, wolves, coyotes. The seasonal churn and harrowings of a Canadian forest worked upon the bones. There were question marks throughout her notes, throughout her life, hanging from her brow like jewellery, always the one to answer the how, the when, the where, but seldom the why people did what they did.

She treated this as a murder-suicide and left it open. Wasn't sure how to connect it with the murders in Toronto, the snake and the skin.

In the store the dog gnawed on her tennis ball. The constable held her leash and talked in the kitchen about the smell of the basement, not able to articulate this feeling of unease. The house clear for a moment while the others loaded evidence. "I thought people were supposed to smile in those days," said the other officer, looking at a black-and-white photo on the fridge. Two boys and two parents in the 1960s or early '70s.

The dog raised her nose and caught another scent from that rotten Eden.

She dropped her ball and barked.

Her handler pulled the leash. So restless this one. A restless breed.

She reared up and stretched. Barking louder now. Protective. Fearful.

"*Heel*. What is it? What's there?"

Out in the hallway. The two men and the dog tried to see, the place brightly lit by Forensics.

The smell still poured out from one of the side rooms and emerged fully into the hall, solid, redoubtable.

The dog's bark sounded like a panic.

"*Sit*. What is it? There's nothing."

Down the hall, slowly strutting and contemplative, Night

dragged his forehead and jowls along the walls. Dried blood on his haunch that would have been visible to the officers if they hadn't been behind him. Dried blood in the room they found later, where he had waited for the boy.

A train of muscle and memory.

Under banished stars he'd languished in the cold those nights when frenzy lingered, when he and the vultures skinned the corpses, ate the pigs, and the nameless predators tried to find their purpose among the trees and died. He lay with the stiff and rotting body of his master and watched as coyotes and raccoons came into the hangar, tiptoed and hunched and half-ashamed like poets at a free buffet. With every darkening of the sky a new parade of creatures coming to suck and haul out bones and he fought and witnessed all manner of struggle and death. Eventually a settling, just the sound of his breath, and his eyes swelled and burned like the moon.

With a full belly, every creature will ponder. The after-dinner dog. Thinking of companions, present or lost. Hand on the back. Missing the hand on the back. That eager little face by the candleflame. Night listened to the lunatic calls of barred owls, part cuckoo part ape, and the howls of wolf packs, calling for what.

He went back to be with Oliver.

He was four feet tall at the shoulder and nudged the sides of people in the city, people who insisted there was a spirit unknowable, forces greater, an angry earth mother saying this, no this, is the last indignity. Nudged off their path and filled with chills. The only one with the full picture of death is the killer, and in this body that walked down the hall was a wisdom greater than his age, greater than he ought to have gathered in months but gathered nonetheless by hearing those desperate calls at night, by the sights in the woods, by killing. Knowing hunger indiscriminate and now able to rein his appetite, aware of the difference between killing for practice and killing for need, killing for fear and now afraid of nothing.

He stalked invisibly alongside Oliver. As a protector. Holding sentry like the Sphinx outside his house, watching the house of the girl, walking with the unwitting boy. He watched him fly and searched the horizon for threats wherever he might land. He sat with the girl and the boy in daylight, and was shot. Licked his blood and stayed in the room where all he'd wanted was the candle and the sleep, and he waited. He waited.

He walked now through the open door of the store, through the crowd of police. A chain swung from his neck that no one noticed, limp and rhythmic, a chain like that of a censer before a priest who has seen it all, the suffering and the miracles, no belief in prayer. He slouched on quiet paws down the sidewalk, no longer curious about all the little birds.

THEY DECIDED TO meet halfway between their schools. There was a maze of alleyways between Indian Grove and Indian Road Crescent. The backs of houses, their detached old garages all meeting here like miniature houses themselves or like barriers to the private lives beyond. Some of them originally built as stables. Nobody came here in the middle of the day, the garages opened in the morning and let out the cars, welcomed them back in the evening. Nobody watching two kids who wanted to hug.

It made you quiet, this feeling. Made you think about every word or wonder why bother talking. Shoulders touching.

"This way," said Oliver. On a map the alleys would look like the letter H. Left here, right there, left there, in the middle of the H like a maze. So quiet. They walked slowly with their hands in their pockets and both stared down at nothing in front of their feet. Feeling like something was going to happen, chests getting hotter and the rising blush, other eyes watching again but nobody around, they knew it.

Oliver stopped first. Too shy to look.

It was the longest kiss yet and it gave them time to see each other with their eyes closed. Garden of velvet, hot peace in the heart. A dream, memory or vision, like when they held hands, he saw his image as real as if he could hold it, a tall and handsome young man, looking happy. What he would look like when he had reasons to love the world. And he didn't want the wings, didn't want them, didn't want them. What he would look like to someone who loved him.

He stepped back and there was a funny sound. Suzi jerked a little and an arrow landed on the snow beside her. She cleared her throat and tried to swallow, looked like she was going to ask him something. There were holes on either side of her neck and blood poured down her front like a scarf.

THE PLAN ALL along was to hunt him. Track him down. Even those deer he saw in the videos, the ones with huge antlers like some figure from mythology. Glorious. Even those could be outsmarted and taken down by a hunter. Taught about who is superior. Mankind rules the forests and the oceans and the sky, every corner of all of it, and within mankind there's an order, a hierarchy. Some were meant to rule, others to be ruled, and when there's a disruption of that, when somehow the weak overcome the brave, that's a perversity. We're hunting, thought Murdoch.

Jonathan's dad always left early to work. Murdoch went over to his place as planned before school and put the crossbow and two arrows in his backpack, clothes wrapped over the butt-stock. Stowed it in his locker and couldn't stop thinking about it all morning. At lunch Jonathan kept an eye on Mickey and went ahead while Murdoch got the backpack.

It's about surprise. Mickey acting all tough now at school, but catch him when he's not ready . . . Maybe those bucks in the woods heard something that made their ears twitch, but still they dipped their heads and ate. Because they needed to eat. Because we all do what we have to. Because the weak will always do something stupid.

Jonathan texted him. *At Keele gate.*

When Murdoch ran into the schoolyard with the backpack he saw Jonathan at the gate gesturing with his hands, *slow down.* They held on to the fence and looked around. Teachers monitoring the little ones, and some of the other kids drifting off grounds to go home for lunch.

"He's up there," said Jonathan. He was wandering up Glenlake, and they followed slowly.

"We'll stay behind. Don't cross."

"The fuck's he going."

"It's good, it's good."

All these days of waiting to catch him. Hoping for some time when Jonathan's dad was at work and when they could get Oliver off school grounds. It was perfect.

Cresting the hill on Glenlake and out of sight for a second. They ran ahead and saw him turning on Indian Road Crescent.

"We have to get the arrows." Jonathan said it a thousand times. Scare the little fucker, hurt him, whatever you want to do, but no matter what, get the arrows. With no arrows there was no proof of anything. And with them back in the cabinet no one would ever know.

"There's debate about where to aim for the one-shot kill," said Murdoch. "With a bullet I saw a guy saying you draw a line from tear duct to tear duct and aim three inches above that. On a deer."

"You don't want to kill him," said Jonathan.

THEY SAW OLIVER meet a girl and walk with her close, into the quiet part of the neighbourhood and those alleys where Murdoch used to practise catwalks on his bike. Questions in Jonathan's mind about how the girl now figured and a clean feeling of determination in Murdoch. He peeked around the corner of the garage and saw the backs of Mickey and the girl, more garages facing him from the other end of the alley. Like his prey was in a box, an easy shot.

He pointed across their end of the alley, wordlessly telling Jonathan to go over there, and he slid the backpack off. Quietly pulled out the clothes and took out the crossbow. Jonathan crept twenty feet across to the other side of the alley's entrance, watching the backs of Oliver and the girl when he ran, and he stood beside the wall of another garage, opposite from Murdoch. Watched his friend put his back to the wall. Put an arrow in the track and his foot in the stirrup to cock the bow.

Murdoch lifted it to the crook of his arm, bigger than he remembered, and stretched his thumb to flick the switch from Safe to Fire. He stepped into the open and tried to measure the wind and remember the videos he'd watched, reckon on the bow kicking back unless you squeeze your shoulder tight and be its master.

Suddenly couldn't decide where to aim. For the leg, the lungs.

Oliver and Suzi were kissing and it was disgusting.

When he opened his eyes the girl was on her knees and holding her throat. He got the other arrow and crouched behind the garage again with the stock against his armpit. Pulled up. Get it right. Shoot low this time. Be smarter, he told himself.

Jonathan saw that Murdoch had shot the girl and he too put his back to the garage as if he had his own bow, and the bow he had was his dad, and they both had smart dads, they'd figure this out. Get the arrow. Head racing to explain, they thought this kid was going to hurt this girl and they followed them and fuck there was no way to explain.

He could see the arrow on the ground beyond the girl and ran towards it when Murdoch fired the next one.

A shot precise down a windless hall, nowhere for it to go but exactly where it intended.

Heard a noise like it hit, a roar, and Oliver was on his knees with the girl on her back.

The arrow was stuck low down in nothing, moving on its own. Air made of meat and the meat moved, bleeding. The arrow still but turning now on its point like it was looking for a target.

Murdoch ran away.

"SUZI?"

Blood kept pouring from her neck and she held it. Oliver held it. Surges with each squeeze of her heart, arteries on both sides of her windpipe severed. She couldn't find her breath or speak, the blood dark and hot on their fingers.

"Please," he said.

He couldn't understand.

Jonathan emerged from behind a garage like a halfwit character you were not meant to expect, this whole thing some shameful pantomime no one wanted to be in or watch. He ran towards them looking at the closest arrow that had drawn blood from nothing, the arrow moving when he got close to it.

"It wasn't me," he said looking quickly at Murdoch running away. He reached for the arrow feathers, trying to understand how they floated and moved and where that blood was coming from.

Oliver stared up from his knees and saw Jonathan's head leap off his body, like he'd walked into some invisible harvester, the body at its business for a second before collapsing forwards, tipped like a cup of blood.

Night made the sound that starving lions make turning on each other, lungs full of murder. He put his mouth to his haunch and pulled the arrow out of his muscle. His own blood and the boy's betrayed his transparency and he stood now breathy and dripping, nosing Jonathan's head on the snow two times like a toy he'd just grown tired of.

YOU CAN SEE it from above.

His future emptied.

Her eyes emptied and reflecting two grey suns.

No moment of comprehension, comfort, benediction.

Blood dark and thick beneath it all like it was leaking up from an abyssal well.

See the haunch and mouth of an otherwise invisible beast, old friend found, looking up and walking away.

Black and grey rooftops. A neighbourhood of graves.

All of it getting smaller.

MURDOCH COULDN'T DECIDE whether to run home or back to school and he slowed.

Tried to think. Jonathan would get the crossbow. He'd get the arrows. They'd figure it out.

Nothing happened.

He bounced on his feet and started jogging. Go back to school like normal.

Nothing happened, he insisted.

The truth is how you say it. Believe whatever you want and say it hard enough.

Jonathan would clean it up, for sure. Oliver's word against theirs.

He jogged and swerved and thought.

His hair was pulled at the crown and he lost his footing. Lost the sidewalk. He grimaced at the pain and tried to understand how he was lifting. Kicked and struggled like a toddler who doesn't want to be picked up.

He clutched onto wrists above his head and raised his eyes. Started screaming.

SEVERAL PEOPLE SAW it.

Downtown in the air between the six black buildings of the TD Centre.

Looked to Oliver like a space to write a final curse.

A bird with something hanging from it. That thing squirming, alive.

A woman who watched from her office on the fifty-second floor saw it rise up, drop the thing it was carrying, dive down and catch it again, like it was playing. She filmed it on her phone. It flew out of sight.

Her rectilinear days reflected in these buildings, the lake a painted backdrop. Down to the food court and up to make some money. She leaned against the tinted window and looked at the February sky. The bird came back in view and she dropped her phone.

A terrible noise on the window like it would break, and a sight unseizable. Hovering there was a half-naked boy with wings, holding another by the hair and pants. Vomit on the jacket, slamming into her window.

The boy with wings flipped the other like a baton, caught him by the ankle and swung him. Beat him like a stubborn fish against the glass and the mullions on either side. A sound that made her jump each time and she tried to tell him to stop. The dangling boy twisted and swayed, sometimes the back of his head and sometimes the front, slamming like a clapper of meat on a bell that wouldn't ring.

Blood started smearing on the glass and she saw the boy's face lose shape.

Oliver flexed and hovered there.

He felt the twitching stop, Murdoch giving up.

Saw Suzi not speaking and nothing to go back to.

He was limp for a second and dropped, then flexed his wings and pumped. He lifted Murdoch and held him by the collar and thigh, his broken face and tongue lolling in front of Oliver.

He flew hard towards the building and slammed Murdoch's spine on the black steel mullion, felt the snap and knew he had halved him in his skin.

She watched through the stains on the window. Boy with wings flying up and away, dropping the other. Flying out above taller buildings and up over the lake, a speck.

So high he couldn't breathe.

The Beginning

To Sorrow
  I bade good morrow,
And thought to leave her far away behind;
  But cheerly, cheerly,
  She loves me dearly;
She is so constant to me, and so kind:
  I would deceive her,
  And so leave her,
But ah! she is so constant and so kind.
                    —John Keats, *Endymion*

1

HOW GARISH WOULD this world look, not least the sky itself, if you were born in the darkness above it. All these colours. Could you ever find peace, even when the sun was hiding.

A spark rose up to that darkness, once, past a medial world where balance reigned, and kindness, people with torches gently calling the hours while they knew this frenzied corpus was hurtling towards extinction. And the spark was once a woman. Upwards.

"Remember she was in her room, with the balcony over the street, an aging woman in layers of clothes, mumbling through the apartment? The flower had withered outside and a clipping of it was floating in a bowl of murky water.

"You have to see her now, once she took hold of it. A soggy flower in her hand that she smelled first and paused over. Smell of failed conquerors on a field of dead horses.

"Do you remember I told you that the first flower on earth was this one that emerged from the water? That the Black Dove was eaten on primordial banks and a fire was lit in every creature's eyes?

"It was the flower itself that had always dreamt of water, to return to the place it came from. The girl's yearning for the ocean had simply been giving voice to that of the flower. And whenever it was soaked, it carried not only strength but the deepest wisdom. Knowing what it was like to lose its home, what it meant to return.

"Despite the smell, she put the flower to her wrinkled mouth and she lipped it, nibbled, her teeth and gums, the world, receding. Magic. She collapsed and transformed into a heap of clothes and the clothes themselves became dust, and the dust blew outside and caught fire in the sun and a speck of it wouldn't burn out. Kept rising.

"Enough wisdom in her now that even that medial world seemed foolish as she travelled through it, that even kindness seemed a denial of truth, and that light, however dim, was always a diversion. Up in the darkness the magic ceased. No sage with a lantern to guide her. No training ground of superior souls heading for other planets.

"The spark blew out and she flailed, thinking she still had arms and legs, touching and holding on to nothing, suspended, an emptiness thick and embracing and far from the milk of the stars. She was immersed, contained in a soft struggle as if she swam in an upper Dead Sea. Oil-black water where her eyes used to be. And if she was sad when she had lost her son and lover, sad when she remembered what might have been, it was nothing compared to this. The very architecture of the dark, the meat and blood of the absence surrounding her, was sadness. Moans and tears were shallow and worldly. This was the true ocean.

"She finally understood.

"Surrounded by numberless souls, each an invisible speck. Souls who every day rain down on the wise to remind them that there is no happy ending, that there is beauty and solace in truth and a braver way of living.

"These specks fall down and bloom like pollen, black as space," said the man.

He and his son had travelled onwards, through the desert

and settling in that city, and he told his son stories every night like they did around the fires of the used-to-be. Tales of guidance and comfort and warning. Don't go into the gorgeous woods. The stories were about the boy's mother, her yearning and failures. About creatures savage and fantastic and people equally so.

"These seeds, these specks, these letters, dust. Our mothers and our fathers."

He tried to explain that they were everywhere, she was everywhere, death was in the ink of every story and there was strength in tales of sorrow.

"We are animals and we will die, and in the journey of each animal is some small triumph or a path surprising and if all we can do is celebrate and sing our struggles in the dust, our fights and wants and eyes so pretty they cannot simply be eyes, then that will be music enough."

OLIVER'S DAD SAT in his study with the door closed, curtains drawn over the window. Picturing the snowstorm that never came, that turned to rain and tried to wash the filth of winter away.

The floor was covered in paper, leaves from the tree of ideas. A dim lamp with a crooked shade was alight in the corner of his desk and he sat on the couch across and stared, at the light, at the walls, the books on the shelves and the TV. He thought of other writers he knew and their spaces, one who rented an office with two-way glass through which he watched pedestrians all day—people passing who looked at their own reflections without knowing a writer was lurking beyond. Another who devised a window of constant rain, water falling down it all day and the sound of a gentle storm. The sound he heard out his window now.

Drown me.

Carry me to the river.

On his walls were mementos of some of his novels, a fan letter from a favourite painter, a photo of a chimp, and the walls were painted green, dark and unfreshened now for at least twenty years, the green of the dreams of a long-dead baron, moss on his collapsing castle, moss on a hollow tree. It was that colour alone that made him want the house, and he could see her standing there now against it, on a lazy noon, naked as a bone.

All around were the books that guided or enflamed him. Made him want to write like *that* or do the opposite. His eyes taking in their letters and their letters tumbling down and flashing from black to white as they fell inside, lightning over the red swamp of aching flowers he was nursing and longed to present. I am me, made of you. All of us made of stories.

He wandered the empty house. Hadn't had the radio on for a while.

Made lunch.

His ideas came to him most brightly in the morning, and lunch was always some kind of banal punctuation or alarm. Remember you get hungry. Remember you are a body.

Old houses are never silent.

THE PAGES ON the floor had character sketches, lines he liked, a range of possible endings. He still wrote in pen sometimes.

> *Oliver thought he couldn't breathe but he kept flying higher. Thought his lungs had burst but they only got hotter and he filled that sky with shrieks. The screams tore his ribs and throat and blood turned his breath to pink steam, and his grief completed his transformation. The flying boy who shouted fire at cruelty and*

injustice, no dragon, hellbird or avenging angel: the fears we couldn't name were the ones that haunted deeply.

He flew above the city for years and let rage be his lord, landing on the shoulders of late-night swine, politicians stumbling from restaurants, watching the fat in their faces melt beneath his screams and flying to lakeside cottages to burn bullies in their beds. The cheats, the ones who built nothing, everyone who had taken from the rest of us. Dreamkillers.

He avenged until he felt guilty and killed to distract his guilt and his screams for Suzi made good people moan in their sleep and sit up. The greater his rage, the brighter that fire from his mouth, up there above the midnight clouds when he could no longer bear to see people. A boy a little younger stood by the window in his bedroom while his family slept, wondered what those flashes were. Darker than lightning. Should I be brave, he wondered. Should I try. All the things out there he couldn't control, under that sky of grief.

Oliver up there forever, now, among the pantheon of mutilated heroes.

AS MUCH AS he loved stories, he longed for a world of directness. Honest conversations and self-awareness. Tell me why you're sad, just tell me. If you want to leave, tell me, I can take it. If she had talked to him instead of drinking.

He'd spent years writing realistic stories and dismissing the need for escape. Dragged down through middle age getting tired of people's need to make things up. Yet watching his boy, his lips moving in the backseat talking to no one—conjuring creatures and friends. Something changed. Something gave him energy again, a choice between creation or despair. The shadow of an airplane over the highway that could have been a massive bird. Oliver talking to himself and seeing nothing that was in front of him. If this was the world and the world will be what each individual wants to see, why not wonder. Why not make things up. That may not have been a giant bird that cast the shadow, it was an airplane. But what is an airplane if not a story about people who wanted to fly.

THERE WAS STILL a lot he needed to figure out. What does the future look like on the other side of those woods. The civets dashing out with diseases in their mouths. Wolves that were bigger than wolves. Does the world keep looking weirder for everyone who survives.

He got so lost in his mind sometimes he would go to the grocery store and suddenly wonder if he was wearing clothes. Maybe it was a kind of addiction, his work. His own need to escape reality, the burdens of being a parent. He liked to believe it was a way to connect with reality more deeply.

When you sit on your own for years you have to ask yourself who is this sitting and why. What are these legs, this flesh. And you put those legs on as many journeys as you can imagine, testing them, wearing them out till they are bone, and you learn what those are, those bones in you. Reduce the world to ash and try to find the beauty in that bleakness. Tell yourself that you can't bear another loss, sing that pain, and find yourself losing again, still singing, until your lips are thin then gone and the world is truly empty, skeletons lying sere in an asthmatic wind, and you still, lying among them, hope the wind will sing through the holes in you. Truth is found in the dark places, and darkness resides not in its discovery but in the effort to avoid it. So you lie there as a skeleton among the others, enlightened.

She was his muse for their life together, the beauty he chased while he walked through all that blanching country in his mind, and he lost his ability to wonder when he finally realized that she was miles away and he simply couldn't catch her. She didn't want to be caught, and she wasn't who he thought she was. She drank when she woke up and passed out in the afternoons. She drank through birth and more thereafter, the presence of a son conjuring her own childhood and all she wanted to do was drown that child within.

OLIVER, YOUR MOTHER was abused by her brother, her father cruel and drunk, and love was a sharp and twisted vine for her. Houses were haunted, kisses were tainted, and a parent, herself, would never make it right. She always tried to forget her past and I always tried to understand how alone she felt, but I could simply never hold her the way she wanted to be held, and in the end she didn't want to be held by me or by you or by anyone. She did not want to give you a sibling. And a brother is someone who can make things better, who can lie in the dark with you, fight for you and listen to you cry. That's what a brother should be, but that was not a brother to her. All those nights when you wished you could have had someone to talk to, someone who could answer your questions, what made Mom leave.

She drank herself to death. She left the hospital and wandered and I heard from her sister after a year that she'd rented a room at the Peacock and was found in a chair up there.

And I don't know what your memories truly are of her, whether you remember she was cruel to you and petty. I know you don't want to remember, but I want you to know everything. You can read this now or when you're older.

I felt like someone took her away from me. Maybe that's where part of this story came from—an arrow out of nowhere, taking away my love. Her eyes in your head. She loved that idea of water instead of streets and hated being told what to do. Who she should have been.

Maybe most people make up stories about who their loved ones are, and we never really know each other. I thought of her not as that bloated thing in a hospital bed but as the beauty I had dreamt of even when I was a kid. Think of the girls or boys you've had a crush on. She was everyone.

HE SAT ALONE, again, in his study, and felt some of the story unfolding.

The very first Amon forsook the lord. He burned the book and let spiderwebs grow on the altar. He had a son who had a son who had a son who had a son, and some were punished and some shone in glory and were kind. And would you believe the reach of this diaspora, from the murderous reckonings and threshings of the Levant to the car staying warm by a postbox in Aklavik. This younger Amon I speak of, the snake, he stretched from there to there.

On the dirt floor of the Taylor basement he awoke.

A fang.

Not two of them but the one that governed from his groin. Pulled up through his insides, its curve feeling soft and compelling, it seemed to spring out just when his eyes reopened. The rhythmic hiss of the boiler and the fetid warmth of his family home. I miss you, my brother, and there's killing to be done.

He shed his skin for the last time in that room, and the fang led him on a journey before the police arrived.

He ate as his city rose and spread its edges, and he

wandered chased by dogs, and at different times he
and his brother travelled from place to place. Neither
of them the kind to write their names on rocks because
they knew they would outlive most. The younger a
bright-eyed and gentle halfboy with venom in his
fingers, he acquired a thousand names. He stayed the
same age, re-adopted and admired, and was raised by
parents who always died. And on separate paths they
neither had to work nor suffer, relying on charm or
a knife, the snake came and went through any room
while the halfboy read all imaginable truths and saw
dramas frivolous and large in the houses of well-mean-
ing strangers.

    And they met. On a hill, of course, because whether
it was flood or war the survivors found the high places.
Both of them so old inside.

    "I know you," said Amon.

    "You do," said the other.

    "We used to live together."

    "I've had so many families."

    "I've seen many things," said Amon. "I watched
a ship catch fire and sail into port and it burned an
entire city. I stood there and saw a man kneel down
with his very hair on fire and I stabbed him to stop
the noise."

    "I think I read that story."

    They sat on the hill and became friends, the only
people they had ever met who didn't die when touched,
and their friendship went through seasons until they
concluded they were brothers. And after these hundreds of years they did not share many enthusiasms,
but they met now and then on that hill, with similar
eyes and little to say, bound by the sins of their parents.

SO FAR, OLIVER, this is all I've written down. Still so many questions. The invisible friend with blood on his haunch. The murders. The bird and the boy with wings. Does he fly even higher and transform like that. His first love taken away from him. Does he kill or come back to earth, change back. Does he know that no matter what he does, no matter his mistakes or failures, he can always come home to his father.

HIS DAD WALKED quietly to Oliver's room, a memorial to the age of twelve. Still a plastic sword over there that would never again be called into battle. Morning light coming in earlier now through the window.

He picked up the letter from where it had always rested, untouched.

Only a writer would believe that he could get through to a twelve-year-old by writing.

> *I feel like my life started when I met your mother. Maybe that would be a good place to stop. Or the day we first kissed. Or if I held the world around those days when I wrote things I loved and could celebrate with her and with you. The day you were born.*
>
> *And you see that if I stopped at one of those days, to avoid some later sadness, the others wouldn't have come.*
>
> *I wanted to give you this letter along with the novel, but I haven't finished it yet. The novel is for me as much as for you. My portrait of twelve. My life and yours reimagined. I don't know if you'll read this or even read the book when it's done, but this is me trying to tell you something. Something that is in the book, but that I want to make clear.*
>
> *It's OK to be sad.*

I know I wanted to tell you a true story that has a happy ending, and I will, I promise. But I want you to know in your heart that it's OK sometimes not to be happy. Not to search for escape at the cost of all reason and wish that you had wings. It's OK to know, even to focus on the fact, that you will be hurt and lose people you love, and that life will often be hard.

Do difficult things and learn the sad histories. Look at your demons in stories and you will be strong for it. Stronger than anyone who cannot face those truths.

Oliver woke up and saw his dad standing by the bed. "It's time for school," he said.

CROCUSES GREW FROM the snow, like bright and fragile hatchlings opening their mouths for their mother. The spring melt was soaking through the holes in Oliver's boots and he told himself he should get a paper route or some kind of job this summer. Buy his own clothes.

Maybe he was feeling that feeling a little less, the one where eyes were watching him. Thinking more these days that the world was interesting, not scary: full of things he didn't know, but he wanted to get out and know them.

After this summer a lot of new kids were going to come to his school from other places. And then he'd be in high school somewhere and almost everything would be new.

Get some new shoes to take him there. Join a club after school, for real, and see what happens next.

A truck came too fast along Annette Street behind him and bounced loudly over the potholes.

HIS DAD READ parts of "Black Dove" to him over the winter months. A story about people wanting to change their nature instead of bearing the troubles of life. A story meant to scare Oliver so that when he looked out the window he could feel that these days, his troubles, weren't that bad. Not yet. They'd stopped the bedtime ritual a while ago, Oliver preferring to be alone now reading or whatever. But on a couple of cold nights his dad said *let me just try this out on you* and he read aloud parts downstairs in the lamplight. He said he was going to write some of it differently from the way he read it out, and Oliver read a version that was slightly less gruesome.

He looked up *gene editing animals* like he did in the story. Saw the beagles with muscles and glow-in-the-dark rabbits. The story was all pretty possible because some of it was already happening. Babies were getting customized to be better. Better people eating better food and animals kneeling down to serve us.

He spent a few nights on his dad's laptop not looking for grim speculations but triumphs in reality, the course of lives actually being improved by edited genes. Vaccines that saved the world, suffering being edited out of the gene pool, no more malaria, the rot and forgetfulness of old age reversed. He found that girl whose leukemia was completely wiped out, who ran the 10K races. That was a happy ending.

"Don't make her die," said Oliver.

"I have to. I want you to be sad."

IT HAD BEEN three years since his mom died.

He had cried when she left and not much since. When he looked in the mirror he saw the same Oliver, not much change from yesterday or the day she left. But so much changing inside.

Could he imagine an Oliver who wasn't afraid. Maybe not an Oliver with wings, but a guy who could look at things he was afraid of, remember shitty things, stand up tall and say it's okay. Keep going and find a friend, try not to worry about what's going to happen.

One of those nights in the lamplight he went to his dad's chair. Sat on his dad's lap and curled up.

Tried to get smaller, and cried.

THE EAVESTROUGHS CARRIED winter to the drains and lakes. Then it snowed again. Through the city, night and day, more than one person tried to sing a song as wide as the ocean and kids drew pictures of houses on mountains, never worried what the wind might do to them.

One night Oliver saw a cloudy shape moving in the hallway upstairs. His dad was asleep. He stared and rubbed his eyes, saw nothing, remembered those lines in the book about the dust and particles of the dead, everyone breathing their mothers and fathers and no one really dying.

In bed he listened to the trains. Tracks inviting them deeper into night.

There was talk of the world's first day, all those stories, but what about the night that came before it. However long ago. The first night, before the first dawn, stretching back endless, when all the unformed and untested writhed and murmured and knew nothing but their own dreams, no light yet to reveal them each to each.

On the first night everyone was perfect.

HIS CLASS PLAYED dodgeball in gym like they did when they were little. Same rules: six balls, you're out if you get hit or your ball gets caught or you step over the line. No shots to the head. Only difference was Ms. Sodebergh let them referee themselves and she left the gym.

Oliver caught a few balls, got Jonathan out. There was a basketball in the corner and no one saw Murdoch grab it. Much heavier than the balls they were supposed to use. He threw it at Oliver's head when he wasn't looking and knocked him over.

Ringing in his ears and a sting on the side of his face for most
of the morning.

He sat behind the tarp in the afternoon and thought.

*The dust did indeed come alive, wrote his dad. You
breathed not only your parents who died near you but
the parents who died in every place you travelled. The
strong, the weak, the ravishing. Lessons in the dirt and
a nudge of change in every breath. You have to open
your eyes. Bury fingers in the mud. You have to.*

ON A SUNDAY Oliver cleaned up his room. Wasn't asked to.
He dared to look under his bed and saw a carpet of dirt and
furry matter that looked like the surface of some hairy planet.
Wanted to make some space, get some air, throw stuff out. He
went through his books, the piles by his bed and on his desk,
the comics, Black Bolt.

He is a king, but he wakes in filth and darkness.

His dad liked those comic books even more than Oliver did.

"So fun!" he said. "You wouldn't believe how fun it can be
being miserable."

He was vibrating these days, manic. Pacing around the
house trying to find an ending.

Oliver wanted a room that was cleaner than his dad's study.
He put pretty much everything in garbage bags or boxes,
except for the books and comics. Made a cool row of them
around two walls, spine upwards, a tidy forest or a paper city.
Thought he could be an architect.

*Night's shoulders rose invisibly as he strode away from
the store and he walked a path different from the
brothers. He licked his wound and saw it disappear
in the light and the taste of his own blood made him*

hungry. Notices appeared on every lamppost of beloved dogs and cats gone missing.

He climbed a crane to be closer to the sky, the operator feeling the extra weight and looking down to the rigger to see if he'd strung a load without signal. One paw over the next, the boom high and rigid like a deity's finger pointing to the horizon it would change. He rested near the tip and adjusted to the movement as if cradled and swung by a playful parent and he looked to the sky for the boy, and he returned there.

In the construction site below, men found refuge as the weather warmed and they were watched by Night. Something there in the shadows as their tiny polities rose and fell, roofs of rebar and fresh concrete, this one coming with beer and arguing with that one with a vial of something, their hands jumping in their sleep and having to move out at dawn, the workers cursing the messes left behind and wondering why the world didn't labour as they did.

The longer he sat still, the less he needed to eat, but he was governed nonetheless by the soak of drool. His menace was indeed that he hunted in the day and night, the whole city could forever be his captive, yet he climbed that crane and sometimes chose to ignore the burning in his belly. He licked the waves of air, the diesel, stood to defy a helicopter that came near, and when that crane was dismantled he found another, always searching upwards. A shirtless man did chin-ups outside by the lakeshore and he watched him, a rival. If these were the pretenders, his throne was safe forever. And was this the burden of every lone hunter, to be just that, to follow his purpose and walk in solitude down corridors of buildings, corridors of trees?

He took the man down and bit his head off at the thrapple, found another crane and climbed.

Sometimes with his eyes half-open he lifted his nose to the clouds. On legs uncertain he turned to face the other direction, he might smell him coming but had to see, had to see. A tooth hung over his lip in the moon-light, as he dreamed, and never mind what did appear to him. Descending as a glass cup of sun in the morning and otherwise bringing muscle to the night. Never mind the other creatures who came uncanny from the marsh to this feeding ground, down the hill above the city like a fleet of burning ships. Whatever battles he was a part of and perversities he witnessed, a candle lit his mind.

Should he need me.

Should saline waters all become roads and clouds of oil catch fire.

Cures more of a burden than diseases, parades of shuffling mutants and absurdities so constant that every mind be jangled and permanently loosed from sense.

He carried on.

Strong-shouldered on the sidewalk.

Should the boy come down from the sky.

Oliver landed barefoot in a winter fifty from now, a part of and a witness to miracles. Bright eyes and the wisest face you've ever seen on a boy. Rage and grief like two new ribs, sore when pressed and he was stronger for them.

People made marks on anything they could, on tablets and bridges and buildings, depicting them both together. Sometimes the boy flew on his own above Night—they painted fire from his mouth. Sometimes they walked side by side.

Kids in the neighbourhood said Oliver could do anything, fly to a glacier and tear out the suppurating eyes of the demons bringing hazard to our world. Melt buildings. Some said he needed Night. They had seen him when the light was just so, when the boy only cautiously spread his wings, how the chest-high creature leaned in and shared warmth, head raised up as if to say go.

HE WENT OUTSIDE to get his bike from the shed. It was cold out. He still needed gloves if he wanted to ride for long. There were patches of snow in the corners of the yard and his shoes stuck in the mud.

When he was little the shed used to scare him.

He had a key for the lock and remembered that it was rusty and always hard to open at this time of year. His bike was there next to his dad's, neither of them remotely expensive or nice. Oliver was surprised to stand next to them and see that he could actually ride his dad's bike soon. They were entangled by the handlebars and brake cords and he pulled his free and leaned it outside the shed.

He could maybe spray-paint it this summer. Steel frame, heavy for a BMX, he kind of hated it but liked it too. He looked up.

He wheeled his bike to the back alley and felt nervous. Something about this time of year, that sky, like it could still snow anytime, or maybe he was afraid that he had forgotten how to ride, or he was just nervous about what he was planning to do.

Black gravel across the alley spread throughout the winter. He'd fallen on that often and cut his knees.

He balanced on the pedals and did a couple of hops.

The alley went down to the end of Pelham Park, so he had

to go all the way there and loop around, standing on his pedals and gliding for most of the way back down his street, plastic bags stuck to fences and garbage in the gutters.

Talking to himself and not really knowing what he was saying. Imagining things or hoping, saying inarticulate prayers to no one.

It was good to ride again. He looked at the stone angels in the neighbour's front garden and stopped outside his house. He stood and looked across the street.

He'd had a friend in his dreams and when he read the book he wondered. Felt like he knew a lot but didn't really know anything about her, not even her name.

His dad watched from the window.

Oliver checked for cars and rode down over the curb.

His dad saw a shadow from above.

Maybe she wasn't home.

One pump of the pedals and he hopped the other curb, put the bike down at the end of her path.

Maybe she'd think it was too cold to ride and where would they go anyway, the park would be too muddy.

His dad watched him ring the doorbell and saw the door open but couldn't see who answered. Saw it close again.

Oliver went back to his bike and picked it up. He waited, and a few minutes later she came around with hers. A smile that hurried the season.

They both looked happy.

His dad had to imagine what they said and the sounds, maybe songbirds chirping like coins on the walls of a well.

Acknowledgments

Thanks to: Bill Clegg, Hayden Desser, Nicole Winstanley, Charlie, Lola, Joyce and my family out west, and Suzanne, my sun and moon.